THE LOST MUSE

Gavin Canham

To Renée, Jake and Hayley

Vivid and in Your Prime

PART ONE

Dum loquimur, fugerit invida

Aetas: carpe diem, quam minimum credula postero

Time selfishly flies by even as we speak.

Seize today, putting as little trust in tomorrow as
you can

Horace Odes 1.11

One

Cambridge, UK – 1986

She was very old. To a hall full of undergraduates she seemed as ancient as the subject she lectured on. But no one sniggered at her as she carefully negotiated the steps to the stage and slowly shuffled towards the lectern. Her reputation and years of scholarship commanded respect amongst the more diligent students. Her sharp tongue and biting sarcasm struck fear in the rest, many of whom would have usually pinpointed an octogenarian lecturer as ideal target practice.

She went through the ritual of spreading out her notes on the lectern and positioning her empty glasses case on top of them to hold them in place, before peering out over the top of her spectacles to inspect her audience. It was a ritual which she had followed for more years than she cared to remember and had been imitated in college common rooms for almost as long.

'Ladies and gentlemen, scholars,' she began, 'and those who have got lost on their way to Applied Mathematics, good morning and welcome to this lecture entitled "Ancient Literature, Lost and Found". My name is Professor Margaret Hodges and I've managed to do both during my career.'

The audience showed their respect by laughing longer and more loudly than the joke merited. The professor's hearing had more in common with her eyesight than her mental acuity and the reaction of the students came through to her as a dampened hum.

'Some of you may have heard of Oxyrhynchus,' she went on. Again, more laughter. 'Yes, I suppose that means

8

most of you,' she conceded, 'except presumably the applied mathematicians. It was a ground-breaking excavation, figuratively as well as literally, and I was fortunate enough to play a small part, late on, alongside the great papyrologists, Grenfell and Hunt. These two young men, great men, made such an important and profound contribution to our knowledge and understanding of ancient civilisation. And they were so young; in their mid-twenties when they started the excavation. Not much older than most of you.' She paused, as though for breath or to gather her thoughts. 'Will any of you make such a mark on history at such an early age?'

She looked around the hall at the questionable hairstyles and dress sense and seemed to confirm to herself that the probability appeared slight at best.

'Anyway, the site offered the most perfect preservation conditions. There's hardly a drop of rainfall at Oxyrhynchus and no annual flood as there would be in the Nile delta. Perfect conditions, unique even, for the preservation of papyrus. Most of the material came from its time as a Roman garrison town. Ninety per cent of it was government stuff - tax records, census reports and the like. The Romans were jolly interested in their bureaucracy after all. All very fascinating I'm sure but I was after the ten per cent; the plays, the poetry…' she paused for dramatic effect and enounced every syllable of the final word, '…the literature.'

She looked around at her audience. 'Which was the greatest library of the Ancient World?'

She pointed towards a hand raised in the front row, 'Yes, Richard?'

'The library at Alexandria,' the owner of the hand replied to raised eyebrows and collaborative grins. Richard Lewis was universally recognised amongst his peers as a

9

little over-eager in his pursuit of academic excellence.

'Yes, Alexandria. And how many papyri survive from this great library?' Her pause encouraged Richard Lewis to raise his hand again but she answered this one herself. 'Nothing' she said with a sympathetic glance down at the young man who simultaneously mouthed her rhetorical response with a confirmatory nod of approval. The old woman was momentarily thrown by this but pulled herself together and carried on.

'Nothing survives from the great library of Alexandria, the largest repository for literature that the world has ever seen. Mainly as a result, only a fraction of the classical literary corpus survives at all to the modern day - the plays and poems deemed worthy of saving by medieval scribes, those dubious arbiters of quality and taste. Hours and hours spent copying huge tomes by hand, compounding earlier errors with their own distortion of the original text and thereby creating a whole industry of modern scholarship in literary criticism and conjecture. And therefore to them I am eternally grateful for the modest royalties which I enjoy from several of my books on the subject, all of which are included in the reading list which accompanies this lecture and most of which can be purchased at quite reasonable prices from Heffers bookstore in the main square.'

Once again a ripple of laughter washed over the audience.

'But here at Oxyrhynchus,' she went on, 'modern-day El-Behnasa as it is now and Behneseh when Grenfell and Hunt, and more latterly myself, were leading the excavations, here at the rubbish dumps which served the city through Hellenistic, Roman and Byzantine times, we had the chance to find works which were once famous and had since become almost completely unknown. Simonides, Sappho, Alcaeus, Menander; poets and playwrights whom scribes in their infinite wisdom had overlooked.

But there were one or two slightly better-known names as well. Sophocles wrote some one hundred and twenty three plays, only seven of which had survived to the twentieth century. And we found evidence of two more. Two completely new plays by one of Ancient History's greatest playwrights, found amidst the detritus of Oxyrhynchus. Imagine it, ladies and gentlemen. It would be like finding a lost play by Shakespeare. A priceless treasure.'

Once more, she paused and peered over her glasses at the assembled students, many of whom took it as a personal reprimand that they weren't imagining it quite as enthusiastically as she was expecting. As if to prove her wrong, a hand shot up from the middle of the third row.

'Professor Hodges?' She nodded at the questioner to continue. 'Is it true, as has been reported, that your expedition was haunted by a curse?' The young man masked a smile with his hand as his friend dug an elbow into his ribs.

The old lady stared at him for several moments with a puzzled frown on her brow. The grin disappeared from her questioner's lips as he felt the mood of the audience turn against him.

Finally, she nudged her spectacles further down her nose and shook her head. 'Why on earth do you think we would be haunted by a nurse?' she enquired with a hint of irritation.

The whole of the lecture theatre erupted in a howl of laughter, leaving the professor even more perplexed until someone in the front row managed to clarify the question which had actually been asked.

'Oh dear,' she continued after the noise had died down, 'nothing seems to work quite as well as it used to. A curse you say?'

The questioner sat up and nodded, regaining much of his composure, but the relief was short-lived.

'Nonsense,' she barked sharply. 'Poppycock. Where did you read this?'

The young man mumbled a vague answer and shrank back into his seat, wishing for all the world that he had never asked the stupid question in the first place.

'Tales of living mummies and deadly curses simply undermine the work we were all doing in Egypt. Important work. Damn hard work. I met Howard Carter on several occasions, both before and after his marvellous discovery, and I can assure you that he was no more cursed than you or I.'

She stared at the young man who, with little hope of the ground opening up to swallow him, couldn't help but question the appropriateness of his own inclusion in her comparison.

'You do realise that our excavations had drawn to a close some time before Carter and Carnarvon had made their last throw of the dice and struck gold. At the time when we were working, the name of Tut-Ankh-Amon meant nothing to the wider world and those silly stereotypes, curses and the whatnot, were yet to pop into the imaginations of newspaper editors and Hollywood producers. Now....' she adjusted her glasses once more, '.....back to the subject in hand.'

Before she could revert to her notes, another question came from the audience, keen to repair the damage. 'What are the chances of making a similar discovery today, professor?' a young girl asked.

The old lady shook her head and sighed.

'Not great, I'm afraid. But not impossible either. You must remember, I was in the field well over sixty years ago and the digging had been going on since the turn of the century. Things were different then and excavations are much more tricky nowadays; the cost, the bureaucracy, the politics especially. Obviously the Sophoclean passages were not the only celebrated finds from our excavation. The library of Alexandria collated the works of Sappho into nine books. Heading into the twentieth century, and give or take a few lines here and there, we barely had nine poems!' She puffed out her chest with pride. 'That certainly wasn't the number by the time our excavations were over.'

She paused for applause and her audience dutifully obliged.

'There's a very interesting story about one particular fragment of ours. It was incomplete and in such a very delicate state. We transported it back to the UK in a Huntley & Palmer's biscuit tin. After we'd eaten the contents of course! It really was quite a mess – just line endings really – but it recently allowed the University of Cologne to make sense of a similarly incomplete fragment of their own. They had found a piece of papyrus concealed in the bandages of an Egyptian mummy but had been unable to identify the author, or authoress, before cross-checking with our own find. A jigsaw puzzle if you will. Very satisfying. There's plenty of her work still to be discovered, of course. So perhaps we don't need to dig for further finds but simply unearth them in library archives or museum store cupboards.'

'Last one,' she said quietly and nodded towards another hand raised in the audience. Richard Lewis was determined to regain his proper place in the lecture hall order of merit.

'Professor, which of her poems would you regard as the most important you discovered?'

She didn't need to think for long. 'It would have to be φαίνεταί μοι that wonderful description of love sickness and its devastating symptoms. I'm proud of all our new finds at

Oxyrhynchus but this one is surely her finest poem and seems so close to completion. Agonisingly close. Perhaps just a line or two short. Let's hope that, somewhere out there, there's an Egyptian mummy who's got this ending wrapped round a part of its anatomy.'

Richard blushed and pretended to scribble some notes on the pad in front of him but the old lady hadn't finished.

'I want you to recognise that there's bound to be more of the Ancient World for us to discover; art, buildings, literature. Someone, somewhere will make a dazzling breakthrough to rank alongside Grenfell & Hunt, Arthur Evans at Knossos and dear old Howard Carter and his Egyptian tomb. Not in my lifetime I suspect, what with so little of it left, but undoubtedly in yours. There are fourteen years to go before the end of this century but, whether it happens in this millennium or the next one, rest assured it *will* happen.'

She gazed around the room. Every corner of the hall hung on her every word, spellbound by the prediction she was making. Every corner, that is, except the one occupied by one young man who sat at the back, resting lazily on his folded arms, nursing a slight hangover and dreaming of his impending trip around Greece, oblivious to the fact that he was missing possibly the most important hour's information of his life.

Two

Like the sweet-apple reddening high on the branch,
High on the highest, the apple-pickers forgot,
Or not forgotten, but one they couldn't reach…

Athens, Greece - that summer

'Jesus Christ' he said out loud, drawing a disapproving glare from the elderly Greek woman walking past. He flicked the pages back to the beginning of the chapter entitled 'Death of Sappho' and read the passage again.

The reconstruction was rather on the dramatic side for what purported to be a scholarly book and, although the ancient commentators often mentioned Sappho's suicide leap from the White Rock, he had never before read of her daughter trying to talk her mother down. Not that there was much doubt that she had a daughter – 'very Sapphic' Dan had sneered when he had first found out – but her inclusion here in the death scene of one of Classical literature's greatest poets smacked more than a little of artistic licence.

He shook his head and flipped the book over to read the back cover. 'One of the literary giants of Ancient Greek literature,' ran the blurb, 'the power of her verse stands undiminished by the tragically meagre amount which has survived through to this day.' He sandwiched the slim volume between the flats of both palms as if to illustrate the point. This was part of the plan though. There's not much the examiners can ask about Sappho of Lesbos, he had argued, if only a handful of her poems are still extant.

Dan had expected gaps in her corpus of poetry but not quite so many gaps in the poetry itself. Page after page was riddled with missing words, half-lines and truncated stanzas, asterisks littering the verse where the original letters had been lost. Some of the poems actually contained more asterisks than words. This was not going to be as straightforward as he had hoped. His plan was coming unstuck and his dreams, or perhaps his parents' dreams, of a first class degree threatened to float away over the rooftops of Athens.

He stuck a hand up and ruffled his fringe with several vigorous strokes, worried that the shock of hair might conceivably, and embarrassingly, have flattened itself out in the few minutes since he had last enlivened it. He couldn't have looked more like a student if he'd been sitting beside a sign with 'I'm only here for the beer' written on it; the unruly light brown hair with smudges of blonde where he'd squeezed the lemon juice a little too strongly, the faded Smiths T-Shirt which he had washed a dozen times before deciding it looked sufficiently worn-in to warrant actually wearing it. He was a good-looking boy. Or man: he wasn't sure himself. Two weeks earlier, in the queue to get on the plane, it had taken him several moments to realise that the little girl complaining to her mother about the man who had trod on her foot was actually referring to him. He suspected he looked a little more the part at that time than he did now and felt a twinge of regret for the loss of a perfectly good beard which he had painstakingly nurtured right up until the past couple of days. He hadn't grown it to disguise acne or pockmarks – through good fortune, and certainly no other reason, he had managed to avoid that particular teenage plague – but he had always thought a beard made him look older than his years, worldlier somehow. At least he had always thought so until the previous week when a girl at the hostel, Sandy, had told him that patchy fluff and an insubstantial moustache might have made Che Guevara look cool but didn't seem to be having the same effect on him.

Sandy was an interesting character – a committed punk determined not to let the rise of the new romantics steer her away from her chosen path – but, when it came to personal grooming and fashion tips, she was not the most obvious of opinion-formers. With the shaved sides of her head leaving a rather lacklustre dyed-blonde Mohawk in between and with a black vest and trouser combination straight out of the Oxfam winter collection, it would have been entirely understandable for Dan to let her comment wash over him. He could have easily pointed to the various empty beer bottles, already acknowledged as a contributory factor in the thickening of her Yorkshire accent, and highlighted the major part they had clearly played in allowing her suppressed prejudices towards facial hair to bubble to the surface. But he hadn't ignored her words. In fact he had taken them extremely seriously. It was not often that anyone listened to her too closely and even less so that they would actually act on what she said but Dan had shaved his beard off by the next morning. It would be nearly 25 years until he dared put the razor away again for any length of time and then only as a reluctant recruit to a charitable cause.

Rubbing the sharp bristles on his chin and giving his hair one last ruffle, he popped the book back in his rucksack and got up from his seat on the low wall. With a final confirmatory check of the map, he started the climb up to the Acropolis, leaving the jumble of noise and activity in the Plaka increasingly further behind. He had been wandering the hot narrow streets from early that morning, enjoying the attention as waiters vied with souvenir shop owners to claim the drachmas from his pocket. At first he had been amused by their patter – 'everything here is hunky dory' and 'what tickles your fancy, mister?' – and had taken the opportunity to practice the few words of Greek he knew, even purchasing some over-priced ornament in recognition of their charming and innovative sales technique. But when he heard the same pitch from the next four traders, he realised that he had fallen into the sort of trap which even his mother would have managed to sidestep.

Now, as he shuffled up the pathway, he looked down at what were once Italian espadrilles but had degenerated over time into a hideous mutant hybrid of Florentine cloth and Marks and Spencer face towel stitched together on to his feet. He had hoped that they were so bad they were good. But they weren't. They were just bad. Really bad. They granted the street urchins of Monastiraki automatic promotion up to the next rung of the social ladder. In Dan's defence he had no choice in the matter. He was bound by a pledge to his friend Paulo, shoe shop proprietor and supplier of cheap footwear and somewhat less cheap recreational substances to the European backpacking fraternity. During last year's summer holidays, he had sworn not to buy another pair of espadrilles on his travels until he returned to Paulo's shop opposite the Golden Boar in Florence. It was an unusual promise to make but then he was stoned out of his mind at the time. So although he had put his hand in his pocket earlier for a plastic replica of a caryatid, he had steadfastly ignored more legitimate entreaties from the stall-holders to furnish him with a fresh pair of footwear, managing to convert their mock disappointment into genuine and jaw-dropping disbelief.

With the winding path gradually melding the individual voices into a single murmur, the memory of these earlier encounters also subsided and he cautiously congratulated himself on avoiding the more conventional route to the top. His climb up Philopapos Hill the day before had begun as an opportunity to gain a panoramic view over the Acropolis but had quickly turned into a reconnaissance exercise for his own pilgrimage the following day. At first he had thought that the Propylaea, the gates to the Acropolis, were preceded by a twisting avenue of thickly-packed trees, swaying in the breeze, but he soon realised that he was watching a forest of people inching their way upwards from the line of tour buses which had disgorged them below.

Although he couldn't avoid the entire queue, he had bypassed the painfully slow first stretch by taking the route from the Plaka and, as his own path merged with the main trail, he could mark this conquest down as a worthy entry in his little black book, another notch on his well-carved bedpost. One day, he would find organisation and rules liberating rather than constricting but, for now, Dan firmly believed that flair and creativity could only flourish outside the restrictions imposed by channelling contributions towards a collective will. He believed that genius should be allowed to express itself, unfettered by the chains of convention. More importantly, he was ludicrously competitive and, to him, cutting his journey time on the Acropolis run by six minutes was something to highlight on his curriculum vitae. There was no doubt that the tedious pace and prickly heat, which he was now experiencing, would have tested the patience of even the most saintly but it was stepping into line with the tourist hordes which was the real cause of his mounting frustration.

Not that his setbacks were entirely the fault of mindless holidaymakers. They were merely puppets. His true tormentor was the one pulling the strings. Try as he might, he couldn't quite imagine the course of his life being dictated by a Punch and Judy show so he chose to picture his opponent facing him over a chessboard instead. He was very particular about his daydreams – this was life and death stuff after all and he needed to create an environment which would reflect that – but his choice of participants and place was influenced rather too heavily by an over-reliance on sword & sorcery magazines as his staple reading material. As a result, the action would often take place in the middle of a small, cold room at the top of a medieval tower. They would both be seated – his opponent and his own heroic self – on tall granite thrones, hands resting on the heads of stone griffins which struggled in vain to break free from the chair arms. In between them would be a small table on which the chess game was in progress, its ornately-carved pieces, bizarre and fantastic mythological creatures, frozen in combat. His adversary would crouch forward over the playing board, a heavy cloth cowl hanging over his shadowed face and spidery fingers crawling over the stone figures as he pondered his next move. Dan knew him as the personification of what the Ancient Greeks called μοίρα but he preferred to think of him as 'Fate'. This had a lot to do with the sound of the Greek word – it was hard to be intimidated by an opponent called Moira.

The final few steps to the Acropolis ticket booth offered little respite, convincing him that not only was Fate truly the architect of his current misfortune but he was also thoroughly enjoying himself in the process. The young man surveyed the scene and nodded in confirmation. 'It's got his fingerprints all over it,' he murmured. He had already endured the standard 'tour party' ploy in which a group of five or six elderly day-trippers, fresh off the cruise ships, inexplicably forget why they have trooped up to the ticket office in the first place and get increasingly confused by the ticket attendant's insistence that the completion of the transaction depends on them handing over something called 'money'. Next in line was an ex-student, intent on resisting the inevitability of the rat race for a few months longer. His mission was to halve the admission price with the aid of a blatantly-lapsed student union card, the expiry date crudely amended by biro. He had obviously been programmed to argue his innocence for as long as humanly possible, ostensibly to save himself fifty drachmas but with the under-lying benefit of exasperating the people queuing in the baking sun behind him. It was an inventive tactic quite beautifully executed and, even though he was on the receiving end, Dan could not help but appreciate the artistry.

When it was finally his turn he asked for his ticket in impeccable Greek with a casual glance up at the ex-student who was now looking back in begrudging admiration. Unfortunately his accent, albeit with these few carefully-rehearsed words, was also good enough to impress the ticket attendant who decided to engage this fluent-speaking foreigner in a lengthy discussion on the con-tricks exercised by less gracious guests to his country. To the obvious amusement of his disgraced compatriot, Dan's fluent Greek dried up and, with a few mumbled words of English, he pulled the ticket from the grasp of the bemused attendant and rushed, red-faced, past him towards the Propylaea. He could hear Fate's throaty laugh ringing in his ears.

He headed towards the huge gates to the Acropolis, the portal between modern and ancient, transporting the people who passed through them some 2500 years back in time. He had walked up these steps on several occasions already and, every time, he had felt the hairs on the back of his neck stiffen as he climbed up from the gateway and out onto the temple complex itself. It was a mind-blowing experience, judging by the behaviour of many of its visitors. He watched a couple stay barely five minutes before presumably assessing the glimpse of white marble sufficient enough culture to legitimise their headlong dash to Piraeus and the island beaches beyond. Others had no doubt spent so long reading about the centuries-old temples that they rushed around the Acropolis at breakneck speed, terrified in case the buildings should collapse before they managed to see them. For most people, though, knowledge of the Classical ruins came from beautifully-shot photographs in travel brochures and they were determined not to allow reality to spoil this perception. The acknowledged wisdom here seemed to involve avoiding direct eye contact by keeping cameras glued to their faces and then hanging on to their tour guide for dear life as they shuffled from one photo opportunity to the next.

To put some distance between himself and the ticket collector, Dan hurried through the gates today a little more quickly than usual before resuming his own strictly-observed routine. He stopped in front of the Parthenon for several minutes, eager to understand its message but finding it, as always, infuriatingly out of reach. Then he walked briskly to the far edge of the Acropolis, behind the museum, where suddenly the crowds disappeared and Athens spilled out below him. Some cities nestle, some sprawl. With Lycabettos and its neighbouring hills hemming it in, Athens had once settled comfortably between them but, as the city spread further out, the hills became islands in an ocean of buildings and streets. He liked to sit at the very far edge of the Acropolis where the rock jutted out over the city and Athens lay at his feet. When he had first climbed the hill a couple of weeks before, he had seen someone perched on this point like a figurehead on the prow of a ship, proudly facing the brunt of the elements with inspirational defiance. He liked this heroic stance and determined, on subsequent visits, to make the spot his own, sometimes rushing to claim it with such eagerness that he resembled a little boy barging his way to the front seat on the top deck so he could pretend to be the bus driver. Not exactly the image he had in mind.

Today he had been forced to wait several minutes before assuming his rightful place; an outrage which he felt entirely justified the scowl he directed at the portly middle-aged gentleman who finally surrendered his position. With a sigh of relief, he settled down close to the edge and lost himself in melancholic reflections of England and the friends and family over there, no doubt happily continuing their daily lives despite his absence, oblivious to it even. Moments later he was interrupted from his thoughts by a voice behind him.

'Fancy seeing you here.'

He swivelled round and looked up to where the voice originated. The sun was directly in front of him and all he saw for a moment was a halo of light surrounding a shadowy face. In the years to come, if he ever dared to unlock the memories of this particular time – and often he would simply be unable to – this would be the image which haunted him the most; faceless, like some ghostly apparition or dark angel, a chilling portent of what lay ahead.

With his eyes gradually adjusting to the light, the face of a girl began to emerge from the shadows. He took a little while to recognise her. Lara…no, no, Laura. He had met her on the train from Patras the day before. She was on holiday, he was at work; a job thrust upon him by the grateful owner of his hostel as soon as it became clear that he planned on staying put in Athens longer than the usual one or two nights. As one of the 'runners', his daily task was to take the train to Oinoi, the first-stop less than half an hour outside Athens, and meet the Patras train coming into Athens with its cargo of backpackers and students who had transferred out of the ferries from Italy and Corfu. Over the next half an hour, and in competition with the other hostel runners, Dan had to cajole, bully or bribe as many of the backpackers as possible into following him back to his own hostel in the Omonia district. Success came from a combination of laddish banter with the boys and flirting with the girls although, on certain occasions, it seemed to work better the other way around.

His friendly face, however, rarely lasted beyond reception desk back at the hostel. It wasn't because, like some of his fellow runners, he felt that treating new arrivals with casual indifference heightened his own status. Instead he had learned from painful experience that the show he put on in the train would often prove so compelling that he would find himself cornered in the bar all night by an inebriated student who either wanted to arm wrestle him or kiss him or, possibly, both. As a result, his general rule was to steer clear of new arrivals but there was no doubt he would have made an exception for Laura, the girl who stood before him now. She had been on yesterday's train with two friends from Strathclyde. He had instantly liked her, not just because she was pretty – although she undoubtedly was, with long black hair framing a face full of life and expression – but probably because she had seen through his facade so quickly. He had reeled off his usual line about how cleverly they had kept a half-filled cabin to themselves by cunningly disguising their backpacks as fellow passengers and strategically placing them on the otherwise empty seats. She had hardly let him get the well-rehearsed words out of his mouth before holding up a hand to stop him in mid-flow.

'So, let's cut to the chase,' she had said sharply. 'What are you actually trying to sell us?'

For a brief moment, studying her face, he had been

unsure how to react to the stern expression which accompanied such a formal enquiry. But when he noticed the laughter twitching at the corners of her mouth, he knew she was teasing him and he grinned in genuine enjoyment. An intellectual challenge, an opportunity to impress, his professional pride; whatever the motivation, he spent the rest of the journey letting fly a bewildering farrago of unlikely anecdotes, personal insights, genuinely incisive comments and blatant puns. He was too engrossed in his performance to bother about visiting the other carriages but stayed with the three girls until the train pulled into Athens.

So it was with a mixture of astonishment and utter disbelief that, after helping the girls off the train with their backpacks, he watched his Scottish siren persuade her companions to follow their original plan and search out another hostel down in the Plaka area. He was completely lost for words as he listened to their discussions, robbed of his persuasive patter by the unexpected turn of events but, as she set off down the street, he couldn't help but admire the cheeky kiss she blew him. And for her part, although she walked away from him with some regret, the look on his face made it all worthwhile.

'I said fancy seeing you here,' she repeated, 'it's such an unlikely spot to while away the hours in Athens.'

'What, the Acropolis? Yeah, I just sort of came upon it. Don't tell the rest of them.' He pressed his finger to his lips and looked around furtively. 'It can be our secret,' he whispered.

She laughed and sat down next to him. He was dying to find out why she had turned him down but he deliberately avoided the subject, partly as a conscious attempt at regaining the initiative but mainly through fear of what her answer would be. Instead, he pointed out the sights of ancient Athens and talked about the great orators, thinkers and artists whose essence still lingered in the stones around and below them. She enjoyed the passion and enthusiasm with which he brought to life the buildings and sculptures. And, while she relaxed into the easy conversation and listened to the confidence in his voice, she was quietly impressed by his resilience in overcoming her rejection...and slightly disappointed at his apparent indifference.

Eventually he decided to break away from the comfort zone of classical antiquity and venture down potentially more fruitful paths.

'So, have you been to Athens before then?'

It was not a propitious choice of question.

She fixed him with her coldest stare, 'You asked me that on the train yesterday,' she said slowly. 'It was no then and it's still no now.'

He froze for a moment, horrified that he had managed to wreck his chances so early in the exchange. He vaguely remembered his mother warning him that women were fully aware that men didn't listen to them but they just didn't want their noses rubbed in it. At least that's what he thought she had said; the cricket had been on the television at the time.

'Sorry, I know I did. I mean I know it was…' He realised he was digging himself into a hole which he might struggle to clamber out of and took a deep breath instead. 'Look,' he sounded almost confessional, 'I've got this condition you see. I refuse to remember what I've been told, no matter how many times I hear it. I honestly can't help it, it's medical. I'll be asking you the same question in a few days' time.'

She shot him a sideways glance. 'You wish.'

He threw his head back and laughed hard, mainly to

hide his embarrassment but also because he couldn't think of anything to say. He wasn't sure but he reckoned that he might just have got away with it.

'Well at least your train got in during the afternoon. Whenever I travel, I manage to arrive in the middle of the night. It doesn't seem to matter how I'm getting around. Plane, train, bus, it's all the same. This time round, my flight was delayed by seven hours just so I could get in at three in the morning.'

'Your flight?' Laura gave him a look bordering on disgust. 'Serves you right for travelling flash. You wouldn't have had the same problems sitting in third class squalor on the Athens Express like we did.'

'Talking of which, where are your two friends?'

'They're halfway to Mykonos by now. They caught the ferry from Piraeus this morning. I'm joining them later after I've done the sights.' She shook her head disapprovingly. 'They were looking for something a bit more up-to-date on the culture front.'

'Oh yeah, they'll find it there. It's the Ibiza of the Aegean. All disco-dancing and pill-popping.' He shook his head as she offered him a cigarette. 'It's the gay capital of Greece as well. I had to stay there on my own once because it's the only place you can get to ancient Delos from....'

'Or that's your story.'

'....and I sat huddled up in my tent all night, listening to the Best of the Bee Gees blaring out from some disco further down the beach.'

'Frightened you might be tempted out of the closet? God, Danny, it's nineteen *eighty* six, not nineteen *oh* six.'

'No, it was bloody raining. Anyway, it was the Bee Gees for Christ's sake.'

'Well, my friends are a little more liberal-minded than you. They've heard it's this party place and they're going for a week solid on the razz. I couldn't handle the pace for that long so I'm doing the abridged version.' She tilted her head forward and lit the cigarette, shielding the match in cupped hands. 'Anyway, if it's like you say it is, perhaps three's a crowd.'

'So what are you going to do instead?' He tried desperately to sound casual but he knew he had caught his breath as he finished the question.

'I'll spend a couple more days in Athens and then I'll probably do a bit of travelling around the mainland before heading for the islands. Mykonos, Santorini; I don't know, I'll see how it goes.'

Dan knew this was the opening he had been waiting for. He might not always have felt confident enough to take such a chance but he was stirred on by something she had said, something which betrayed her interest in him. She had called him by his name.

'Well, let me help you out with the Athens part of your plans. You've made it up to the Acropolis so far. And that's good. That's very good. Now, have you seen the most stunning building in the world?' He got up and motioned towards the Parthenon behind them.

'Yes, I managed to spot that one on the way in.'

'Ah yes, but did you really *see* it. Did you gaze into its soul? Did you whisper your burning questions and hear history breathe its weighty reply?'

The wind whistled through the stones as if to illustrate his point.

'You're full of shit, aren't you,' she said.

Three

The boy woke with a start. There had been a noise, a crash, as though something had been broken. Not in his bedroom but somewhere else in the house. Or had it just been a dream? He stared into the black night until his eyes adjusted to the gloom and shapes began to emerge from the fog. Out of habit, he pulled the curtain aside and checked whether the mountain towering over his village had begun to glow but it remained as silent and shadowy as it usually did. He was not frightened – he was too old to be scared of the dark – but he was aware that something was wrong. A murmur leaked from the small body next to him as he pulled back the blanket which covered them both.

Slowly he got out of bed, careful not to wake up his little brother, and padded gingerly down the hallway towards his parents' room. He paused at the door. It was already ajar and he was about to push it further open when he heard another crash, definitely from inside, and now raised voices. His fingers flew away from the handle as though burnt and he sank to his knees to peer through the crack in the door. Just a few yards away from where he was crouching, he saw his father and mother standing together by the side of the bed. At first, he thought his parents were hugging and he smiled but then he noticed his father's hand jerk up to his mother's throat and saw the terrified look on her face. His father was shouting, calling her ugly names. 'Puttana.' 'Cagna.' The boy watched in horror as this giant of a man took off his belt, paused and unleashed a sickening blow across the woman's back. She muffled her cry to avoid antagonising him further.

'You want it don't you, whore', he shouted at her, rocking unsteadily on his feet. The boy looked down at the trousers bunched around his father's ankles and assumed they were the cause of his struggle for balance.

'Well? Answer me, bitch.'

His mother was now lying face down on the bed, sobbing but eventually nodding. He saw her lips crack open and mouth a whispered 'yes'.

'What did you say, whore? I didn't hear you.' The man brought his belt down again, this time across the back of her legs.

'Yes, yes,' she cried, her face contorted in pain.

The man grunted his approval and positioned himself behind the woman, pulling off his underpants and fumbling with something hidden from the boy's view. He knew instinctively he shouldn't be watching this but was incapable of moving away. The woman took her hand off the pillow and reached underneath her towards the man.

'Not there, whore. I don't want you giving me another little invalid to bleed me dry.'

The boy winced at his father's words and swallowed hard, misunderstanding the man's reference to his backward brother.

He watched as his father put his hand on the woman's backside and seemed to push hard. The boy stared at his mother's face as she let out a whimper. For the first time, she looked up and saw him. Her eyes pleaded with him not to watch and she gestured to him to leave. But he stayed. He looked across at his father's face, dripping with sweat and leaking spittle on his mother's back. The man's eyes were staring down in front of him as he pushed his hips backwards and forwards. He smiled as he noticed the drops of blood on the sheet.

'Too big for you am I?' He laughed. 'Not anymore, I'm not.'

The boy looked back at his mother who was still staring

at him, gesturing him back to his room. Suddenly, his father groaned and her eyes widened in panic. The boy looked back at the man but his eyes were squeezed shut and his face turned up to the ceiling. He collapsed on the bed. The woman didn't dare move until she heard the steady snoring. She looked to the door but the eyes were no longer there. She softly slid off the bed, wincing in pain as she got to her feet, and quietly made her way to her sons' bedroom. The boy pretended to be asleep. She sat with him for several minutes, stroking his hair, until eventually she headed back to her husband in the room next door.

Four

If she flees, soon she will pursue you
And if she refuses your gifts, in time she will become the giver
And if, for now, she shows you no love
Soon she will love you, even despite herself

For the rest of the day Dan became Laura's tour guide. He was helpful, interesting and erudite but, above all, an outrageous show off. She saw how lightly the Parthenon's roof (or what was left of it) sat on its forest of columns and noted how perfectly proportioned the building seemed to be. He pointed out that there was hardly a straight line in the temple and that the lightweight pediment and perfect proportions were optical illusions caused by intentionally-bulging columns and floors. She admired the creamy white marble of the facade and he told her that the whole building was originally painted a kaleidoscope of reds, blues and yellows. She decried Elgin's theft of the marbles at the same time as he praised the British Museum for its conservation work. For every pile of stones she spotted, he saw a masterpiece.

'Do you have to disagree with everything I say?' she asked in exasperation.

He took a swipe at a small pebble in front of his feet. This did nothing to ingratiate him with Laura as the stone bounced off the tongue of her sandshoe. 'And do you really need to do that?'

He shrugged his shoulders, 'I'm a boy, it's my job.'

And though she tutted disapprovingly, he noticed the slight smile she gave him and felt sure he was making some progress.

They walked down from the Acropolis and he led her through the Agora, the ancient marketplace of classical

Athens.

'This would've been like the Kings Road on a Saturday morning. The place to be. Loads of wannabes parading up and down, toadying to the rich and famous. Aristotle would be the A-lister, the one everyone wanted to talk to…or at least be seen talking to. He'd be seated here,' Dan patted the statue base next to them, 'immaculately turned out in designer toga and Gucci sandals, stroking that cool grey beard of his. Very "in" that would have been at the time.'

Rubbing his chin with a thoughtful expression on his face made him look more like Jimmy Hill than one of the world's greatest philosophers and Laura laughed out loud. She watched in amusement as he steered his way between competing tour groups and parked himself by one of the many columns lying prone on the ground, the discs carefully arranged to give the impression that it had only recently toppled over.

'And Socrates,' he shouted, loudly enough for both tour parties to turn their collective heads in unison and see what they were missing, 'he'd be over here.'

Dan pointed extravagantly at the fluted shaft he was now standing on. Laura came running over, still laughing but urging him to keep his voice down.

'Now Socrates was the one you'd want to avoid,' he went on, a little more quietly this time. 'A notorious drunkard. Bottle of nectar in a brown paper bag clutched tight to his chest. Mark my words,' Dan wagged his finger at her, 'he'll drink himself to death one day.'

Laura groaned and rolled her eyes but Dan was off again.

'See this dent here?' He pointed at a depression in the ground. 'This was the site of one of the most exclusive addresses in Athens.'

'Go on, then.' Her arms were folded in front of her now

33

and she wore an expression of weary resignation. 'Tell me who lived here. Whose house was it?'

'Not a house,' he grinned at her, 'a wine jar. A massive one. It was owned by some property developer, Diogenes, and he'd had it stylishly converted. All the mod-cons.

He wafted his hand in front of his face. 'Perhaps not so strong on the ventilation though,' he muttered and staggered from the site, eyes bulging from the finger and thumb pinched over the end of his nose. Laura took off after him, swearing to sack him as her tour guide and replace him with a proper one. 'And one with a bloody flag as well,' she shouted.

Moments later they found themselves in front of the Temple of Hephaestus, the Theseion. The difference between this black, ponderous building and the Parthenon above was remarkable. Laura was glad for the picket fence which stopped her getting inside the temple because she was terrified that the roof would cave in at any minute, it weighed so heavily on its squat stone supports. Dan could hardly contain himself,

'Look at the columns and the floor, the roof. Look at the lines, they're all straight, they're absolutely dead straight. So you can see the effect on us, the viewer: we think the columns bulge and the roof sags. With the Parthenon, the columns really *do* bulge and the roof's nowhere near straight but, to the eye, it looks perfect. Marble as light as a feather. It's brilliant, isn't it?'

She thought about making another facetious remark but, seeing his boyish enthusiasm and keenness to please, she simply nodded in agreement. He smiled at her and she felt herself smiling back, genuinely and freely, before a flash of self-consciousness twisted her mouth into a sarcastic smirk. Nonetheless, she hooked her arm through his and let him lead her away from the Agora.

They spent the rest of the afternoon wandering round the shops and stalls in Monastiraki.

'What are you looking for?' Dan had asked early on.

'You'll see,' she had said, grabbing hold of his hand and hauling him into one of the nearby shops.

'I'm not going to continue walking around with someone wearing those on their feet for one minute longer,' she had announced, pointing an offending finger at the unholy marriage of face towel and Florentine cloth. 'I mean that style is just *so* passé, darling.'

Despite his protestations about pledges sealed in blood and the hideous tortures which Italians inflicted on those who broke their sacred bond, his opposition was never more than half-hearted. Paulo or Laura? The mob or the moll? It was not one of life's tougher decisions.

So an hour later there he was, surreptitiously trying to scuff his new espadrilles and tone down the bright orange with a modest layer of street dust. And she, for her part, was the proud owner of a heavy plastic statuette of 3 monkeys in the 'see no evil, hear no evil, speak no evil' pose. He had also brushed protestations aside to buy it for her but, unlike his much-needed footwear, she had no intention of holding on to something so breathtakingly ugly any longer than necessary and, by next morning, the monkeys were seeing, hearing and speaking no evil from the mantelpiece of the owner of Hostel Orestes where Laura was staying.

As the last of the sun's rays slipped off the Acropolis, they negotiated Athens' narrow back streets and headed for her pension in the heart of the Plaka. Dan had noticed on previous wanderings that most of the myths and legends of ancient Greece could be played out by taking a stroll around the tourist routes and noting the names of hotels and restaurants along the way, names which systematically spelled out epic tales and tragic stories. He treated it as a form of revision. In the street where the Hostel Orestes stood, the establishments told the story of the House of Atreus. All the classical Greek playwrights had covered this one and he paid particular attention to the places they passed, muttering the names under his breath. Unnerved by his slightly odd behaviour Laura asked him what he was doing. 'It's on the reading list' he replied in such a matter-of-fact manner that she felt certain it was her own fault she hadn't been able to grasp his meaning.

Dan knew that only after every Clytemnestra, Agamemnon and Mycenae had been used up would reluctant restaurateurs and hoteliers further down the road be forced to fall back on more everyday names from the Greek pantheon – the Aphrodites and Athenas. This was a long street but the Atreid was an even longer story and, despite a lengthy walk, the two of them reached their destination well before the drama of the final act.

For one brief moment, Dan had considered heading back to his own pension in the Omonia district to check the schedule for the next day. Years later he would remember how casually he had rejected the suggestion. 'What's the worst that could happen?' he had muttered under his breath.

As soon as they had mounted the steps to the reception, the young man behind the desk got up and made towards them.

'Daniel, my friend, how goes it?'

Dan grinned at the advancing figure, 'Pedro. Bloody hell, so this is where you ended up!'

They embraced and clasped hands in what Dan, with one eye on Laura, hoped looked cool and street-wise.

'It's going well, mate.' Dan carried on, 'Bit tougher on the trains though, now that the has-beens have moved on to desk jobs and your old pension's hired some decent runners at last.'

Pedro smiled and rubbed his fingers together in way of explanation. He had arrived from Lisbon six months previously and had comfortably become regarded as Omonia's best runner. In the short time he had been competing against Dan, he recognised him as a creditable opponent and perhaps even a friend (or the closest that travellers' transitory relationships came to friendship) and Dan's stock with the other runners had risen accordingly. Pedro was larger than life. The respect he inspired in others verged on hero-worship, generating a vast number of 'Adventures of ...' tales which variously depicted him as swashbuckling buccaneer, irresistible charmer or brazen womaniser. Some of these stories were apocryphal, some not. He was widely rumoured, on more than one occasion, to have marched an entire train-load of backpackers past open-mouthed and empty-handed rival runners for whose benefit he would conduct his multi-national troop in a series of chants, American marine style, praising his own pension and pouring scorn on theirs. Dan had only once come off the train empty-handed (and Laura could take full credit for that failure) and so had never been forced to face the full ignominy of a Pedro onslaught. Not that he had managed to escape entirely unscathed. On only his second day in the job, he had escorted a modest contingent of backpackers up towards Hostel Diana only to be overtaken by a horde of European and North American rucksacks obediently singing along to 'You know where the sad guys are, *You know where the sad guys are,* At Diana's in the bar, *At Diana's in the bar.'* By the time he had reached his pension he had lost half his followers to the chanting pack.

'You know Laura don't you, Ped?'

Laura reached for her room keys, 'Oh he should do, I

was one of his groupies in the bar last night. He gave us an evening of Fado music.' She adjusted her skirt which had ridden up as she collected her keys from the shelf. 'Now if you gentlemen will excuse me, I'm going to have a shower. See you in the bar.' And with that she turned on her heel and disappeared up the stairs which twisted towards the upper floors.

Dan and Pedro turned their heads, following her up the steps. As soon as she was out of sight, they snapped back to look at each other, broad grins on their faces,

'I've been with her all bloody day,' said Dan, 'and not a sniff. She's probably a lesbian.'

'Ah, I'm afraid not, my friend. She got through plenty of Amstel last night and the last time I saw her she was heading upstairs with some Italian guy.'

Dan wasn't sure how to take this news. The genuine pang of jealousy was slightly mollified by a realisation that she *was* up for it if circumstances were right (she was dead drunk and he was close by at the time). All he needed to do was to keep a clear head himself. How difficult could that be?

Pedro led the way down to the basement bar and sat down at a table which had just been vacated, seemingly on his behalf. He nodded almost imperceptibly to a young boy in the corner of the room and two bottles of beer were immediately set down in front of them. Dan was barely able to disguise his admiration. Whilst he wouldn't admit it, he was grateful that someone as impressive as Pedro should consider him a friend. The man seemed to have met everyone, been everywhere and tried his hand at just about everything. All he needed for a full set was sand-boarding in the Sahara and beef bashing in the cow fields of England. A little too trusting by nature, Dan was often susceptible to a tall story persuasively told but there seemed little doubt that

Pedro had actually experienced pretty much all the things he claimed to have done.

By popular consensus, this young man was the coolest backpacker in Athens. And Dan was with him having a drink.

He and Pedro were already on to their second by the time Laura came down to the bar. She had scraped her hair back and clipped it near the nape of her neck, leaving the soft lines of skin exposed. Gone were the workmanlike T-Shirt and skirt to be replaced by a figure-hugging dress which left even less to the imagination at the bottom than it did at the top. Not that either of her two companions were complaining; she looked gorgeous. Dan wanted to compliment her, to tell her how fantastic she looked, but he couldn't find words which didn't sound either patronising or desperate.

'Hi,' he finally blurted out, 'grab a beer.'

Pedro was not constrained by such delicate social etiquette, 'Bellissima, your beauty would make even Apollo turn his head.'

Dan looked at Laura, certain that she would scoff at such an obvious chat-up line but instead she glowed at Pedro's words.

'Well thank you, kind sir. And they say good manners are dead.'

Dan couldn't believe it. How on earth had he got away with that? She had fallen for a line straight out of a Valentine's card; puppies, roses and all. The glare he gave Pedro was so fierce that, if looks could kill, he would have emptied both barrels into his Portuguese rival's chest.

Realising the effect his flirting was having on his hot-headed friend, Pedro spent the next hour turning the charm on every now and then just to watch Dan's temperature rise. He even mentioned it to Laura while their mate was getting a round in at the bar and she began to play up to his advances much to Dan's undisguised disgust. But, before the evening was soured by bitter words, Pedro drained his glass and announced a prior engagement which he was loath to break.

'Bring her back here, Ped, we're just getting started.' Dan spoke his words through gritted teeth but Pedro's refusal was polite yet firm. As he was walking away, Dan ran up to him, 'Honest, mate, you don't need to leave to make it easier for me,' he whispered. 'Stay and have a few more beers…..as long as you keep your hands off.'

Pedro laughed, 'Sorry, my friend, you're just not my type.'

This was true. Pedro's type was the young Swedish sailor who was currently waiting for him in Syntagma Square.

Five

He is as lucky as the gods, the man who sits opposite you,
so close to you listening to your sweet voice
and lovely laughter, everything which makes
my heart beat heavily in my chest

Dan turned back to the table with a shrug of his shoulders.

'He says we're so boring that he's had to go off and watch a bit of paint-drying before he fell asleep.'

Laura folded her arms and leant back on the chair. 'Well, you'll have to entertain me then or I'll most likely do the same thing.'

Dan feigned a reluctant sigh, 'Look, Laura, I wasn't going to tell you this but Ped actually said it was *you* who were boring him and that, despite my scintillating wit, he couldn't bear your tedious Scottish droning for one more minute. To be honest, I don't even think he could understand you. Sorry, but you need to know this. It probably explains why blokes fall asleep on you.'

That cold stare made a temporary return. 'No one,' she leaned forward to within inches of Dan's face, so close that he was sure she was going to kiss him, 'but no one….has ever fallen asleep *on* me.' She fell back into her chair with a slight smirk, the emphasis leaving little doubt to what she was referring. 'But be warned, the reverse has been known.'

'What,' he looked at her quizzically, 'they fall asleep under you?'

She laughed and let him win this particular rally, choosing to press on with her original line of attack and disappointed that he didn't seem to pick up from her final comment that the warning could easily apply to him.

'Well, boring or not, that paint-drying's going to become mighty appealing unless you get a bit more interesting.'

Dan considered his options. He could embark on some fresh, original topic of conversation and let it lead him down whichever path it happened to take. This was the high risk strategy. There were plenty of dead ends and blind alleys in the city of unrehearsed soliloquies. Otherwise he could fall back on the easier option of tried and tested anecdotes, stories of previous adventures grown tall in the retelling. It was no contest. He was a backpacker and travellers' tales were part of the job description.

'Ooookay....' The pause was purely to give the impression of an impending off-the-cuff anecdote. Instead he did the storytelling equivalent of pressing the play button on the tape recorder. 'I did some travelling in my gap year between school and University. I was making my way through Egypt with my girlfriend, Nikki. We'd spent a few days in Cairo before embarking on the slowest, longest train journey in the whole of bloody Africa to get down to Aswan where, incidentally, I got Montezuma's revenge five minutes into a three hour taxi ride to the temple at Abu Simbel.'

'Poor girlfriend.'

'At least she knew me. It was the two Australian nurses sharing the taxi I felt sorry for.'

He paused to think back and remembered that, in reality, they were not exactly sympathetic to his plight and he actually had no reason to feel sorry for them at all. Laura had only been half-listening anyway as she prised open a particularly stubborn packet of crisps so he didn't bother correcting himself.

'Anyway, we'd eventually made our way back up to Luxor, getting up at the ungodly hour of four o'clock in the morning to cycle round the Valley of the Kings and the rest of the sites.'

Laura looked at him, a little non-plussed.

'You went by bicycle? In that heat? What was wrong with a taxi?'

He gave her an exaggerated wink, 'Nikki liked me hot and sweaty.'

'Oh yes. And I suppose she didn't have the fondest memories of the last taxi ride she took with you.'

He gave her a sarcastic smile. 'Anyway, the plan was to make our way across to the Sinai peninsula for me to finish off my scuba diving qualification in the Red Sea. Nikki already had hers so we'd only three days to complete the course before our flight back to the UK. We took a bus across to Hurghada on the coast where we'd been told we could get a boat to Sharm-el-Sheikh in the Sinai. As soon as we got off the bus, a young lad latched on to us and hung around for the rest of the day. A hotel? He knew the best in town. A boat to the Sinai? He could get us tickets before dinner. And, yes, he knew the best place to eat as well. It took us hours to shake him off but we finally got rid of him and sorted out hotel, dinner and boat tickets all on our own. Well, things couldn't have gone much worse. By the time we settled down to bed that night, Nikki had got food poisoning from the restaurant we'd found and my camera had been nicked from our hotel room while we were out. At least – and I can honestly remember us actually saying this – we could comfort ourselves that we'd got a relaxing, leisurely cruise arranged for the next day.'

She smiled sympathetically, 'You'd forgotten that bad luck always comes in threes, had you?'

'Nope' replied Dan, 'we'd remembered that.' He took a deep intake of breath. 'But we thought that getting stuck with that street urchin was the first setback and we only had two more to worry about after that.'

'Yep, thank God you got away from him. You wouldn't have been able to enjoy the character-building experiences of losing your camera and most of your stomach lining otherwise. And what would have happened if you'd followed his recommendations then? I suppose you'd have been forced to put up with a gourmet meal and four-poster bed?'

'Dunno. Probably. We never came across his hotel and restaurant – although they couldn't have been any worse than our own choices – but we found out later that the kid's boat had made the crossing in three hours and arrived bang on schedule.'

'I take it that you didn't get there quite as quickly?'

'Not quite.' Dan heaved another deep sigh. 'Actually, we didn't get there at all.'

He waited patiently as Laura dissolved into a fit of giggles which seemed to last forever. In the end, her laughter proved so infectious that he couldn't help joining in himself. He finally managed to continue his story at the third attempt by looking away from his companion as she sat rocking back and forth, her hand clamped tightly over her mouth to stop it exploding.

'We finally got on to our boat two hours after it should have sailed. This was because the Harbour Master spent an hour with his hand on my girlfriend's bum and another half an hour fondling mine. There were fifteen of us travelling on the boat; two New Zealanders who we spent some time with later and then two British couples who looked like an outing from a leper colony. All four of them had come down with some weird flesh-eating disease which put my own condition into its proper perspective. And finally there was a whole group of Asians, the Hong Kong Seven, who'd somehow got detached from their tour party and were now roughing it with the backpackers. I don't think they quite knew what had hit them.

After a couple more hours on a stationary boat we started to get a mite suspicious that not all was going to plan. This being Egypt after all, none of the 'any minute nows' from the crew inspired much confidence. After another hour, it was full-scale mutiny. Me and Nikki were the self-appointed ringleaders. Off we went to confront the captain. Well, yes, there was a slight engine problem, he admitted, but his engineers (by which he meant his two nephews who wouldn't know a boat engine from a bloody fire engine) were close to fixing it as we spoke. Yeah, sure.

We didn't feel too confident but, ten minutes later, the engines started up and the ship moved off in the general direction of the Sinai Peninsula. I don't know who was more surprised, us or the captain.'

'Too good to be true?'

'That would be a bit of an under-statement. Less than ten minutes after we'd got going, there was this almighty explosion from below deck and smoke started pouring out of the main hatch. The boat lurched to one side and we all went flying.'

'Christ, you're joking. Really?' She stared at him until his nodding convinced her. 'Wow, that's unbelievable. What did you do?'

'Panic, generally, and scream. Yes, screaming and panicking seemed the most appropriate course of action. Most of us jumped over the side into the water. It wasn't the Titanic or anything but we still didn't want to get sucked underneath as it sank. As it was, the boat proved pretty resilient and didn't seem in much of a hurry to nosedive down to the seabed. We must have looked pretty stupid after a while, gasping for air and desperately treading water to keep afloat, while the crew stood up on deck in the dry, casually waving to their mates back in the harbour.'

'You hadn't got very far then?'

Dan looked a little sheepish.

'Well, not exactly. In fact we'd hardly left the port. I had half a mind to try and get back on board but within a few minutes another boat appeared alongside to rescue us. Well I say rescue *us*. It seemed pretty clear after a while that he was more concerned with saving his mate's boat. Saving us was a bit incidental.'

'Was everyone OK?'

'I think so. It was hard to tell with the Brits – they looked like the sharks had been at them *before* they jumped in the water. There weren't any blankets on-board so we sat huddled together with towels around us, as if we were just drying ourselves down from a pleasant dip. After a few futile attempts at towing the other boat back into harbour, they finally dumped us back on shore and set out again in a bigger ship. The last I saw of our skipper was him handing over our ticket money to the owner of this tug and threatening to feed one of his nephews to the fish. And off he went, no apology, no "cheerio and good luck". We ended up forking out another king's ransom to take half of Hurghada's taxi rank up north along the Egyptian coast, across the Suez canal and down to the tip of the Sinai Peninsula that way.'

'Oh, comfortable. And did you manage OK this time?'

'Yep…besides a couple of sandstorms, the early closure of the Suez crossing and a detour via Dahab. Oh and the taxis playing chicken with each other round hairpin bends. Apart from that it was all plain sailing really.' He smiled at the irony. 'Exactly what the boat trip should have been.'

He looked at Laura for her reaction. She seemed suitably impressed with his storytelling and leant forward to clink their beer bottles together as if to tell him so. He was relieved to get her approval. He had been worried that he wouldn't be able to remember the story that well, especially since there was only a modicum of truth in it, but these were traveller's tales and veracity was hardly the number one concern.

A song erupted from the sound system, the volume suddenly turned up from the quiet background hum of before, and the whole bar seemed to jump up in unison. Dan glanced nervously towards Laura but she was already on her feet, arms above her head and hips swaying in time to the beat. He knew he was a crap dancer but he also realised that he had little choice. If he had remained in his seat, he would have been the only one in the bar to do so. He got up, kicked back his chair and, with pumping elbows clearing his path, began to slide over towards Laura.

He didn't know the song but, embarrassingly, he seemed to be in the minority. All he could hear above the cheering, on the record as well as in the bar, was the crack of a guitar chord like a drumbeat and he understood straightaway why everyone liked it. Most importantly, Laura obviously loved it.

He watched as she danced, so languidly and effortlessly. Even his own efforts improved by following her rhythm. He couldn't believe his luck. She was wonderful. He had made a few friends in his first week, Pedro notable among them, but none of them made him feel as alive as she did. He desperately wanted to grab hold of her and pull her towards him, or simply just to hold her hand, but he was terrified that she would reject him and so bring their time together to an abrupt end. That would be unbearable.

He tried listening to the words. With everyone joining in loudly but not quite simultaneously, they were difficult to make out. They sounded French and he briefly thought he was listening to that summer's Euro hit but the song sounded too good for such short-lived fame. He began to relax and enjoy the dancing until, noticing Laura looking at him, he became a little self-conscious again. Not enough alcohol yet he thought. The end of the song came with a mixture of disappointment and relief and they sat down again along with the rest of the bar who clearly felt that one good dance tune was quite sufficient for one evening. Even the volume was turned back down again.

They looked at each other and laughed. It really did seem like the crowd's reaction had been carefully choreographed.

He leaned towards her. 'What's it called again, that song?'

He couldn't quite hear her reply, or at least he hoped he hadn't because it didn't sound too complimentary. He asked her again.

'Psycho Killer,' she said more loudly, a frown creasing her brow.

His slow and sagely nod of confirmation seemed to suggest that either he had suffered a brief mental block or that she had passed his musical trivia test but in reality he was none the wiser…..although when he returned to college for the new term, it was a song he wouldn't be able to avoid hearing, always bringing back the memory of a cellar bar in Athens and a beautiful dark-haired girl.

'Anyway, Laura, now it's your turn. Entertain *me*.'

'Oh, a half-decent bedtime story and you're getting all cocky are you? OK then, smartarse,' she thought for a little, 'ok then, three weeks ago we were staying in Venice at a friend's flat on the Grand Canal….'

Dan burst out with indignation, 'You were staying where?'

Laura smiled. She'd taken the location for granted while she was there but her companion's reaction had brought home the exclusivity of the address.

'This friend of ours, his dad is chairman of some huge multi-national. One of his properties, only one of them mind, happens to be a flat directly over-looking the Grand Canal. Works of art on the walls, the latest TV and Hi-Fi systems, instructions still in the cooker and a washing machine unsoiled by anything as downmarket as dirty laundry. He used to send his maid out to collect his meals and sort out the service wash. Well, the three of us turned up to see him and so did a few other friends who'd been travelling around Italy. We had a ball; MTV on full blast constantly, drinking ourselves stupid, constantly. At one stage, all of us were leaning out of the window, chucking up into the Grand Canal at the same time. And Franco, our friend who owned the flat, was hilarious. He disconnected his phone to stop his parents checking up on him and banished his maid for the week by greeting her at the door with nothing on but a floppy white hat. He also decided to allocate jobs to all his guests. The girls were to do the washing, cooking and cleaning while the boys were in charge of watching telly, operating the remote control and cleaning up the beer.'

'Sounds fair enough to me: play to the appropriate strengths.'

'Hmmmm, well we got our own back. We washed his ciabatta and pasta in Fairy Liquid and cooked his underpants in olive oil. He didn't give us any more jobs after that.'

Dan was sceptical about this last claim but felt that he wasn't on the firmest of footings to make a comment and so wisely kept his own counsel.

'Anyway, one morning, there was a loud banging at the front door. Seconds later, armed police came bursting in. They pulled us out of our beds and herded us into the lounge. We didn't know what on earth was going on. They kept on prodding us with their guns and firing questions at us. Franco was the only one who could speak Italian and he was nowhere to be seen so they must have thought the rest of us were being deliberately obstructive. They searched the apartment inside out as we got more and more paranoid about Franco's role in all this. At first we thought he'd simply gone out to the shops but, as time went by, we grew suspicious that the police raid was his idea of a practical joke. After a few more minutes though, someone came up with the worryingly plausible theory that his bloated body had been pulled out of the canal at dawn and one or all of us would be spending the rest of our lives in an Italian jail as a result.'

It was Dan's turn to express his amazement.

'What, Midnight Express all over again?'

'Yes, Italian-style. Better-dressed prison guards and all that. But, I tell you, if they had been half as inept as the police, we'd have escaped in two minutes flat. You see they eventually found Franco. Not dead, not even close….unless you count a bad hangover (which I do). No, he was very much alive and in the flat all along. He'd locked himself in the toilet the night before and had fallen asleep in there. And this crack police search team had taken nearly half an hour to discover his ingenious hiding place. No wonder the mafia are Italian.'

Dan had only just put the bottle to his lips but, at this final comment, he stopped in mid-flow as he rewound her words to check whether they made any better sense second time round. He concluded that they didn't but, by that time, she was already pushing ahead with her story.

'Anyway after he'd explained a bit about who we were and what we were doing, the police eventually calmed down a little and ordered us to get dressed. We were frog-marched down to the station, past all these cafes of people-watchers who clearly thought their hours of nosiness had finally paid off.

They interviewed each of us separately and it became obvious after a while that there was some senior politician in the flat below who had got convinced that a bunch of terrorists upstairs were planning an assassination attempt on his life. Quite how playing loud music and throwing up out of the window constituted planning a covert attack I'm not entirely sure. I suppose the police had to be seen to be taking it seriously though, so they sped over in search of our hidden arms cache. If it had taken them half an hour to find a bloke asleep in a toilet, I doubt they'd have found an arms cache if it had been laid out on the hall table by the front door with a big sign saying "WEAPONS" propped next to it. To be fair to them, when they finally realised we were just a bunch of innocent students, they had a great laugh about the whole thing. In fact one of them even had the cheek to chat me up and ask me out.'

'Did you say yes?'

'A free dinner? Of course. What sort of mug do you think I am?'

She sat back in the chair and took a swig of her beer, looking at her companion for a reaction. With the alcohol starting to take effect, Dan's response was a little more exuberant than it might otherwise have been.

'These stories would make a great book,' he announced with the hint of a slur.

Her frown betrayed some slight scepticism which only served to spur him on.

'I'll get them published. Mark my words. I'll rope Pedro in as well. Between the three of us, we'd easily fill a few chapters.' He grinned at Laura. 'The rest we'll just make up.'

He spent the next few minutes championing the virtues

of independent travel and emphasising the character-building nature of experiences like theirs. The beer was starting to have an effect on Laura as well and she joined in enthusiastically.

'That was a mad few days in Italy, for sure, but you've got to grab whatever opportunities life throws up and see where they take you. Carpe Diem, boy, that's my motto. Who knows what tomorrow's going to bring? If I ever have the option of doing something positive or sitting on my backside as the safer option, I'll always think, "Fuck it" and go for it. No compromise, no surrender. No easy life. I've never sat by the phone and thought, "Shouldn't I wait and see if he rings *me*?".'

'So I'll expect a call then, shall I?' He caught his breath as he waited for her reply, unable to play down the importance he'd already attached to her response.

She raised an eyebrow to look up at him, 'Yes, even you'd get a call,' she smiled.

And as he sat facing her in this Athenian pension, he imagined the phone ringing in his study at Cambridge and her soft Scottish voice saying, 'Told you I'd ring.' But, although they would swap telephone numbers later in the trip, she would never ring and every now and then he would come across her number in his address book but decide against using it. If he had have done, he would have found out that she had been killed in a moped accident on Santorini just a few days after she had left him to head off to the Islands.

He gestured at the bar, 'Another beer?'

'Hell, why not live a little' she replied and skulled the final few mouthfuls from the bottle.

Six

She half-smiled with satisfaction as the last smear of crusted food finally yielded to the energetic wipes of her cloth and disappeared down the plughole. She rinsed the pot and placed it upside down in the sink to mark the completion of her task.

The welts across her back and legs still stung with pain when her clothes caught them but she accepted her punishment as a reminder of her failure. As a mother, probably as a wife as well.

Her youngest son, Tommaso, sat by her feet, rocking to and fro and murmuring the same words over and over again. She bent down and put her hand to his chin, nudging his face to look up at hers.

The child avoided his mother's eyes and put his head back down to stare at the floor. She knew that something was not quite right, a loose connection, some missing wiring. She saw how her husband looked at their son. She read the shame and disgust in his face and later she bore the brunt of his anger.

The nursery teachers said that he didn't do as he was told, that he was disobedient; either a disruptive influence or else away with the fairies. But she knew he couldn't help it. Looking after him was a constant chore and one with little obvious reward. But it was not his fault.

'You're not a bad boy are you?' He looked at her blankly. 'You love your mother don't you?'

She sighed as he settled back into his rocking motion and she crossed to the window. The street below typical of Naples at that time, clogged with uncollected rubbish from yet another dispute, the foul vapour arcing its way up and tangling itself with the clean washing strung out between adjacent houses above.

She saw her elder son walking up the street with the young girl from two doors down. She was just about to call out to him, to tell him to hurry up for tea, when she saw that there was something not quite right. They were exchanging angry words and now her son was shouting at the girl. His companion was visibly frightened and was looking around anxiously. The woman caught her breath and watched helplessly as the boy pushed his companion away from him. The girl stumbled to the floor, shocked and disorientated. She tried to get up but the boy was standing over her with his foot on her chest, preventing her from moving.

'You whore, you bitch,' he spat out the words. 'Come on, fight back, you whore bitch.'

The girl couldn't understand what he was saying or why. She mumbled that she didn't want to fight.

'Too big for you am I?' he screamed at her.

And his mother buried her head in her hands and began to cry. Not yet seven years old and she knew she had lost him already.

Seven

For, as soon as I look at you, even for a moment,
I no longer have the power to speak, my tongue stops working
Straightaway, a subtle flame steals beneath my flesh,
With my eyes I see nothing, my ears are humming,
I'm in the grip of a clammy sweat, trembling seizes me all over,
I am paler than grass and seem to be not far short of death

The sun was already bright and hot by the time he woke up. He lay still for some time, requesting a status report from every organ, limb and nerve ending. He only stirred when he was totally reassured that, despite a thudding in his temples, no lasting damage had been done. He tried to look around and find his bearings but his puffed-up eyes refused to open onto the stinging sunlight. Finally, by sitting up and looking down and away from the light, he managed to work out that he had spent the night on the hostel roof. He slumped back onto the thin padding of his nylon sleeping bag, the material already uncomfortably hot from the morning sun, and tried to cast his mind back to the previous evening.

His headache allowed only snatches of memory to surface. Pedro had left, early. And then what? They'd chatted and drunk and told each other anecdotes. And then, oh shit, he'd got into a fight. He was sure he had. But had they ended up in bed together? Again he looked around at his immediate surroundings but there was no apparent evidence pointing to such a successful conclusion to the evening. He gazed down at his tatty sleeping bag. His faithful companion had seen better days and, even through the haze of his hangover, he was capable of working out that it didn't represent a particularly alluring option. Not for a girl like Laura.

He decided to get dressed and go down into the hostel to look for her. This was not a lengthy process as he hadn't actually managed to get out of his clothes the night before but it still took him several minutes to find his shoes. He was beginning to worry how he would explain to Laura that he had mislaid the new espadrilles she had bought him until finally, lifting up his sleeping bag, he realised that he had slept on top of them all night. He took some comfort from the fact that at least they looked a little more worn-in than they had the day before.

It was the third consecutive day he had worn the same clothes and he recognised the feat with a congratulatory grunt of approval. He shuffled unsteadily towards the stairs and paused at the doorway to murmur hello to the Scandinavian couple playing cards on the ground nearby. Their strangely-muted response made him think that he had confused them with his use of the colloquial Greek 'yas' as a greeting but, halfway down the stairs, it occurred to him that he might not be looking his best that morning. After diving into the toilets, it only took a quick glance in the mirror to understand what his fellow roof-mates had found so unnerving. He looked dreadful. It took several splashes of water to his face and a vigorous towelling to his hair to render him anything like presentable. He still looked pretty awful but he resigned himself to the fact that he'd reached his maximum level of improvement.

He trudged down the final few steps into the breakfast bar where Laura was sitting in front of a plate of omelette and chips. Stopping at the doorway, he watched her for a few moments. Although she was eating on her own, she was sharing conversations with several other tables. Even with his hangover, he couldn't help but admire how enjoyable she made it for other people to talk to her. She laughed at their jokes, encouraged them if their English faltered or they ran out of conversation and smiled so brightly it was impossible not to smile back. He looked at the people she was speaking with and watched as, one by one, they fell in love with her.

Finally he stepped into the room. 'Hello,' he muttered, 'how are you then?'

She looked up at him, fork poised midway between plate and mouth, 'My hero!' she grinned and settled back to her breakfast.

Good God, he thought, what the hell did that mean? The sex? The fight? He couldn't exactly ask her and the wave of nausea which just hit him suggested that now was not the best moment to try. He groaned slightly and put a hand to his mouth.

'What did you say?' she looked up at him again.

'Just going to the loo,' he replied and headed for the door.

By the time he returned she had finished her breakfast and was gingerly sipping at a hot cup of coffee like a bird pecking at a worm.

'Not too hungover then?' he ventured.

'Not too bad. You sobered me up pretty quickly after all.'

It must have been the sex.

'Were you OK about it?' He tried to adopt the new man approach, concerned yet casual.

'Well it wasn't too enjoyable at the time but I'm glad you did it.'

Damn, please let it be the fight.

'How did it all finish up?'

'Don't you remember? They chucked him out of the hostel and carted you up to the roof. Apparently you turned into Larry the Lamb and curled up asleep in no time.'

His spirits sank and he realised that he would rather it

had been the sex even if she hadn't enjoyed it.

'Who was he then?'

'Oh some jilted Italian lover. You know how it is.'

'Not really but I can try and imagine. Who won anyway?'

'Well, to be fair you were probably coming off second best but you know what Italians are like in fights – he suddenly couldn't decide which side he was on and started punching himself.'

'Very funny, Laura. You just carry on taking the piss while I come to terms with my impending brain haemorrhage. I'd hate to spoil your day by collapsing into a coma on you.'

'Well, I wouldn't get too worried. Neither of you looked capable of doing each other any serious injury. In fact the best punch you threw was at the end when the barman pinned the bloke's arms by his side.'

Dan puffed his chest out proudly. Laura looked at him, clearly unimpressed.

'He was only trying to break up the fight for God's sake.'

Dan was undeterred, 'A clever move on my part and entirely within the Queensbury rules, I think you'll find.'

'That may be but they were ready to throw both of you out until I stepped in. I told them that Antonio was the creep who'd been bothering me the night before and had a problem with girls who said no. You were purely coming to my rescue as any English gentleman would do.'

'Did they believe you?'

'Course they did, I'm very believable. Racial stereotypes aside, it's not a million miles from the truth. He's not a bad guy but he's definitely got anger management issues. Anyway, hadn't you better get back to your hostel to pick up your bags? You're going to smell pretty bad if you live in those clothes for another few days.'

He looked at her blankly.

'You do remember don't you, Danny? You're escorting me around the Peloponnese before I meet up with my mates. And don't look at me like that, you were pretty adamant about it last night. A couple of hours as my tour guide around the Acropolis yesterday and you thought you were Thomas bloody Cook.'

'And I agreed to this? What about my job?'

' I think your exact words were "Georgios can stick his job where the sun don't shine". Of course if you're wimping out I'm sure I can rely on my Italian stallion to step in to the breach.'

'Give me an hour and I'll see you back here.'

He gave her a wave as he turned to the stairway, taking the steps two at a time and heading towards reception and the way out. He paused briefly to look for Pedro but, seeing no sign of him, stepped out onto the street and joined the noise and bustle of late morning rush hour. On the way, he walked right past the young man checking out at the desk, failing to recognise his opponent from the night before. But his rival had not failed to recognise Dan, carefully watching every step of his departure from the hostel and swearing a patient revenge so quietly and coldly that, had Dan heard him, the words would have sent a chill to his very core.

Eight

Like the rosy-fingered moon after sunset,
surpassing all the stars.
Its light extends over the salty sea
and the fields of flowers alike

The bus dropped them off just after they had crossed the isthmus of Corinth. Dan had completely missed this wondrous feat of engineering, despite eagerly anticipating it, and it was Laura who had glanced out of the window to look down on a distant strip of bright blue water hemmed in by high cliffs of shadowy rock.

They trudged back past a run-down old restaurant to the road bridge which spanned the isthmus and which indicated that the Peloponnese peninsula was now actually all 'insula' and very little 'pen'. The channel of water flowed through a cut in the land no more than 100 feet in width and 4 miles in length and so clean a cut that it was as though one of Greek mythology's many giants (presumably a lesser-known gardening variety) had driven his spade through the narrow neck of land holding Pelop's island to mainland Greece. Dan had recently scanned his map of the Hellenistic world and had come to the conclusion that the Peloponnese bore a remarkable resemblance to testicles nestling behind Attica's dangling member. Understandably in this context, imagining the impact of the giant's spade thrust brought tears to his eyes.

Laura's voice jolted him away from such toe-curling thoughts.

'It's very dramatic isn't it? You just couldn't be ambivalent about a view like that.'

Dan winced at her comment. He hated people misusing

'ambivalent' when they really meant 'indifferent'. It was the same with 'reticent' and 'reluctant'. He knew it was not the most popular course of action but he could rarely stop himself from correcting their English, generally encouraging an immediate improvement as they informed him in no uncertain terms what an irritating little pedant he was. This time though he bit his tongue. He didn't want to risk saying anything critical of Laura, certainly not if it made her think less of him. He clenched his teeth and, to his great relief, only a strangled grunt escaped his tight lips.

She looked at him as he rested his arms on the railings, his whole body juddering in time to the traffic which rolled over the bridge, but he had mumbled his reply without turning to face her.

'It really is fantastic, isn't it?' She tried again to engage him but he didn't acknowledge her at all. She couldn't fathom him. Part of him was warm and approachable but there was another side where the shutters were closed and the 'No Entry' sign hung forbiddingly as a warning for anyone who tried to get too close. She assumed he liked her but what she couldn't quite work out was whether he liked her in the way she wanted him to. They had spent nearly thirty six hours together and, in her own limited experience, that was usually plenty of time for a bloke to make his feelings known. Generally, thirty six minutes was quite sufficient.

Perhaps not quite as self-assured as the image she liked to project, she had still spent far more time fending off unwelcome advances or gently discouraging the nicer ones than taking the initiative and orchestrating the pursuit herself. This one might be different though. This could be more of a challenge.

She was still half-turned towards him. Without making it too obvious, she conducted a quick appraisal, reassuring herself that he was worth the effort. Certainly, he was good-looking. Not ruggedly so but very easy on the eye nonetheless. The shock of light brown hair seemed to hover over his face, casting a light shadow over his eyes and, in her own mind, shrouding his thoughts from her. And he was bright too. Perhaps very bright, she wasn't sure yet.

He seemed so deep in thought as he stared down at the ribbon of water beneath them. She wondered what had managed to secure such a hold on his attention; the beauty and ingenuity of their surroundings or, and she took in a sharp breath at the thought, the strength of feeling for his companion. Was he imagining the construction of the isthmus in classical times, admiring the contrasts in colours and textures between the earthy cliff face and the blue sea below? Or was he searching for the inspiration, or the courage, to find the words which would bring the two of them together?

Finally he noticed her looking at him and he grinned.

'Two hours before the test starts,' he announced.

Laura tried hard not to let the sudden surge of panic show in her expression. Christ, what did he mean? What would she have to do? Was this what he'd planned all along – a series of challenges which she'd need to overcome to prove herself worthy of his affections? And, if she managed to pass his test, what on earth was the prize?

She scrunched up her brow, urging him to shed more light on his plan.

'The second test at Lords,' he clarified helpfully. 'I'm hoping we'll bat first this time.'

She didn't make much of an effort to hide her irritation at his remark and he realised that his comment had been insensitive and poorly-judged…..without being entirely sure why. They were slightly subdued as they made their way back to the bus stop, each wrapped up in their own thoughts, each thinking about the other one. Olympia had been their planned destination but the first bus to arrive was on its way down south. They looked at each other and, with a shrug of the shoulders, climbed on board, finding themselves an hour later in the tiny village of Palea Epidauros on the South East coast of the Peloponnese. Most people came to the area to visit the ancient theatre, either to see an actual production or to test out the world-famous acoustics themselves, and were promptly whisked back out again to neighbouring Nafplion or Mycenae. The village where the bus had abandoned Dan and Laura was some way from the theatre site and not exactly on the tourist trail. The only accommodation open to them was a small campsite by the water's edge. This would have been perfectly adequate if they had remembered to pack a tent but, without one, it didn't seem such an enticing option. Their unlikely knight in shining armour came in the unappealing shape of the campsite owner whose greeting had been quite a few degrees less than warm but who, against all odds, had fished a nearly-new tent out of a cupboard in his office and handed it, free of charge, to the two travellers. The outlook brightened even further for Dan when they quickly realised that the 'tent' was not much bigger than a sleeping bag.

'But it's hardly been used' was Dan's counter to Laura's horrified reaction to the size of their sleeping quarters.

'I don't care how new it is. You're bloody well sleeping outside,' she replied indignantly.

'Well, I'll just have to pour a few beers down your neck and hope you change your mind.'

Dan chanced his arm and was relieved to get away with nothing more ferocious than a sarcastic smile. Things are definitely looking up he thought. And, behind that dark-eyed glare, so did she.

An hour later and with some torturous tent-erecting behind them, Dan and Laura flopped onto the wooden benches drawn up either side of the trestle table outside reception and settled down to their first beer of the evening. Their only company was a gang of scrawny-looking cats which sat on adjoining tables, ears pricked up as if eavesdropping on the conversation.

Many years on, but well before the events of this trip had come back to haunt him, he would return to this spot with his girlfriend, the woman who would become his wife. They would visit this same campsite, or one which looked very like it, but would move on as soon as they realised that either it was no longer as idyllic as Dan remembered or it never had been.

They too would spend some magical days together here. They too would be oblivious of the dark future which lay ahead of them both. But they would still have longer to enjoy life than Laura. As the sun began to set, signalling the end of another day on the east coast of the Peloponnese, her own allotted time was drawing to a close.

With the sound of the Aegean lapping at the shore and the cicadas sending their Morse code messages to each other, Laura suddenly felt vulnerable. She was a long way from home and alone with a guy she had only just met. Dan sensed her nervousness and his conversation dried up. For a moment he was helpless, desperately hoping for one flash of inspiration from her to kick-start the evening's entertainment.

She took a long swig from the bottle and considered her companion. 'Hell,' she thought, 'he's a nice bloke. Better than a few I've come across lately.' She took one more sip and slammed the bottle down on the table, her decision made.

'What are the wildest places you've had sex then?' she demanded.

Dan rocked back on the bench and leaned against the wall of the reception building. He stared at Laura for a moment. This sounded very much like boys' talk and Dan felt confident that this was a language in which he was supremely fluent. He leant forward again and his expression became earnest. 'Shagged only or does foreplay count?' He wanted the rules to be clear right from the start.

'If it's not the full monty then you'll have to be in a pretty wild place to get any points from me,' came the adjudication.

'OK then. A girlfriend of mine did a pretty convincing impression of the 'When Harry Met Sally' orgasm scene on top of a double-decker bus.'

Laura looked dismayed. 'So what?'

'She was sitting on my lap at the time.'

Dan started laughing first. Laura desperately tried to avoid giving him the satisfaction of joining in but soon they were both bent over double, giggling helplessly and uncontrollably.

'That….is….pathetic.' she managed to blurt out between the sobs. 'Wishful thinking does *not* count.'

'OK, so maybe it was more friction than anything else but we still got thrown off by the bus conductor.'

'Oh well done, Romeo, where else?'

'Well, I've obviously got a thing for buses. I got a blow job at the back of one full of commuters leaving New York at rush hour.'

'Anywhere that doesn't involve buses or any other forms of public transport?'

Dan thought for a while. 'Oh God, yes. I was in the loos at the back of the Green Man being serviced by one of the barmaids.'

'That's not particularly adventurous.'

'Oh yeah? We were in the Ladies, she was married and her husband was in the gents next door. I was terrified.'

'You were drunk.'

'Hmmm, probably. But not as much as she was. Actually, I seem to make a habit of it. I did the same thing outside a villa in Corfu while mum and dad waited inside for their angelic daughter to bring the towels back in. I've never done it so quickly'

'Good God, boy, that's not much of an advert is it?'

He laughed again. He felt more relaxed with her than with any other girl he had known. In fact he had never met anyone quite as easy to talk to as she was. Strong but not intimidating. He gazed at her smile as it lit up her face. She really was wonderful.

'What about you then?'

He expected an equally light-hearted run-through but Laura took this game very seriously. He winced as she told him how some biker had fucked her on the back of her own motorbike in the car park outside a niteclub, how she had given her boyfriend a blow job in the upstairs toilet of someone's house while the party was in full swing around them and how some stranger had slid his hand under her skirt at a football match and played with her for the entire second half. He pretended to enjoy her graphic accounts and threw in some suitable expressions of amazement and incredulity, as if to spur her on, but in truth he hated every word of every confession. He couldn't bear to think of other men pawing over her, violating her, and even less to picture her enjoyment of it. He knew it was totally irrational to react like that but he was helpless to stop it. He began to think he loved her.

'Have you done the dirty with any blokes then?' she asked. 'What about Pedro? He's a good-looking guy.'

'It would be a pretty pointless exercise trying to turn old Pedro' Dan laughed. 'I don't think I've got the patience.'

Laura looked a little sceptical but she let the comment pass.

'The closest I got,' Dan continued, 'was with Big Jack. One of the more respectable football hooligans at college. He's the spitting image of John Belushi and eats twice as much. Great company but you just need to keep your fingers well away from his mouth at dinner time. We were watching the FA Cup final a few weeks ago, having some lunchtime beers in the college bar. Liverpool, Everton – an all-Merseyside final. Great atmosphere, nearly a hundred thousand fans at Wembley.'

It was clear from Laura's expression that this was already far more information than she was looking for.

'Sorry, anyway we were one down – Liverpool that is – and then put three past them in the second half. Fantastic finish – the third one, which sealed it, was only five minutes from the end. I saw Jack at breakfast the next morning and sat down opposite him. I was desperately trying to drag out the memory of the previous afternoon and evening through an absolutely vicious hangover.

"Here, Jack," I said. "You were at the game yesterday weren't you?" I got a grunt in return. "Did I jump on you," I asked, "when we scored the equaliser?" He looked up at me from his boiled egg & toast soldiers and raised one black bushy eyebrow in confirmation. "And when we scored the second," I went on, "am I right in thinking I gave you a big hug?" Again same glance, same arched eyebrow. "And," it was all coming back to me by now "when we scored the winner, I've got a horrible feeling I gave you a full-on kiss on the mouth?" This time he leant back and stopped chewing on his toast, "Yes," he said, "and you can thank whichever god you believe in that you didn't score a fourth." '

Dan threw his head back and laughed out loud. This time she happily laughed along with him.

'That doesn't bloody count,' she protested. 'That's not a confession it's just another one of your bloody anecdotes.'

'Well, that's as close as I get to hot homo action. What about you then? Any Sapphic experiences?' He tried to keep a straight face but a broad grin eventually gave him away. Laura looked at him slightly cautiously. She was tempted to mention her drunken kiss with Maureen the night they arrived in Athens but decided not to encourage him down that path and shook her head instead.

'Too bad,' Dan said with genuine disappointment and headed inside for fresh beers.

'So is this how you want to spend the rest of your life then,' he asked when he came back, 'one sexual adventure after another?'

'Well, it doesn't sound like a bad idea does it? But I think I'm a bit of a traditionalist at heart. A white wedding in a lovely old village church for me. Mum and dad dressed up to the nines and proud as punch.'

'What, meringue dress, bridesmaids and the works?'

'Oh yes, the full monty. Why not go to town? It's your day. You're the centre of attention. Make the most of it.'

For a few moments she was there, laughing at the speeches, cutting the cake, dancing with the guests.

'And afterwards, when I'd risen as far up the career ladder as my male bosses felt comfortable with, I'd give it all up and start my own brood.'

'Kids! Are you serious?'

'God yes, I'd love children. Six of them in all – four boys and two girls. I'll call one of them Danny if you like?'

'As long as it's one of the boys' he muttered.

Laura ignored his comment and carried on. 'You see I

come from a big family – staunch Catholics you know – and we get on with each other really, really well. If I bring up a family which is half as close, I'll grow old happy.' She took a sip of her beer. 'So saying, I'll probably fall down dead tomorrow.'

Dan felt a chill cut through him, 'Don't say that' he replied and he meant it.

Laura looked at him intently, touched by his reaction.

'What about you, Danny? How's your family situation? What sort of parents could possibly claim responsibility for you?'

'Only my mum's alive now.' He took off his shoe and banged out the little pebbles on the bench besides him. 'My dad died when I was young. Ages ago.'

Laura immediately regretted her flippant remark.

'Oh God, I'm sorry. That's dreadful. How did, well, what happened…if you want to of course?'

Dan performed the same operation with his other shoe, this time not to remove some irritating grit but to stop the emotions getting too strong a grip on him.

'Heart attack.' He tried to sound casual and matter-of-fact. 'A real shock. He didn't really smoke much or eat a lot of crap. I was 11 and my sister was 9. We were in the house with him. Mum had gone shopping and dad was having a lie-down. He said he was feeling a little under the weather.'

'Did you see him? What happened?'

'See him? We heard him. I don't suppose you know what someone dying sounds like? All you can hear is this wheezing, like air escaping from a balloon, as they battle for breath. We rushed in and saw him half out of the bed and hanging over the side. We were helpless. If we'd have been older, we might have known what to do. I don't know, perhaps we could have saved him but we just didn't know how.' He slipped his other shoe back on and looked at his companion for the first time since he had begun recounting the episode. 'Instead, we just stood there and watched him die,' he said and turned away as a tear threatened to spill over the lip of his eyelid.

Laura leant over and took both his hands in her own. She watched him struggling to hide his emotions and murmured comforting words which said nothing but meant everything because of the tenderness with which they were expressed. Eventually Dan sat up and made a big show of pulling himself together.

He smiled at her and slapped his stomach. 'God, I'm hungry,' he said.

'Me too' she laughed and they ordered a large slab of moussaka to share.

Dinner duly arrived lukewarm and consisting of meat so tough that they systematically counted the neighbouring cats to make sure none had gone missing. Over more beer they continued to talk to each other with a frankness more easily reached with passing strangers than apparent friends. She shared her feelings about her parents, her brothers and sisters, whilst he talked about job aspirations and whether he'd be able to avoid the conveyor belt of a business career long enough to pick up his true vocation. Unfortunately he couldn't decide whether his true vocation was to write for a national newspaper, produce arts programmes for BBC2 or play professional sport – though he certainly couldn't think of a sport which his level of proficiency would allow him to take up professionally so that at least seemed to narrow down the options. They took their final beer out on to the beach and sat in silence listening to the waves lap the shore at their feet and the fish splash in and out of the water further out to sea.

'What's the point of all this?' Dan finally asked. 'What are we all here for?'

Laura looked at him quizzically as he stared out into the blackness. 'That's pretty profound,' she said with a laugh.

'You see, you can live your life to the full, fantastic experiences and a scrap-book crammed with cuttings, and what for? Unless you're Einstein or Thomas bloody Edison, you're no more likely to be remembered than someone who's bored their way through life, not ruffling a single feather or raising even an iota of interest in anyone else. I mean, I don't go in for this life after death stuff. As far as I'm concerned, you only live on in the memories of the people you leave behind. Your friends, family. In a hundred years' time, when me and my sister are long gone, who'll remember my dad? It will be as though he never existed.'

'No, no, you're wrong. Well, I mean, I think you're fundamentally wrong anyway. I genuinely believe there's something for us after all this. But, even if I didn't, people live on through their children, and through their children's children. You can trace a bloodline with DNA testing. That means there's always something of someone which survives. That's our legacy. That's our purpose. We help form future generations, either directly through our own children or else through our brothers' or sisters' children.'

Dan turned this thought over in his head.

'So, we're all made up of hundreds and thousands of our ancestors then.'

'And perhaps a little bit that's unique to us,' Laura added.

Dan nodded in acknowledgement but carried on.

So, I could be made up of a concoction of Genghis Khan, Attila the Hun and Ivan the Terrible?'

'Hmmm, possibly.' Laura looked him up and down. 'In fact, make that probably. There'd need to be some well-travelled mums in your bloodline to have collected that lot of DNA though. But wouldn't it be more interesting if it were the forgotten people of history? How about if you were related to the waitress who served the disciples at the last supper or the man who nailed Christ to the cross.'

'Or Christ himself.'

Laura turned to Dan, expecting him to be grinning back at her, but he looked deadly serious. 'Oh come on, Laura,' he went on. 'You honestly believe that he and Mary Magdalene were just good friends?'

She stared at him, open-mouthed, until he realised he'd taken things a little too far. 'Well, it would make a good book,' he said apologetically.

He leant forward, hugging his knees. 'Anyway, it would be nice to think that dad lives on, that we've got a chance to keep something of him alive.'

He took a deep breath and exhaled slowly. 'Hell of a responsibility' he said with a nervous glance towards her.

'I'm sure you're up to it,' she said reassuringly and put her arm through his. They stayed motionless for what seemed like a lifetime. Finally she stirred, kissed his cheek and got up. 'I'm going back to the tent. Are you coming?'

This was the moment. It was now.

He looked up at her and smiled with genuine affection, 'I'll just be a few more minutes, you go ahead.' The moment was gone.

He squeezed her hand momentarily before turning back to the gentle swell of water in front of him. Aided by the alcohol, he lost himself in his own thoughts about his father, his future and finally about Laura herself who had made such a strong impression on him in the short time they had been together.

If he had headed off to the tent to be with her when he had first intended, he would have found her waiting for him, ready to give herself to him. But, by the time he had finally reached the tent, some half an hour later, she was fast asleep.

'Never mind,' he thought, 'the future's bound to offer plenty more chances. I'll probably end up being the one to marry her.'

Nine

The woman stepped out on to the side of the bridge along the pathway which separated the rail tracks from the giddying drop below. She beckoned to the young boy to follow her.

'Come on, Tommaso, it's OK. I'm here.'

The boy remained on the gravel track, held there by his own fear despite her gentle coaxing.

'I can't, mama.'

His worried eyes shifted nervously between her face and the fingers which rested on the low stone safety guard beside her. The woman stretched out her hand towards him but he stayed where he was, hugging the grass bank for safety.

She looked at him protectively. It was not his fault he was born different. Perhaps it was not her fault either, despite her husband's cruel words and punishing beatings. But she was tired. So tired. Years of fighting the system and the specialists, of suffering those knowing looks – sometimes sympathetic, often accusing – from everyone she ever came into contact with. Years of protecting him from his father, from himself and for such meagre reward.

Eventually she took a step towards him and lifted him into her arms. He was small for his eight years but the woman let out a deep groan at the strain of picking him up.

Slowly she shuffled back to the centre of the span and looked over her shoulder at the deep gorge below. It was a long way down. The boy buried his face deeper into his mother's jumper. He could feel her heartbeat thumping through his temples and wondered for a moment whether it was his instead.

'I love you, my little soldier.' She kissed the top of his

head and stroked his hair with her cheek, dislodging a single tear as she did so and watching it drop onto the stone path at her feet.

'You're a good boy, sweetheart, a good boy. Mummy loves you very much.'

She gave him one final squeeze and fell back gently and silently over the side of the safety wall, her son cradled in her arms.

Ten

The beautiful way she walks
and the bright sparkle of her face
I would rather see than all the war-chariots in Lydia
and the fully-armed infantry

The next morning the roles were reversed. He woke up to find her gone. He felt a slight pang of panic as he wondered whether she had left him in a fit of pique at his late arrival to bed but even he wasn't arrogant enough to believe she would be quite as put out as that. Anyway, he could see her rucksack at the foot of his sleeping bag.

He emerged from the tent, blinking at the sunshine like a mole clambering out of its earthy home. Laura was sitting on the shingled beach gazing out to sea, much as they had done the previous evening. He walked over to her and watched the reflection of the sun in the water dance over her arms and legs. She looked up at him and smiled, 'Hi, what time did you get in last night?'

Bizarrely he felt like apologising to her, telling her he was sorry for standing her up and begging her to give him another opportunity that night.

'Not long after you but you were already snoring your head off.' Not quite what he had in mind.

'*Pretend* snoring you mean. Just in case you decided to try your luck.'

'Oh, you were quite safe there. Far too much beer for me to be a threat to anyone.'

'Well in that case, you'd better stick to the soft drinks tonight.'

She grinned up at him and her eyes sparkled as she spoke the words. He smirked back at her knowingly but in truth he was confused. He thought she had given him a buying signal but he wasn't totally sure. After all she could have been simply pulling his leg in a jokey 'just good friends' way. Imagine the excruciating embarrassment, he told himself, if he were to make a lunge for her just as she was about to tell him how refreshing it was to come across a bloke who was happy to be friends with a girl without trying to jump on top of her every two minutes. He wished she had been a bit more direct, that little bit clearer. To be fair though, the only way she could have been much clearer was if she'd hitched her skirt up and told him to come and get it.

Later that morning they trudged along the beach towards the headland and the views over to the closest of the Saronic Gulf islands. They passed a wiry man sitting on his haunches over a yellowed newspaper. They both stopped suddenly when Dan's polite 'Yasu' was returned by a 'Hello there' delivered in an unmistakably Scottish accent. With an eagerness which struck Dan as a mite unwarranted, Laura seized the opportunity of chatting to a compatriot and embarked upon a wide-ranging discussion, covering places they both knew, people they didn't and mutual experiences which neither could fully remember. Eventually Laura got round to enquiring about the turn of events which had taken her fellow Scot from Glasgow to Greece.

It seemed that Ian had got involved with a children's charity in Scotland and had volunteered to set up an offshoot in this out-of-the-way area of the Peloponnese. Dan was unsurprisingly sceptical of such an unlikely chain of events, deciding that drugs, alcohol and prison had played a more important part in Ian's exodus than the well-being of international Under-10s.

'Why did you come here of all places?' He couldn't help himself.

'Why not?' was the enlightening response.

Ian turned back to Laura.

'So you've turned up to see the theatre, have you?'

And while Laura was mumbling something about jumping on any old bus and being emptied out here, Dan, still smarting from his earlier curt treatment, saw his opportunity for a bit of points-scoring.

'The theatre's actually quite a way from here at Epidauros itself. We're going there later today.'

'You're wrong there, son. Palea Epidauros has got its own theatre, years older than the one up the road.' Dan reddened at Ian's rebuke. 'It's on private land. In fact it was going to make way for the owner's new barn until he made the mistake of informing the authorities and they slapped a fucking preservation order on it.'

Laura laughed. 'Should've just kept his mouth shut and got on with it,' she said, her Scottish accent growing noticeably stronger as the minutes went on.

'And not just that. This area has got so many fucking unexcavated ruins that the government can't afford the funds to begin digging. All the locals know where they are and they reckon some of the sites are even bigger than Delphi.' He looked at each of them in turn, waiting for the enormity of his revelation to sink in. 'Anyway, what the fuck do you think that is?' He pointed at the thick stone column lying on the shingle behind them.

Laura looked over at Dan, 'Well, is it the real thing?'

Dan looked a little uncomfortable. He was pleased that Laura had turned to him for a judgment but he was wary about how much Ian really knew on the subject. The best he could do was hedge his bets. He bent down and ran his hand over the smooth stone surface.

'Christ, yes, well......I'm not an expert but.....well, yes it certainly could be. It really is so difficult to tell when they've been exposed to the elements for so long.'

He could feel Ian smirking and stared at the object for a few more moments to avoid meeting his eye. 'It's certainly pretty old, that's for sure,' he finally pronounced and looked up at Ian for his reaction.

'Too fucking right it is. And there's loads more.' Ian jumped up to stand with them. 'Just climb up to the top of the acropolis over there and look down at the water. You can see the ruins of the old harbour stretching out to sea. Clear as day. And do you see where those two trees are over there?' He leant over Laura's shoulder, a little too close for Dan's liking, until she saw the spot on the beach where he was indicating. 'Straight out to sea from that point are huge fuck-off amphorae. Big enough to swim in and out of. And right next to them, mosaics of wild animals and gladiators. I've been down there loads of times.'

'You're joking.' Dan couldn't believe what he was hearing. Genuine Greek and Roman antiquities, unexcavated by the authorities and his to discover.

'You'll probably find more stuff on the acropolis. No one goes up there much. Have a root around but don't get caught. The government doesn't give a flying fuck about all these artefacts unless someone else finds them and tries taking them out of the country.'

They said their goodbyes with instructions from Ian on how to find the theatre and a promise from them to return for retsina in the evening.

Even with these clear directions, it still took Dan and Laura over an hour of wrong turns and dead-ends before they came upon the theatre. Most of the site was open and unguarded but there were several randomly-placed patches of barbed wire hanging between thin fencing poles, presumably placed by the local authorities so that they could claim with some semblance of justification to be providing adequate protection for their cultural heritage. The ruins themselves were not especially dramatic. Most of the theatre's proscenium had long since been dismantled by the local townsfolk for building material and the carvings which remained were only of average quality but the secrecy of the site sparked a frisson of excitement in the two explorers as they clambered over the stone seats.

'Laura, quick, come here.' Dan was crouched over one area of the terraced seating, poking at a crack between the stones. 'There's something metal down here. I think it's a coin.'

She ran over to where he was kneeling and watched his patient attempts at flicking his find from its safe home. Finally, encouraged by the probes of a sliver of fencing pole, a small, grey object flew out from between Dan's feet and clinked down the steps with Laura in hot pursuit. With a lunge of her foot she stamped down on the coin, cutting short its stick-injected journey and causing Dan to wince at the clumsy effort and its potentially damaging consequences.

'For Christ's sake, Laura, it could be two thousand years old,' he pleaded in exasperation.

Laura picked up the artefact and inspected it briefly before looking up at him.

'Probably not if it's got 1, 9, 8 and 3 stamped around the edge of it,' she replied cheerily.

He looked so crestfallen that she couldn't help but feel sorry for him and suggested that they make their way up to the acropolis. They scrambled over a raised bank and found the route leading up the side of the hill, negotiating the erratic placement of barbed wire along the way. The path was steep and overgrown with bracken which acted as a natural safety barrier between the walkway and the sea below but obscured any view across the bay until they had made it to the top.

'What did Ian say about the ruins up here?' Laura shouted at Dan's back as he surged up to the summit. Her question reached him just as he rounded the final bend leading to the open hillside of the acropolis.

'Wow. It's not the ruins up here. It's the ones down there he was on about.'

He pointed to the sea below just as Laura joined him on top of the hill. It took her a moment to focus not on the water but on the stone shapes beneath the surface. What revealed itself was an incredible latticework of low walls and pavements in what must have once been the ancient harbour. There was no indication from the shore that the sea had captured such a fantastic historical tableau but, from a bird's-eye vantage point, the waves readily surrendered their secret.

They sat down on the grass and tried identifying the buildings and landmarks below them. The sea walls and jetty were easy enough but they were less sure about a series of adjoining rooms. Dan argued passionately for 'hospitality rooms' which the sailors would use to entertain local prostitutes but he was finally over-ruled by Laura's rather more prosaic suggestion of quarters for the harbour officials ('same thing' he had muttered under his breath).

Still relatively pleased with their archaeological efforts, Dan swung the rucksack off his back and placed it on the ground in front of him. He pulled out his camera and turned to Laura,

'Stand over there by the edge.' He stood up and gestured her back. She put her hands on her hips and looked at him disapprovingly.

'Yes, yes. Don't tell me, "back a little, a bit further, a bit more" and I drop off the side of this precipice and impale myself on those rocks down there.'

'The old comedy cliff photo routine? You really have got a low opinion of me haven't you.'

He adopted his best look of resignation and raised the camera to his eye, framing her figure within the blue background of the sea. The shoreline cut through her neck like a garrotte and threatened to sever her laughing face from the slim body attached. He tried to stop the line from touching her by changing the angle of the shot but he couldn't seem to find a position which succeeded in shifting it sufficiently so he took the picture as it was.

At the click of the shutter, she unfroze from her pose and threw herself down on the ground, rolling onto her back and linking her hands behind her head. He lay down on his stomach alongside her and offered her a crisp from the packet he had bought in the campsite.

'So who's your favourite band then, Danny?' She turned back over and shuffled closer towards him.

'My favourite band?' His ruffled his hair, brushing against the elbow she was leaning on as he did so. 'The Smiths, by a mile. Morrissey & Marr are right up there with Lennon & McCartney, Bacharach & David, Lieber & Stoller…..'

'….Gloom & Doom. Oh come on, Danny, the Smiths are such a miserable bunch.'

'Look, they're not bloody miserable and it really gets on my nerves when people say they are.'

She rocked on to her other elbow, away from him, either a little hurt or a little put out. He backtracked hastily.

'Sorry, I'm not having a go at you personally but Morrissey's lyrics are genuinely funny. Black definitely but funny, no question. "I was minding my business, lifting some lead off the roof of the Holy Name church", "I want to live and I want to love, I want to catch something that I might be ashamed of", "Spending warm summer days indoors, writing frightening verse to a buck-toothed girl in Luxemburg"…..'

'My God you really are an anorak Smiths fan aren't you? Calm down, you're getting yourself all worked up over Mr Morrissey. Do you want a hanky?'

'I'm not too fussed about Morrissey the man. I mean I don't necessarily agree with a lot of his views but there's no doubt that he's written some absolute gems as far as lyrics go. In fact my personal mantra is a Morrissey line. "Vivid and in your prime". It's a state of mind. At least that's how I like to think about it. I hope my life always lives up to the billing – it's a really inspiring thought. And what about you? What's the lyric which sums up your life then?'

She raised herself up onto both elbows and stared at him defiantly,

'I will survive.'

Eleven

He had not cried for years. Ever since he followed the coffins of his mother and brother down the street. He didn't think his father had either though he had found renewed comfort in the bottle. They had never been close but there had always been a chance that mutual grief and a need for comfort would bring them together. It didn't. As far as he was concerned, he had lost his father long before his mother and brother.

Now they lived separate lives in the same house. He sometimes cooked for them both but only when common sense rather than kindness dictated. That was the only time they ever sat together and talked and, even then, they covered only superficial topics and matters of routine.

Despite the space and the freedom, he felt suffocated and claustrophobic. The walls inched further inwards by the day and the blankets & bed-sheets hung heavier on top of him. He needed to get away. Anywhere. Jump on his motorbike or just stick out his thumb on the autostrada and see where it would take him.

He was 18 years old, just. His father hadn't even acknowledged his birthday. If he had any friends, he doubted whether they would have done either. The one person who might have remembered had abandoned him.

There was barely a moment when he didn't feel angry, always on the brink of losing control and lashing out. He saw himself mirrored in the ancient volcano which loomed over his home-town, solitary and unpredictable. Dangerous. The build-up of pressure forced his temples to pulse and his forehead to ache. He needed a release. They used to think that drilling a hole in the skull was the cure and he could understand why. The rage which was boiling up through his body needed an escape route. And, when it found one, somebody was going to suffer. Like he had.

He really needed to get away. Head south to Brindisi and the boat to a new world. Away from his father. And away from the painful memories which provoked him constantly during the day and shook him awake at night.

He thought of his mother. There was no warmth in the memories. Just bitterness. He could understand that bringing up a son like Tommaso was tough but she had *two* children not one. You were not supposed to favour one over the other, no matter how needy one of them appeared to be.

When she took her own life, she had decided to end his brother's as well. For her, he felt no pity, no compassion but, for Tommaso, his over-riding emotion was one of envy. One question kept nagging at him, as it had ever since he first heard the news so many years before.

'Why did she choose him and not me?' He spat out the words and struck the table with his fist, over and over until blood wept from the knuckle.

Twelve

*If you hungered after what is honourable and good
and your tongue wasn't conjuring up
something dreadful to say,
shame would not fall upon your eyes
and you would speak with justice on your side*

They lay on the hilltop for the rest of the afternoon, playing trumps with song lyrics – Dan's "I'm as honest as the day is long, the longer the daylight the less I do wrong" by Madness narrowly losing out to Laura's favourite Billy Bragg line, "How can you lie there and think of England when you don't even know who's in the team."

They talked non-stop, mainly about her. She was hardly well-travelled but there was a certain worldliness about her, surprising in such a hometown girl. Her knowledge of international affairs embarrassed Dan. He had made a throwaway remark about the Graeco-Turkish frictions in Cyprus and she had responded with a concise, salient and balanced deconstruction of the key drivers behind the present situation. The intention was clearly not merely to parade her knowledge in front of him – she had a genuine interest in the subject – but Dan struggled even to provide enough interjections to justify describing this one-way flow of information as an 'exchange'.

He shifted uncomfortably on the grass as she effortlessly drew parallels between British intervention in Ireland and South African apartheid, between Australian aborigines and American Indians. She didn't notice his minimal contribution. Like many people, she assumed academic intelligence was a proxy for general knowledge which, in turn, equated to common sense. She had a short memory.

Dan's approach to erecting the tent should have dispelled that particular theory.

As the afternoon wore on, he dragged the conversation back within his comfort zone and treated Laura to topics as diverse as whether the moon landing was a propaganda-fuelled hoax and could Top of the Pops be described, by any stretch of the imagination, as cutting edge music television. The sun was already nudging the horizon when they finally decided to make their way down from the hilltop. As they walked along the shore, they saw Ian at the door of his beachside house.

'Hi, are you coming in then?' he shouted.

Laura looked at Dan, 'Sure, why not. I'm dying for a drink.'

As soon as they got in, Ian poured out three full tumblers of retsina. Dan excused himself and made for the toilet. When he got back he saw that Laura had already downed most of her glass. He took a sip from his and quickly came to the conclusion that, thirsty though he undoubtedly was, it would take a week without water in the Gobi desert for him to enjoy such stunningly atrocious wine. He also realised that half a packet of crisps and no lunch was not the best preparation for an evening of alcohol. He looked at Laura as Ian refilled her glass. If she was sharing Dan's reservations, she was doing an impressive job of hiding it.

'So what's the plan from here, Laura?' Ian sat down on the couch next to her. 'Heading back to Scotland?'

'God no, not yet. After this gentleman has finished escorting me round the Peloponnese, I'm going to head off to Mykonos to meet up with some friends from college.'

'And then where?'

Oh, I don't know. Naxos? Paros? Santorini?'

Ian allowed himself a slight smile and leant back into the

cushions, swinging his hands round to the back of his head with the 'been there, done that' air of a seasoned traveller faced with the naïve questions of a wide-eyed and innocent schoolgirl.

Dan had seen these signs before and knew what was coming next. 'What a wanker' he thought.

'Laura,' Ian finally sighed, 'don't waste your time on any of the other Cycladic islands. I've been to them all and Mykonos is the best by a fucking mile. You're better off bypassing those other two you mentioned and heading straight down to Thira afterwards. You'll know it better as Santorini. The capital, Thira town, sits on the rim of a *caldera* – that's a volcanic crater. I tell you, the view from the Minos restaurant is top-fucking-notch….and the food's not bad either.'

Dan looked at him in disbelief. 'What a *complete* wanker.' He almost said it out loud.

Again he glanced at Laura but the second glass of retsina, downed nearly as quickly as the first, had obviously dampened her senses because she made no reaction to Ian's speech and he sensed she could usually smell bullshit a mile away.

'I'll have a word with the girls,' she said, 'and maybe we'll make a beeline for Santorini…..' she paused and grinned at Ian, '….Thira,' she corrected herself. 'It was on our list after all. You sound like you've travelled a lot, Ian. Where else have you been?'

'It might be quicker to run through where I *haven't* been!'

By now Dan was standing on his chair, with a flag in each hand, spelling out WANKER in semaphore to Laura.

'China and Vietnam are probably my favourites. Not the friendliest people in the world but it's understandable, they're not used to tourists over there. The scenery's pretty spectacular but, for really fucking A1 landscapes, the South

Island of New Zealand is the dog's bollocks. The Kiwis are fucking nutcases too. They've got all these mountains, waterfalls and rapids and what do they want to do? Helicopter on to them, you know, raft over them, bungee into them. Fucking nutcases.'

He finished this last little insight with a snort of a smile and a shake of the head. Dan was close to exploding. Laura was nearly collapsing. Ian mistook Dan's look of anguish as a signal for a refill and raised himself off the cushions to top up his guest's glass. He turned to smile at Laura as he sat back down on the couch, noticeably closer than earlier, and leant across her to pour the retsina into her own glass again (did his fingertips touch her breasts?). His hand rested on her knee and he gave her leg a squeeze,

'So, are you two together then?' he asked, nodding towards Dan.

Laura looked at him blankly, 'Together?'

'You know what I mean. *Together.*' The growl which Ian bestowed on the word left little doubt about the sort of "together" he had in mind.

Dan opened his mouth to speak but couldn't find any words. He realised he was a spectator not a participant here, watching the drama unfold before him but playing no part, powerless to alter the direction of the plot. He stared at Ian's hand resting on her knee, the knee which he, Dan, should have been caressing. He'd had his chances, God knows he'd had plenty of them. She had definitely given him the green light but he had stalled and stuttered, failing to take the opportunities on offer. And then this foul-mouthed stranger, this skinny, tattooed Scot, within half an hour had got further than Dan had managed in three days. But how would Laura react to the question? What would be her response?

She knocked back the rest of her wine and looked across

at Dan, 'No, we're not together.'

Dan sat stock still. His whole body was tensed rigid and his joints had locked in place. He thought he had groaned his disappointment but the sound stuck in his throat. Even his stare was frozen, remaining fixed on Ian's hand as he watched it begin its slow journey along her thigh and up to the hem of her skirt. Here it paused as its owner created some diversionary conversation to distract attention from the straying fingers. Dan couldn't take in what Ian was saying. Instead he saw the hand start to stroke back and forth along the golden skin of Laura's thigh, inching her skirt up and up with each caress. And every time the hand returned to her knee, it had travelled a little further inwards so that its return journey took it increasingly along the inside of her thigh and closer to its intended target.

Still Ian's words murmured in the background, the sound of static drowning out all other noise and heightening the electricity created by the sweep of his hand. Even Ian himself appeared to pay little attention to what he was saying. He too was concentrating solely on the skin beneath his hand, his speech on auto-pilot to make the journey smoother.

Soon Dan could glimpse the white triangle of Laura's knickers, slightly darkened by the shadow of hair within. He couldn't decide whether he was appalled or fascinated by the scene. But there was no doubt that he was excited.

The alcohol buzzed in his head so loudly that he was sure the noise must have been coming from something in the room. For the first time since the seduction began he looked at Laura. She was staring straight at him – he felt as though she had been looking at him for some time. When he returned his gaze to Ian's hand, he noticed that it was now obscuring his view of the white triangle, having reached the highest point of its climb so far. Dan suddenly realised that, for Ian to have reached this point, Laura must have parted her knees slightly to ease his path. The next sweep of his hand would doubtless take Ian to his target. Dan caught his breath. Again he looked over at Laura and again she sat staring straight back at him.

Without warning she lifted herself from the couch, letting Ian's final sweep of the hand land onto his own crotch. The tension dissolved in a split-second.

'I'm just going to the loo.'

Ian glanced up at Dan casually and shrugged, settling back into the cushions again.

'Worth a go,' he laughed. Dan just smiled.

When Laura returned, she grabbed her companion by the arm and pulled him towards the door.

'Come on, Danny, we should be getting back.'

Muttering their thanks and goodbyes to Ian, they staggered out of the door, Dan barely able to keep Laura upright as she draped herself around his shoulders. As soon as they were clear of the cottage though, Laura straightened up and put her arms around his neck.

'Turn you on did it?'

And with that, she leant forward and kissed his mouth, pushing her tongue between his lips and pressing her breasts against his chest.

When they pulled apart, he saw a familiar grin twitching at the corners of her mouth.

'Not as drunk as you thought I was, am I?' she said, the grin broadening into a smile which lit up her face and set her eyes sparkling.

He grinned back and pressed his mouth against hers again. His hand reached down behind her and he pulled her towards him so that she could feel him. His fingers caressed the fleshy tops of her thighs under her skirt until he suddenly realised that she was no longer wearing the knickers she'd had on earlier. He broke away in surprise.

'When the hell did you take those off? That was nothing to do with him was it?'

'Oh no, that was just for you. How long would you have left them on for anyway?'

Dan was taken aback by her directness and smiled in embarrassment. Perhaps Laura was more drunk than either of them thought because she mistook this sheepish grin for a dirty leer and pressed herself against him once again.

They didn't even make it back to the tent, stumbling over onto the grass verge between campsite and beach and somehow discarding or nudging aside enough clothing to facilitate a frantic, exhilarating and, ultimately, successful union. It would prove to be the last sex which Laura would ever experience and, if she had known this, she may well have been content to finish in such a fashion – unfettered, untamed and alive.

Thirteen

Margaret Hodges was a young woman who had just spent most of the Great War reading books. Old books. As old as anything the library of her Oxford college held. Manuscripts by poets and playwrights from the Ancient World, some so obscure that her fellow students had a better chance of finding their way to the Americas or the Orient, the New World, than coming upon the shelves where these works were hidden.

As a result, she had survived the war fairly comfortably. The German bombers weren't minded to make it past the capital and, when she returned home to the Shropshire countryside, the one suspected spy her local village had managed to uncover turned out to be a former postman from Shrewsbury searching for a quieter place to spend his retirement. Clearly she hadn't taken an active role in the war effort, letting others with greater dexterity handle chemicals and explosives in munitions factories, but survival was still an achievement for many of her young age. It wasn't that she felt less strongly than others about making a contribution, it was just that she felt far more strongly about making an indelible mark in her own struggle, the scholarship of textual criticism; more like detective work than study, a search for the truth when truth was no more than an opinion shared by a collection of self-appointed experts.

It was solitary work which meant she had few friends. Or possibly it was the other way round. Either her obsession with her subject matter made people over-look her dry sense of humour or her straight-talking drove away anyone other than the most ardent admirer. Of which there were very few.

She was not untouched by the war and nor was she indifferent to it. Several of her former classmates had not made it through the conflict – a victim of disease in a rat-infected trench or skewered on the end of a bayonet thrust. A girl she knew had been buried under the masonry of a collapsed building, just yards from the safety of the shelter. These events hurt her but they didn't shock her. The horrors of war were brought viscerally to life in many of the texts which she spent long days poring over and, whilst they didn't insulate her from the shock and despair of the current struggle, they no doubt helped generate a certain detachment and robbed the news of some of its power. Any historian, which by proxy Margaret could lay claim to be, would treat media headlines announcing this as 'the war to end war' with reluctant contention. She treated them with something closer to disdain, drawing a sharp 'poppycock' whenever they landed on her desk.

So, whilst many of the boys from her old school were hunkered down in water-logged ditches or flattened face-first in the mud as bullets whistled above their heads, she had been fighting her own war in rooms full of books, either at her college, where the authorities were all too eager to retain a semblance of normality and a sense of continued relevance in a world-gone-mad, or at her parents' home on their modest estate where the war seemed only to have provided little more than a fresh topic of conversation around the breakfast table and a little less variety on the table itself.

During the conflict, it never occurred to this feisty young woman that she was shirking her responsibilities to her country in its hour of greatest need. If she had given it any consideration, which was unlikely given the sheer quantity of Greek lyric poetry she had to work her way through, it would have genuinely surprised her to think that anyone would consider her own contribution as warranting any less merit than the soldiers and the support staff themselves. They were all working for a greater good.

After the war was over and her undergraduate course was complete, she had been able to take her passion out into the field to help source the actual material she had spent several years studying. That meant Egypt. This was her second spell with the expedition and it was hard, back-breaking work – so tough that one or two of the team who hadn't got to know her too well during her first stint hadn't expected her to return for another. Too lengthy a journey to pop back for Christmas (even if the festive season had ever been marked in the Hodges family calendar as a time for great celebration), she had been working on-site since the previous autumn.

And now it was spring, a season which she always regarded so fondly back in England, a time of new growth and fresh hope. But not in Egypt. Here it was a season to dread. It always arrived innocuously enough but, by the time it had run its course, all the vitality had been drained from the land and its people. It signalled the transition between mild winter and the oppressive months of summer. In cities and towns along the Nile, the cooling waters of the great river offered an increasingly welcome source of relief but away from the delta, in the vast plains which stretched out on either side, the inhospitable nature of the desert was gradually revealed. Gradually but inevitably. Ever-greater extremes of temperature, ushered in during the spring months, presented their own challenge but it was the introduction of the sirocco that the more long-standing members of her party feared most. With no trees or buildings to break their relentless march or provide shelter from their stinging cargo of dust and sand, these gale-force winds made the twin deserts of Egypt one of the harshest and most unforgiving environments on the planet.

This was especially true at night when temperatures plunged like a stone and darkness cloaked what would otherwise have been tell-tale warning signs that the winds were approaching. It was now late March and the worst of the sirocco was yet to come but the change in weather over the past week had been noticeable to Margaret and every one of her companions: the heat of the day had, for the first time in months, been dry enough and hot enough to burn the throat and, after dusk, the gusts had become far stronger and more frequent than at any previous juncture.

Some of the tents had already been packed up and shipped back to England, along with several of the excavation team. Many of the local workers had been laid off for the summer when they would need to search out less labour-intensive work for their income – it was difficult enough to concentrate in such sweltering heat, let alone dig – but many would find little employment before re-joining the expedition on its return to Egypt in the autumn.

This night, the winds had reached their most violent level yet and the occupants of one of the few remaining tents remained grateful for the sturdy canvas which protected them from the worst of the elements. Margaret and her older male colleague sat facing each other at a dining table composed of three separate trestle tables of varying heights. The fact that the local servants, with the best of intentions, had sought to mask the joins with a large white cotton tablecloth simply made the placing of plates and drinking cups a hazardous exercise to negotiate.

The man eyed the arrangement suspiciously, grateful that he would only be required to tolerate such hardship for a few more days. He extended a strained smile to his companion who, after struggling through two courses of tedious conversation, found herself thinking much the same thing. The tent flapped incessantly to fill the silence. Margaret looked up from her food as he voiced yet another bland question and raised her eyebrows.

'Oxyrhynchus? It means the City of the Sharp-Nosed Fish, a creature sacred to the god Osiris.' She paused for reflection and leant forward. Released from the shadows, her face took on an eerie glow in the flickering light of the gas lamp. 'It must have been pretty sharp-toothed as well because apparently it managed to bite off his divine penis.'

Harold's fork stopped its upward trajectory and hovered just below his wiry beard. He stared at the woman in astonishment.

'Really, Margaret!'

He shook his head in disapproval, causing him to lose most of the contents off his fork as he brought it back up towards his mouth. He didn't understand why the younger generation these days chose the language of the gutter to litter their conversation.

'Oh, don't be so old-fashioned, Harold. We're in the twentieth century now after all.' The gale picked up again and pulled the flap of the tent away from the pole it had been roped to. 'And you can fasten that thing back up. We don't want half the Western desert in our food, do we.'

Within seconds the wind had snatched the flame from the lamp, plunging the tent and its occupants into darkness as it howled in triumph. Harold got up obediently and began to struggle with the canvas door as the gusts threatened to deposit both it and him across the sand dunes and halfway to Cairo. Eventually he conjured up a knot which promised to hold longer than the trip back to the table; a marked improvement on his previous two efforts. He waited until his companion had re-lit the lamp and then sat down once again at the table. He noticed the light dusting of sand which now covered his food and, with a weary sigh, he pushed the plate to one side and put his hat down in its place in front of him.

'What I don't understand, Margaret – and I know I'm not a Classical scholar like you and Hunt and the rest of them – but if Oxyrhynchus is so damned important, why aren't you excavating the city itself instead of digging around the rubbish dumps outside the walls?'

The young woman fixed him with such an intense stare that he was forced to look away from her and down at his hat where his fingers flicked at the band around the brim. The wind tore at the fly sheet but the rope held firm. Then suddenly it died, drowned out by a silence every bit as disconcerting as the howling it replaced. The woman caught her breath.

'Treasure!' she whispered with fire in her eyes.

He glanced up at her nervously and wondered whether she was pulling his leg. She was far younger than him, in her early twenties, but with an intelligence and maturity which often managed to unnerve him and which had originally brought her to the attention of Grenfell and Hunt at Oxford. She was the only one who had been allowed to help them sift through their finds over the summer in England when the Egyptian climate became too unbearable to work closer to the excavation site itself. She had originally joined the expedition in Egypt itself along with a senior member of the Classics Faculty but one season had proved too much for him so, for her second spell, her parents had laid down the condition that she be accompanied by Harold, long-term family friend, loyal and trustworthy…..but rather too easily intimidated. Their daughter, on the other hand, was robust, forthright and more than capable of looking after herself. To many on the team, he was in far more need of a chaperone than she was.

'But I just thought you'd be after something......' he paused to gauge her reaction, '....a little more valuable?'

'More valuable?' She bellowed out the words with such ferocity that he dropped his hat on the floor. 'What could be more valuable than rubbish?'

His unease grew and he shuffled in his seat. 'You're not making fun of me are you Margaret?'

He bent down to retrieve his hat and banged his head on the under-side of the table as he straightened back up again.

'Now why would I have reason to do a thing like that?' she asked, arching her eyebrow as he rubbed the back of his head, letting his hat fall on the ground once more.

'Well, it's just I thought, you know, gold and silver. *Real* treasure.'

Her eyes narrowed. 'Gold and silver? No, no, Harold. Pots and paper, *that's* the real treasure. Documentation, official papers, literature. Everything that gets thrown in a rubbish dump. Worthless at the time – read, used, discarded – but priceless to us. Absolutely priceless. It's a literary graveyard, a cemetery full of lost masterpieces and fragments of life.'

She pushed the food around her plate with the fork but found little that had escaped the sand.

'This was a prosperous society, Harold, have no illusions about that. One of the most important in Egypt in the Hellenistic period. And that means government records, high-brow reading material, quality decorative pieces.'

She leaned forward towards him and dropped her voice to a whisper. 'Have no doubt, this is valuable stuff. Museums would pay handsomely for it and some people would even kill for it as readily as they would for gold and silver. Our Egyptian bodyguards aren't here to protect us from the locals. They're here to save us from our own kind.'

Harold shivered and the candle flickered in response. 'Why Oxyrhynchus though? Why did Grenfell and Hunt start looking here? We're in the middle of nowhere. All the other sites are right next to the Nile.'

'Exactly.' The woman smiled at him, clearly pleased with herself, and then abruptly her smile vanished, as if wiped clean on a blackboard. 'What was that?' she hissed urgently.

They sat in silence, she upright and alert, alive to the slightest sign of danger, he hunched over the table, desperately trying to make himself as small as possible. The seconds ticked by and the woman began to question whether she might have been mistaken. It was not something she was prone to do very often. She slowly began to relax and turned back to her companion. All she could see was a pair of startled eyes peering at her from underneath the hat which had been hastily jammed back on its owner's head in an attempt at some form of camouflage. She had to employ all her concentration simply to stop herself from laughing out loud.

Suddenly the flap of the tent flew open, causing both of them to start. Harold sighed and made to get up to close it but this time there was a man in the doorway, filling the opening of the tent.

'Miss Hodges…..sir' he nodded respectfully towards both of them in turn. 'Mr Hunt has asked me to fetch you. He says it's important.'

The woman pushed her plate to one side and stood up abruptly.

'Pick up your hat, Harold, we're off.'

It took them almost twenty minutes to cross the three hundred yards of sand to their destination. Not so long before, the route would have been punctuated by a chain of tents, similar to their own, which offered a semblance of shelter from the elements. Now though, with most of the expedition team decamped back to England, their journey took them across an increasingly empty landscape and they required frequent stops to re-adjust the scarves and hats which protected their faces from the harsh wind and biting dust it carried with it.

They found Arthur Hunt in a pit framed by panels of corrugated iron and accessed by a short wooden ladder, the rungs bound by thick twine. Sheets of corrugated iron had also been roped together to form a make-shift roof raised on wooden poles high above the walls and with a large enough gap between the two to afford a clear view of the pit itself which was brightly-lit by a series of electric lights powered from the generator. The space was alive with industry, barrow-loads of dirt appearing every few minutes only to be devoured by figures emerging from the shadows and retreating back there again moments later. In the centre of this flurry of enterprise stood Hunt. All the activity seemed to revolve around him. Despite his trademark flat cloth cap, he had something of the military about him, not just by dint of the rich handlebar moustache but in the way he strode across the pit floor, inspecting the progress of the local workers who brought their finds to him.

'Ah, Margaret,' he beamed, holding the lantern in front of him as he looked up at them. He nodded curtly at the man, 'Stebson.'

The woman was already half way down the ladder. 'What have you got, Arthur?'

Still beaming, he picked up one of the wicker baskets which were lined up in front of him and which had originally been used to bury the documents they carried. It was covered with a heavy cloth to protect the contents from the wind.

'I thought this one was full of court records. Well, most of it was. But there's one in particular I think you'll like, Margaret. I've cleaned it up as best I could. Obviously we'll be able to do a better job back in Oxford but still…'

As he spoke, he walked towards a small tent which took up one corner of the pit. When he and the woman had squeezed inside the cramped space, he gingerly handed the basket over to her and watched as she placed it on the table top between the two of them and carefully peeled back the cloth. There were no chairs so both of them hunched over the basket instead, shielding the contents from Harold who stood at the doorway to the tent as if waiting for an invitation to step inside.

Margaret gazed at the scrap of papyrus which sat on the top of the pile.

'The bugs have had a good go at it.' Hunt seemed almost apologetic.

She nodded. 'All the left hand margin's been eaten away. Shame. But it's really not in bad shape'

She bent closer to the papyrus, deciphering sometimes a whole word, sometimes only an odd letter.

'Well?' Hunt said expectantly after a while. 'Who do you think it is? I'm pretty sure I don't recognise it but, if there's anyone who'll know it, it's you.'

Margaret's cheeks flushed with pride. 'Well, Arthur, that's very kind of you but really I don't…..' Embarrassment reduced the final words to a mumble before she managed to collect herself again.

'Leave it with me for a few minutes,' she announced firmly. 'Let me have a good look at it and hopefully I'll give you some answers.'

Her companion smiled at her and nodded his agreement, planting an affectionate but slightly clumsy pat on her shoulder before turning on his heel and heading out of the tent. He marched purposely towards the waiting throng but, just as it threatened to envelope him again, he seemed to remember Harold's presence and paused.

'Move yourself, Stebson,' he barked. 'I know she's on her own in there but I'm sure she won't come to any harm.'

Margaret heard his comment and tried to stifle a laugh, not quite successfully enough to prevent her chaperone from hearing. Out of the corner of her eye she watched him stare at her for a moment before following the other man's instructions and heading away from the tent.

Now alone, the woman felt a sense of relief that she could fully focus her attention on the task in hand. Hunt and Grenfell had spent many years at this remote site before her arrival and, over that time, they had sifted through thousands of pieces of papyrus, some in well-preserved rolls but many existing only as flimsy scraps or fragments caked between layers of dirt and sand. In the process, they had become remarkably adept at identifying those finds with the greatest potential importance.

She knew she would never have been able to filter the material so quickly or so accurately but, now that this had been done for her, her own particular expertise in textual and literary criticism could come into play.

Her fingers trembled as she carefully smoothed out the papyrus on the trestle table in front of her, conscious that one slip or heavy touch could obliterate whole words or lines forever. As soon as Hunt had shown her the writing, she'd picked up on the Aeolic language, a helpfully obscure Greek dialect, and had a strong feeling about its provenance. It's what had impressed the expedition leadership in the first place – her uncanny ability, especially at such a young age, to hone in on her target once she had been given the scent. To her, though, it was less of an art than a science. There were always clues, clear signposts to anyone who had immersed themselves in classical texts for much of their teenage years as she had. Taken step by step and following a simple and logical process of elimination, the possibilities could quite quickly be narrowed down to just a handful of options. Perhaps, she would concede, that's when the art came in; the feel for style and language, far more subtle clues, which could reveal the fingerprints of the true author.

She took out her notebook and carefully jotted down any of the letters which she was able to recognise, just as they appeared on the papyrus. Any gaps or markings she found difficult to decipher, she left a space and underlined their position on the page. When she felt she had pulled out as much as she could from a first run-through of the text, she placed the fragile scrap of papyrus with its faint markings back into the basket and re-covered it with the cloth before turning her attention back to the notebook.

She loved this part of the process. By making vertical slashes to separate the more obvious words, whole phrases and then entire lines would gradually appear out of the jumble of letters on the page. Where the meaning remained opaque, she would go back to the papyrus to see whether she should revise her original interpretation of the script. At this stage, and in less than ideal conditions, all she was trying to do was to get an initial feel for provenance. She was certain it was poetry now, not easy to recognise when written in one continuous block of gap-free letters, and could even discern the metre, another clear indicator of its origin. Her heartbeat grew faster as more was revealed.

Harold was the first to see her emerge from the tent and shouted at Hunt to let him know. The workers scattered as their boss hurried over to where the woman was standing.

'Well?' he asked. 'Was I right in thinking I'd not seen it before?'

She looked at him without expression. 'Yes,' she replied, 'I think you were.' She handed the basket of papyri over to him, almost reverentially. 'In fact, if I'm correct, you're certainly not alone. No one's seen this for a very long time, centuries.'

She took out her notebook and showed him the markings.

'It's dactylic hexameter,' she went on, 'and it looks like 6th century judging by the language.'

'So, it *is* poetry then?' Hunt interjected.

Margaret blushed. 'Oh yes, sorry, it's verse. Quite beautiful from what I can make out.'

'Doesn't that mean....?' He trailed off as she finally looked up at him. Her eyes burned brightly.

She could hardly contain her excitement but the showman in her controlled her urge to blurt out the answer.

'Go on, Arthur, say it.'

His words came as a whisper so that Harold had to strain to hear them.

'We've found her.'

Margaret smiled at him in genuine delight. 'Yes, Arthur, I suspect we have.'

Harold was growing increasingly frustrated at the exchange.

'God damn it, who is it then?' he blurted out.

The woman looked over at him, acknowledging his presence for the first time.

'The greatest female poet of Ancient time, possibly all time,' she announced, her eyes ablaze with excitement. She stabbed her finger at the page in her notebook.

'These, my friends, are almost certainly the words of a genius.' She paused to collect her breath and reached out a hand, slightly melodramatically, to steady herself on her companion's arm.

'Unless I'm very much mistaken,' she exclaimed triumphantly, 'these are the lost words of Sappho.'

Fourteen

In that spot, cold water babbles through apple branches
and the place is all shadowy with roses
From quivering leaves deep slumber falls down

There was no embarrassment the next morning, no awkward attempts to avoid eye contact, no tacit agreement to wipe the events of the previous night from the memory. Instead he had adopted the 'sleepy little boy' role – all dozy, disoriented and vulnerable – and she had happily assumed the maternal mantle, ruffling his already-tousled hair and cradling him in protective arms.

After several minutes, she eventually pulled away from him, kissing his half-opened eyelids and smiling as her hair flicked his face and his nose wrinkled in response.

'I'm going diving for treasure,' she declared emphatically. 'I'll see whether they've got a mask and snorkel at the desk. I might not bother wearing anything else.' She gave Dan a hugely flirtatious grin. 'Do you feel like coming? Again.'

'Later,' he mumbled and buried his head into his makeshift pillow of T-shirt and shorts, oblivious to her innuendo.

'Suit yourself,' she said (although, muffled by the pillow, the words sounded unnervingly to Dan like 'shoot yourself') and reversed out of the tent, zipping the flaps back down with a satisfying 'thhhwip' – a fitting V sign flicked at the slumbering figure within.

But Dan hadn't gone back to sleep. Instead, he opened one eye and waited for her footsteps to register sufficient distance before rolling over and replaying the key moments of the previous night in his mind. He couldn't quite believe it had happened, readily acknowledging how unlikely such an outcome had appeared at one stage. Whenever he thought of Laura's incredible teasing of him with Ian or her trick with the vanishing underwear, he would shake his head with a mixture of amazement and admiration....and then rewind the action to see whether he could find the events any more credible second time around. He would never experience an episode like that again. No one would. It was pure spontaneity, a one-off and brilliant because of its uniqueness.

By the time he eventually wandered out to the shore, Laura had already made several trips down to the seafloor and had amassed quite a collection of ceramic and stone fragments, placing them neatly in rows on top of her discarded T-shirt at the water's edge. It was actually *his* T-Shirt, the cover of a Smiths single, Big Mouth Strikes Again, depicting a young James Dean astride the obligatory motorbike but wearing an unlikely combination of spectacles and sweater. It had been appropriated by Laura first thing that morning as some sort of trophy for their love-making and he had been in two minds whether to let her keep it but the silt and dirt from the pottery, smeared over the pale purple image, made the decision a little easier to make.

He bent down and examined one of the pieces. It certainly had colour on it, presumably a tessera from a mosaic by the shape and size of it, but meaning nothing without the whole it was once a part of. He placed it back in its position amongst the rank and file and picked up a mottled-brown piece of smooth pottery which had caught his eye. It had writing on it. He had thought it a pattern of some sort when he first noticed it but, now that he held it close to his eye, he could make out distinct letters, Greek letters, which ran across the width of the ceramic surface.

He traced the lines with his finger; ωσγαρ. He couldn't make out the sixth letter at the fractured edge of the shard because the discoloration, which the sea had administered in generous proportions across the entire surface, was particularly impenetrable at this point. He picked over the other finds and came across one more piece which had similar letters, fainter than the first, two o's or perhaps οὐ, he wasn't sure. He heard splashing and looked up to see Laura making her way towards him.

'Where did you find all this?' he asked as she gingerly stepped over the shingle and out of the water.

'Exactly where he said, mosaics and all.' She looked extremely pleased with herself as she placed her latest spoils on a spare piece of the cloth. 'He did bloody well to make out animals and warriors but you can definitely see shapes and colours of some sort. And the wine jars, Christ they're incredible. Not complete anymore, about half the original size I guess, but you really can swim in and out of them, you really can. They must have been gigantic. They still are.'

She was buzzing. Really excited. He had to wait several moments for her to pause for breath long enough to allow him to get a word in edgeways.

'And where did you find these two?' He pushed his up-turned palm carrying the inscribed pottery towards her. 'They've got writing on them. Were they with the mosaics?'

She peered at the two pieces he was holding.

'Oh those, no, I found them early on with the other bits and bobs here.' She pointed at a couple of rectangular stone fragments. 'It's a bit further to the jars than I thought it would be. I probably scoured half the bay getting there.'

She plucked one of the pieces from Dan's hand, 'Do they really have writing on? I didn't realise under the water. I thought it was a pattern.'

Dan stripped off his top and waded into the water.

'Come on, Laura, there's probably a jar down there with a whole bloody novel on it and it's not going to be easy to find the rest of it without you.'

'But what about "take only photographs and leave only footprints"?' She seemed genuinely concerned. 'This lot belongs to the Greek people. It's their heritage.'

Dan paused, weighing up her words against the strong compunction to continue his quest for treasure. After a short while, he turned back towards her, his decision made. 'Bollocks to that,' he snorted and dived under the water, determined to drive yet another nail into the coffin of conservation.

Eventually she followed him in but her presence didn't seem to make quite as much difference as he had hoped and, after fifteen minutes of fruitless searching, they still had not come across any sign of the rest of the vase. Finally he caught sight of some coloured fragments in a hole below him. Only when he dived down for a closer look did he realise that the hole had sides and that these sides were as tall as his torso. Several of these wine jars sat together amongst the shingle and seaweed. It was an incredible sight, reminding him of photographs of ancient shipwrecks which his books on Greek art plundered with tedious regularity to bring their dreary texts to life. Any regret at the failure of their original mission was rapidly submerged under waves of childlike exuberance as the two of them took turns to plunge into the cavernous wine jars, transferring the cracked swimming mask from one to another in between each dive trip, leaving the other to tread water on the surface. Laura was the first to suggest they head back and they began to make their way slowly to the shore. Dan's progress was made slower still by having the pockets of his shorts weighed down by fragments of mosaics, pottery and glass, all of which he assumed were ancient Greek but which in reality covered time periods spanning from Late Roman (the mosaics), Early Byzantine (the pottery) and Mid-Eighties (the glass which a German tourist had skimmed, ducks and drakes-style, into the water and landed quite inadvertently into the jar on the third bounce).

Dan had totally forgotten about their earlier search until Laura, who had ended up with the mask and snorkel and was scanning the rocky seabed behind him, tugged at his foot several times until he turned to face her.

'This looks like the place I found your novel,' she spluttered, taking in a mouthful of water as her tired legs proved less and less effective at keeping her afloat. She pulled off the mask and handed it over to Dan. 'At least as long as that big crab down there has stayed put for the last hour or so.'

Dan's eyes widened through the mask, reminding Laura briefly and unnervingly of Mr Magoo. He took a deep breath, made an OK sign with his fingers and pulled himself downwards to the sea bed below. He spotted the creature pretty quickly. It was difficult to miss. 'Big' seemed to be an understatement for this particular crustacean and he gave it a wide berth, keeping a cautious eye on it as he flicked at the rocks and pebbles in the surrounding area. His scuba diving training made him extremely efficient with the snorkel, shooting a blast of air out of the tube just before he surfaced and avoiding the effort of taking a breath above water as a result, but, by his third dive down, fatigue began to take a grip on him as well.

'Who'd have a crab as a bloody marker?' he thought, his frustration mounting as he hovered above his target and scoured the sand and shingle below. 'It's probably gone walkabout since she last saw it. Or it comes from a large family of identical giant crabs who all live in the same neighbourhood.' He nervously looked over his shoulder to check that one of its brothers wasn't sneaking up behind him.

Just as he was on the verge of giving up, he finally caught sight of a brown tube standing proud of the rocks and pebbles, the smooth curve of something more man-made and considerably closer to the clawed monster than he had hoped to look. Gingerly he picked at the find, hoping to avoid attracting unnecessary attention from the guard nearby. After a few gentle tugs, the piece finally freed itself from the sand and he stared at it in amazement. It was the lip of a vase, obviously so with a small piece of the body tucked underneath it. Dan brushed the surface lightly with his fingers. It didn't seem to have any writing on. 'Too near the top' he thought to himself.

He headed back to the surface and presented it to Laura in triumph. She seemed genuinely pleased with his success, not least because it gave her an excuse to head back to the shore.

'I'll be along in a moment,' he said. 'I'm just going to say goodbye to my mate.'

Having taken a little while to adjust his mask, he dived once more under the water and swam towards the crab, closer than he had been since his search had begun. The monster stared at him menacingly. It had not moved one inch in all the time he had been uprooting its garden. Hard as nails. He shifted his gaze to its claws. They were resting on a smooth rock which served as its nest. He looked closer. Suddenly he realised that it wasn't a rock but a curved piece of pottery, far larger than any he had found so far. Dan almost groaned at his luck. He took one last look at his adversary before heading up for air. He was sure it was smiling at him.

After breaking the surface, he turned towards the shore and saw Laura walking the final few steps through the shallow waves. He looked at her helplessly and thought of calling her back but she was too far away to hear him even if she had have been the slightest bit inclined to drag herself back into the sea again. 'Bollocks.' He slapped the water with his hand but received only an insipid and unsatisfactory splash in return. What could he do? He couldn't go back to the shore to pick up a stick – he would never find the bloody crab again. He suddenly became acutely aware of how tired he was. But he couldn't ignore his treasure. He had put too much into the search to give up now. Taking a deep breath, as much to calm his nerves as fill his lungs, he sank down to meet his fate. He dropped to within two feet of the beast. One look at the giant claws told him he needed to be armed as well and he picked up the largest stone he could find before approaching his adversary. He considered whether to smash the stone onto the crab's back but only had the nerve to hold it vaguely above his target and drop it like a depth charge. It missed the crab by a sufficient margin not to make it flinch. Either that or it really was a particularly tough bastard. Dan picked up another stone and made towards the crab. Its claws seemed to beckon him towards it. 'Come and have a go if you think you're hard enough'. He decided to break for air instead.

Down he went once more and tried to use the stone to flick the crab off the treasure it was guarding. So pathetic were his attempts that he didn't even touch the creature, conscious all the time that he would need to withdraw his fingers with lightning speed should the claws decide to strike. He reached the surface and pulled himself together for one last foray. He took several short breaths as he psyched himself up for battle and, with a reassuring glance at the rock in his hand, disappeared beneath the water for one final time. With renewed purpose he approached the beast and, with a war cry disappointingly muffled by the plastic of his snorkel, he stabbed the stone underneath its rib cage and gave it as hard a push as he could muster. The crab seemed to scuttle across the floor before resting on its back, one detached claw left carelessly abandoned at its guard-post. For a moment he thought he had killed it before it dawned on him that it had been dead all along. With a huge sense of relief, he collected the pottery and, as an afterthought, grabbed the claw as spoils of war. It briefly crossed his mind that the dead crab could have been left as bait by an even bigger sea creature and he hurried to the surface before there was any chance of the trap being sprung.

A few minutes later, he emerged from the waves close to the shore like a triumphant gladiator, fresh from battle. Instead of the welcome he felt he deserved, he was horrified to see Laura sitting on the beach with a bottle of water from the tent, alternating between taking sips herself and pouring small amounts on the finds. Within moments he was out of the water and emptying the contents of his pockets into a pile on the shingle. With a groan of despair, Laura shuffled across to incorporate this untidy accumulation into her neat rows allowing Dan the opening he was looking for to slide into her position and take over the inspection of their treasure. He related his tussle with the sea monster with false modesty - false because he omitted to tell her it was hardly in a position to fight back - and started to sift through the various pieces in front of him. It was relatively easy to pick out the shards which belonged to the jar in question but many of the pieces had either lost their markings from centuries of erosion under the sea or never carried them in the first place. He was glad to see that the large piece, which he had wrestled from the giant crab, was particularly rewarding – 4 lines of relatively clear writing covering the brown surface. He could even translate some of the words from the ancient Greek: ἰδρὼς ψυχρος 'cold sweat' and τεθνάκην δολίγω which appeared to mean something like 'near death'.

'It sounds like a poem,' he offered, 'some war epic. A passage from the Iliad probably.' He glanced over at his companion. 'Homer's Iliad,' he added helpfully.

Laura stared at him with barely-disguised disgust.

'Yes, thanks for that, you Oxbridge twat.' She picked up a pebble from the beach and threw it at him, bouncing off his shoulder and eliciting a feeble 'ow' in response. 'In case you didn't realise, Scottish cultural appreciation doesn't begin and end with the fucking Krankies you know!'

Dan's upturned palms signalled conciliation. 'Sorry, sorry.' The look on her face made it clear that any attempt to laugh his way out of this would not end well. He looked her straight in the eye. 'Sorry. That sounded patronising and it wasn't meant to.'

She remained sceptical until one final 'sorry, honestly' was considered sufficiently contrite to allow the matter to be put to rest.

'God, you're infuriating though,' she muttered and looked down at the pebble she'd thrown at him. 'Can't believe I missed your mouth by the way – it's a hell of a target.'

It felt like the right time to head back. He picked out the pieces of interest and collected them up into the folds of the T-shirt, leaving several of the finds (including, thankfully, the fragment of beer bottle) discarded on the shore.

Arms around each other, they headed back to the campsite and sat down at one of the wooden benches. Making a rather bold assumption of interest on her part, Dan took her through the provenance of every single find, managing both to reaffirm his academic credentials, which had slipped a little since Athens, and at the same time mislead her utterly with his error-strewn attempts at art history.

She saw through his pretension but enjoyed indulging his passion. He half-suspected this – despite the blinkers his ego inevitably imposed – but he loved talking to her, seeing the sparkle in her eyes and sensing the teasing grin never far from her lips.

'You're a proper little classical scholar aren't you?' The comment seemed to come from the top of her head as she bent over the fragments of pottery, shuffling them around like a card sharp playing 'find the lady' in her efforts to piece them together, jigsaw-fashion, on the bench in front of her. 'So, what makes you think the words come from Homer?'

Dan tried to help with the jigsaw but was rewarded with a slap on the hand for his trouble.

'Well, it sounds like he's writing about war and you'd be hard put to find a passage in the Iliad that didn't hark on about the subject. Not that a military theme exactly narrows down the options. Half of classical literature seems to have been obsessed with war and death.'

'What about the other half?'

'The gods.'

'And what did they get up to?'

Dan thought for a moment, 'Well, I suppose, war and death too......and a dose of deceit thrown in for good measure,' he conceded.

Laura paused from her task and looked up at him, squinting at the sunlight. 'Are you actually any good at Classics?'

She didn't mean it aggressively and he didn't take it as such.

'Good question. I've got a decent memory so can retain vocab but I'm not entirely sure where it's leading to be honest. The subject's definitely grown on me. I was probably just looking for something which would end up delivering BA Cantab after my name and I heard that Classics was under-subscribed compared to Maths or English.' He was almost apologetic. 'I know I should have far better reasons but that's me I'm afraid, a bit of a pragmatist and not much of a risk-taker.'

Laura smiled and took his hand. 'That's why we're such a good couple, lover. I'm the ultimate risk-taker.' She thought she saw him blush. 'Why else would I have shacked up with you?'

'Good point,' he laughed. 'I better switch to medicine, something vocational. I won't be able to afford your expensive risk-loaded lifestyle otherwise.'

'Hold your horses for a while yet.' She unclasped his hand and pointed at their treasure trove of pottery fragments. 'I still need the classicist for a while longer until we decipher this lot. Where's he gone? Still with us?'

He definitely blushed this time and Laura instinctively warmed to him all the more.

'You were droning on about war and all that but what about love?' she asked, quickly adding 'you know, *luuuurv*' when he caught her eye and she suddenly felt it her turn to redden.

'I'm not sure if the Greeks were too bothered about all that soft stuff you know. Not half as much as the Romans anyway. They had a whole production line churning out poetry on the subject: Catullus, Tibullus, Propertius, Ovid.'

'They don't sound much of a romantic lot. Not with names like those.'

Dan laughed, 'Yeah, you're right. They sound like a bunch of thugs, don't they. Except for Propertius. He sounds more like a toff to me. Probably got his man-servant to write his verse for him.' He leant over towards her, warming to the subject. 'Some of their poetry was fantastic though,' he went on. 'Especially Ovid.' He picked up the pottery fragment again and traced the lines of verse with his finger. 'He really was top-notch. A lot of Latin writers just copied the Greeks and blindly followed all the conventions they'd laid out centuries before. But not Ovid. He stuck two fingers up at tradition and took the piss out of the conventions. He was hilarious.'

Laura looked sceptical. 'Hilarious?'

'No, honestly. He was genuinely funny. A real superstar in Rome when Augustus was Emperor. You know we get told that such and such is the new rock 'n' roll? Comedy, cookery, football? Well Latin poetry is the *old* rock 'n' roll. And Ovid was Elvis Presley. The King. *Uh huh huh.*' The corner of his mouth lifted in a sneer of comic proportions. 'All his predecessors followed the Greek rules of Love Poetry. To the letter. The lover – that's the poet – he's always wasting away out of unrequited love. And he's always locked outside the door of his mistress' house, begging her to pull a fast one over her husband and let him in. It's called *'paraclausithyron'*....'

He looked up to see Laura struggling to stick with the conversation,

'....it, er, means "standing outside a locked door". Bit odd I suppose but there you go.'

His helpful translation didn't seem to have much effect on his companion but he pressed on regardless.

'Anyway Ovid twists all this formulaic stuff round. He'd still have his poet sitting outside the locked door but this time he'd whisper to her just to open it a fraction because he's now so thin he'll be able to slip through the crack.'

It was as though the colour had drained from Laura's

face.

'So that's your idea of hilarious is it?' She lit a cigarette and took a long drag on it.

It finally dawned on him that he had been getting a little carried away with himself and he put his hands up in surrender.

'OK, so maybe it's all relative. It was certainly funny compared to Livy or Cicero. I mean all these poets made up the names of their lovers and pretended they were for real. But Ovid quite happily tells us from the start that Corinna, his girlfriend, is a figment of his imagination.'

'Now stop it, Daniel. Just stop it.' Laura spoke the words slowly and deliberately. 'We can get you help.'

'Sorry, sorry, sorry.' He banged his head on the table top. 'Anyway, out of the blue he got sent into exile. Guess that wiped the smile off his face.'

Laura's interest was momentarily raised. 'How come he got sent into exile?'

Dan seized on this encouraging sign and leant forward in conspiratorial fashion. 'Well, it's a bit odd,' he replied, lowering his voice so that Laura also had to lean forward to catch his words. 'None of the classical texts shed much light on it. He refers to it in his own verse only as some sort of 'indiscretion'. What sort of indiscretion is anyone's guess – and most scholars have tossed in a suggestion or two at some time or another. I mean he always sailed pretty close to the wind with his poetry so there's a good chance that what he wrote got him into trouble with the Emperor.'

'Bloody hell. It must have been bad if it got all the way up to the Emperor.'

Well, he was a pretty high profile character don't forget. Honestly, poetry in their day was like our pop music. Superstars and fame, groupies probably as well. His exile to the Black Sea must have been front page news. Like Wilde being sent to Reading gaol.'

'How long was he there for?'

'Who, Wilde?'

She raised her eyebrows in mild irritation.

'Oh Ovid. He died there. Can't remember when but he'd certainly been stuck there for a few years. It was the middle of nowhere. He wrote loads of stuff out there but most of it was rubbish, "I'm cold", "I'm bored", "It's black", that sort of thing.'

'You'd have thought being separated from this Corinna woman, real or otherwise, would've got his creative juices flowing.' She wanted to prove that she had been listening earlier despite her remarks.

He nodded. 'She was his muse.' He swallowed hard, knowing that he felt the same about Laura.

'Typical bloke.' She took a drag on her cigarette. 'Two minutes after he says goodbye he's completely forgotten her.'

They sat for a while in silence, conscious of the relevance of this comment to the present situation and contemplating their own imminent parting.

'Do you think we'll remember this time, remember each other?' he finally asked and watched her shrug her shoulders and sigh a hollow 'Who knows?' through a sad smile.

'It's just that a few weeks ago I met an old girlfriend from school. Well, sort of girlfriend. We used to hang around together, play about a bit. Never anything serious though.'

He paused out of misplaced sensitivity in case Laura found it difficult hearing about his past relationships. This had never occurred to him a couple of days ago when he was bragging to her about his sexual exploits but, after last night, everything had changed.

'Her name was Susie Richards,' he went on, 'and I bumped into her in my local college pub. I hadn't seen her in ages. We got talking about 'the old days' and I reminded her of one or two little incidents, just silly things to laugh about. Like when we slept together...literally. I kept my Y Fronts on, she kept her bra on and neither pair of hands strayed below the waistline all night! And I was babbling on about all these old stories. Like the time when she and her mate, Emma, brought a porn video over to my house when my folks were out and all three of us watched it together like it was a Hollywood film. You know; the odd critical comment, some mention of the poor plot and the diabolical acting. And not a hint of it triggering any adolescent activity. I mean there we were, sixteen years old and seething with testosterone, hormones and God knows what else, watching steamy sex all on our own in an empty house. And what did we do? Turn into a bunch of Barry bloody Normans.'

A wave of embarrassment hit him and he looked down to finger the pieces of ceramic on the bench in front of him.

'I was laughing, really enjoying reliving the memories. And she just looked at me blankly. As though I'd made it all up. No recollection, not the faintest blur. I was absolutely gutted. I mean how could she forget it all so quickly?'

He looked up as her sad smile returned. 'As you say, who knows?' he murmured.

They sat together in silence for a while, watching those cats fortunate enough to have escaped the previous night's barbecue use up more of their allotted lives by teasing campsite dogs whose skeletal appearance suggested that fun wasn't uppermost on their minds. Dan looked back at Laura and watched her flick the dying cigarette onto the ground. He knew what he wanted to say but somehow he couldn't get the words out of his mouth. He desperately wanted her to stay, for it not to be over, but either nerves or pride prevented him from telling her. Instead he gave her a slightly forlorn, apologetic look which, if he had actually been able to see it reflected, would have made him slap himself in the face at such a pathetic effort.

Laura traced the graffiti on the bench in front of her with her finger. Names and dates, mostly English and all made in the last two years. Why didn't he say anything? Did he care whether or not she left? She glanced up and saw him staring straight at her with an expression which suggested nonchalance and indifference rolled into one. She had been steeling herself to ask him whether they might get together in the future but now she hesitated, fearful of the response his look seemed to predict. She took a sharp intake of breath. 'Carpe diem' she whispered to herself.

'We could always meet up again. In a couple of weeks' time? After I've seen the girls. I've only got Mykonos and now Santorini on the list as definites. We could see some of the others together. Or perhaps more round here?' She saw his expression change but couldn't tell if he liked the idea or not. 'That is, if you want to?'

He briefly considered playing it cool but decided he couldn't risk her calling his bluff. Anyway, her courage deserved something more enthusiastic in terms of response.

'Yeah that would be great. Really great. Well, to be honest, it would be a crime against literature if we didn't get together again. We've got to work on our Travellers' Tales collaboration haven't we? I'm relying on you to provide a couple of chapters at the very least.'

Relief made her laugh out loud. 'OK, you're right. It would be selfish of us not to publish. The book-lovers of the world deserve better.'

He reached across to take her hands in his. 'Two weeks?

122

I'd still be in the Peloponnese by then….if you want to make it back to this neck of the woods? I mean it's up to you.'

'Sure. No problem. I'm coming this way anyhow to head back to the UK. And it's not as though you've shown me very much of it so far, is it?' She shook her head in disappointment. 'Some tour guide you turned out to be.'

He smiled at her and leant across the bench to kiss her.

'But you got your money's worth though, didn't you?' he whispered as he drew away before she reached up to grab his neck and pulled him back towards her again.

Identifying where and when to meet proved a less than straightforward exercise as he rejected several locations due to practicalities and she dismissed a number more because she didn't like the sound of their names. They finally settled on the entrance to the museum at Olympia at 4pm in two weeks' time to the day. She said it was indelibly etched on her memory, he wrote it down in case he forgot.

Later that night in the tent, Dan lay on his side next to her and gently stroked her sleeping face, trying hard to commit the lines and curves to memory as his fingers traced a path along the arch of her eyebrow and over the ridge of her cheekbone. She was so beautiful, he thought, a fresh and pure sort of beauty and one which couldn't be conjured from the cosmetics counter. He was not naïve enough to believe that she was definitely 'the one' but he felt sure they had a future together. A picture of them sharing breakfast in an apartment, their apartment, kept occurring to him. It was an image that felt natural and comfortable and he thought about it so often that it became almost real to him. It was an image that cropped up often as he sat outside the museum in Olympia, waiting for her to arrive. Three hours on the first day, three more on the second and two on the day after that. He played out every scenario in his mind for her no-show – the unreliable Greek ferries, a different museum at a different site, a family bereavement – without touching on the true cause.

On the fourth day he finally moved on, leaving the details of his travel plans with the ticket attendant and a message for him to pass on to Laura. With no photograph and only the scratchiest of descriptions to go on, the likelihood of success was never too high but the attendant was keen to help any fellow mortal who spent longer sitting outside his museum than most other people spent inside.

Every night for the next week Dan would lie awake retracing the curves of her features with his fingers as the memory of her face slowly slipped away from him. Only on his return to England would he discover that memories were the sole souvenirs of this wonderful girl left to him. Every set of prints, the full record of his three months in Greece and Europe, were totally blank as each film had never once been properly wound onto the spindle of the camera in the first place. He was crushingly disappointed, as much for the loss of stolen flash photos of statues in gloomy museums (and how he had agonised over taking those illicit shots) as for the disappearance of the sole image of his Scottish muse taken on that hilltop in Palea Epidauros.

There were times to come though when, relating a characteristically-exaggerated version of this current trip, he would grow wistful at the memory of the dark-haired Laura and frustrated at his inability to recapture her features. All that remained was the image of her on the Athenian Acropolis, her face shrouded in shadow and the bright sunshine forming a halo of light around her head.

PART TWO

You ought to thank your lucky star

That here in England where you are

You'll never find (or so it's said)

A scorpion inside your bed.

....

The moment that his tail goes swish

He has but one determined wish,

He wants to make a sudden jump

And sting you hard upon your rump.

Roald Dahl 1916-1990

Fifteen

Home Counties, UK – Today

There was still heat in the sun but, the moment it disappeared behind a cloud, the air took on a chilly edge which served as a reminder that summer was over. Soon the days would be shorter, the wind and rain more frequent and the sun less hot, less often.

The road at the bottom of the avenue, quiet by inner-city and even suburban standards, still conducted a fairly steady stream of traffic past its wide tree-lined tributaries. Most people used it to connect one or other of the two nearby town centres to the motorway but a small proportion, an affluent one, would turn into one of these side-streets to come home.

The houses on the avenue had no numbers just names, a practice which tended to play havoc with delivery drivers and infrequent visitors but, as compensation, bestowed a certain caché to the address of those who lived there.

The young girl trudged past these properties without a sideways glance, oblivious to the sense of privilege she was supposed to feel. She was wearing a heavy coat, collar turned up, and jeans tucked into knee-high boots. Dressed like this, she would not have looked out of place if she had been struggling home the day after a large dump of late winter snow. But then she was a teenager and such a defiant dress code, matched by a similar attitude, went with the job.

She paused at a gate, halfway up the avenue, and punched a code into the keypad. The gate clicked open and revealed a house which, whilst impressive enough, was not quite able to live up to such a grand entrance. It was a

Victorian property originally but had been extended several times over the previous few decades to mask the period cottage at its heart. The girl had lived in it for almost as long as she could remember. In that time, as far as she could recall, her father had done nothing with it structurally. In fact, apart from having a couple of rooms decorated, he had done nothing with it at all. It was a house not a home, convenient enough to deposit him within minutes on to the motorway or the train to London to get to his workplace but far enough out of the city for him to keep his white shirts whiter for longer and save him blowing the dirt and detritus of the city air into his handkerchief every night.

It was probably not the best place to bring up a teenage daughter, especially with no mother around to act as tutor and confidante, but the boarding school looked after her during term time and the towns were close enough and sufficiently lively to provide entertainment during the holidays.

The girl plucked a set of keys from her pocket and opened the front door. Once inside, she kicked off her boots and threw her coat over one of the hooks which lined the wall of the cloakroom. She noticed it slide back down to the floor but continued through to the hall anyway.

'Samantha?'

The voice came from the study. It always came from the study. She didn't answer and went into the kitchen, switching on the kettle and fishing a coffee mug out of the cupboard above her.

'Yes please.'

She tutted but went back into the cupboard to find a second cup.

Her father was sitting at the desk in front of his PC and she set the mug down on the coaster beside him.

'Thanks, sweetheart,' he said and smiled at her.

'It's hot,' she replied, twisting the handle around towards him.

'How was Becky?'

'Fine.'

'Did you go out?'

'Yep.'

'Late?'

'Not really.'

She took her own mug and wandered into the lounge next door. He shrugged his shoulders, resigned to this chapter of his daughter's life, and went back to reading the background notes of one of his cases. He knew his clients would settle before the start date. They almost always did. It was a shame because, after a quiet couple of months, the fee from a long and complicated trial would have been useful.

As one of the more senior members of chambers, and certainly one of the more competent ones, he would have expected to enjoy more regular and lucrative cases than he actually managed. But then his outside interests had taken the edge off his career ambitions and the income from his legal work had remained comfortable rather than astronomic. It was also fair to say that book publications, blogsites and TV appearances, even at his modest level of fame and output, were sufficiently off-putting to alienate clients, colleagues and the clerks on whom he relied for work. It may not have been a deep-rooted yearning for celebrity status which had driven his successful approach to publishers but he had certainly hoped for some level of recognition. Even though he had accepted, with some reluctance, their advice that the appeal of the work was likely to be confined to a fairly small niche, no one was more surprised than him when interest proved somewhat more mainstream.

That said, and whilst protesting the opposite view, he thoroughly enjoyed his invitations to participate in high-brow TV arts programmes or provide the odd interview to the broadsheet Sunday supplements. He was one of the cultural elite, an opinion-former and respected commentator. It was official. His membership of the Groucho proved it.

It was hardly fame with a capital F but he felt an obligation to make the most of it. For his own sake, certainly, but mostly for the sake of his daughter. It had brought with it financial security but at such a high price. Both their lives had been thrown into turmoil, his little girl's before it had ever really begun. He wished she had a mother to shout at and go shopping with, to share secrets and turn to when she was upset. This was his biggest regret. But he also wished his wife was still with him to share the success which had come their way. It didn't seem quite as meaningful without her.

The telephone rang and his daughter's voice shouted 'I'll get it.'

Moments later, she walked back into his study and handed him the phone.

'It's for you,' she said with a touch of resentment, 'long distance I think.'

He frowned and took it from her. 'Hello, Daniel here.'

He heard the man's voice and motioned to his daughter to push the door to. She pulled it towards her and then resumed her interrogation of his CD collection, pretending not to eavesdrop but keeping one ear on the conversation. The person on the end of the line had known her. He had called her by her name.

'What do you want?'

She had rarely heard him sound so short on the phone before. She could hear the other man talking until her father cut him off in mid-flow.

'That's not going to happen. End of story.'

A pause, a few words from the other end of the line.

'I'm sorry but I have no intention whatsoever of doing that. I do not have anything which belongs to you. You know that really, don't you.'

A few more seconds went by and then his voice quietened to a whisper so that she had to lean closer to the door to make out the words.

'I gave you money for you to clear off. That's not an admission of any rights you might think you have. I made that perfectly clear at the time.'

Another pause.

'Listen, she didn't love you. She hardly even knew you. She....' He was obviously interrupted but only briefly. 'She didn't need to tell me. I spent a damn sight more time with her than you ever did. How do I know that there's even an ounce of truth in any of your story? You saw my name in print, recognised a tenuous connection and thought you might make some money out of it. And you did. Well done. Even if what you've told me is true, you made a brief appearance at a time of upheaval in our lives. That hardly constitutes a legal claim for custody. Pursuing this will only cause pain and aggravation to all those concerned, including you.'

The voice on the other end of the line seemed to get louder.

'Not a threat. I'm just telling you how it is.'

Louder still.

'Do you want me to get the police involved?' Her father spoke calmly and quietly. It was either the question or the

131

tone in which he posed it but the volume seemed to drop away and she could hardly hear the man speaking now.

'I'm sure you do miss her. Do you think I don't? How easy do you suppose it's been for us? Pull yourself together, man.'

She wished she could hear the other person's words but instead she waited for her father to speak again.

'OK, I understand. No problem.' He sounded more conciliatory. 'But, Tony….. don't ring again.'

She heard his finger depress the off button and then a deep sigh as he slumped back into his chair. He didn't come out straightaway as she thought he would so she pushed open the door and gave him a questioning look.

He threw a reassuring smile back at her.

'Just a case I'm working on. Getting a bit hairy. Nothing I can't handle though.'

She nodded, not entirely convincingly, and wandered back into the lounge.

He felt bad using this excuse on her, especially since he had employed it several times with her mother. He settled back in his chair and ran his fingers through his hair. They seemed to meet less and less resistance as every few weeks passed.

He shook his head as he thought about the phone call. 'Drunken idiot,' he muttered under his breath.

This man was a chancer, an opportunist. His claims were several and incoherent. He'd struggle to get them to stand up in court. Daniel of all people would know that. But, as an extortion device, they were surprisingly effective. The last time the two of them met was to hand over an envelope of £50 notes. It was far more preferable than some drawn-out legal process to establish the facts and rights, news of which would take precious little time to reach the media, chambers….and his daughter. He had decided that the transaction was purely a practical choice, morally and legally unjustified but a sensible course of action in the circumstances. But two people he had cared about deeply were no longer around to put their own case forward and he was always left with the nagging suspicion that, as much as pragmatism was the acceptable explanation for his action, it was guilt which actually drove his decision.

'Why have you still got these things?' His daughter stood at the doorway and waved a handful of CDs at him.

'Hmmmm?' He looked up at her over the top of his glasses. 'Oh, for when my iPod bursts into flames or decides to conquer the world, taking my music library with it. Anyway those things,' he nodded at the plastic sleeves in her hand, 'may well come back into fashion.'

His daughter stared at him with a mixture of contempt and pity. 'Back into fashion? That's hardly likely, Dad.'

'Anyone my age or above,' he said as he lowered his head back into his papers, 'would have said the same thing about vinyl.'

She knew it was what made him good at his job but she hated him having an answer for everything. She stepped back into the other room and took a look at the CDs in her hand. She opened one of the cases and put the disc in the music system.

'At least you had decent taste when you were younger' she shouted and pressed start.

Daniel heard the familiar guitar riff and leant back in his chair. He put his paper down and slid both hands behind his head. His daughter's voice floated into the study. *'Can't seem to face up to the facts.'*

This song took him straight back to a basement bar in Athens many, many years ago. Laura, Pedro.....for a moment he smiled but his face darkened as more painful memories forced themselves forward.......the fight. He had no better memory of it now than he did nearer the time. How could something so apparently inconsequential have such a far-reaching effect? And how ironic that she should play this song, given the phone call he had just received.

'*Psycho killer, qu'est-ce que c'est,*' she sang.

He shivered involuntarily. More than ironic, almost prescient.

It was one of the most important and far-reaching chapters of his life. More than that, it was a pivot, an episode which shaped the direction his life was to take. Everything that came afterwards seemed to have been conceived, altered or infected by those few short weeks. One chance encounter, one remarkable girl, one drunken disagreement and the path of his life fundamentally shifted.

How naively he had yearned for a life full of excitement and thrills. 'Be careful what you wish for,' Pedro had written in a recent email exchange and he'd been right. Daniel hadn't commented in his own message back – he'd been pleased enough that Pedro had made the effort to track him down once he'd been published in Portugal – but he couldn't help wondering how this young firebrand had ended up settling back down in his home town, taking up accountancy for a living and working out of an office in his parents' house. Lost potential or sensible decision-making? The answer wasn't as obvious to him now as it once might have been.

He looked out at his daughter as she danced around the room. He had suggested 'Laura' when they were searching for a name but his wife was having nothing of it. She was probably right, he conceded, but remembered being a little more stubborn at the time.

The song ended and his daughter took it as a sign to head purposely into the study, as though her dance had been a warm-up exercise for this exchange. She fixed him with a determined stare.

'I want to go travelling next summer. With Becky.'

He couldn't help but let out a slight groan. 'Oh, Sam, you're far too young. Surely you realise that.'

It was the answer she had been expecting.

'God, you're such a hypocrite. You were my age when your parents first let you go off on your own.'

'I was older than you and anyway your grandparents, bless them, didn't know what I know.' He got up from his chair and perched himself on the edge of the desk next to where she was standing. 'And what do Becky's parents say. Has she told them?'

'They'll say yes.' She knew this wasn't necessarily true but she was angry. 'They're a lot more chilled than you about this sort of thing. What's the worry anyway? 'Fraid I'll end up like your Scottish girlfriend?'

She realised this was a pretty low blow and instantly regretted it. It also handed the moral high ground to her father. Many years ago, especially with her mother, he would have taken it but, instead, he stood up and stepped towards her, reaching out a hand to hers.

'Well, yes, I suppose so. Amongst other things. The world is a scarier place than it was in my day. What happened to Laura could happen to anyone. She wasn't stupid or naïve you know.'

The girl pulled her hand away from his.

'What, like me you mean?'

He tried to explain but she carried on over the top of him.

'No, she was just marvellous wasn't she?' The sarcasm was heavy and obvious. She wanted to hurt him. 'Isn't she my surrogate mother? Hasn't she paid for all my nice clothes, my education. For all this?' She theatrically spread her arms out and slowly spun round on her heel.

'It was her idea for a treasure hunt and I wouldn't have got anything published otherwise so I guess we've a lot to thank her for.' He paused and took a sharp breath. 'But a lot which we wish could have been different too.' He slipped off the desk and slowly made his way back round to his chair. She had lost the exchange and knew she would get no further by arguing. At least not now.

'Ok then. I'll give Becky a ring and apologise for having such a dickhead for a father.' She was already on the stairs as she spat out the final few words. For a brief moment, he considered storming after her and forcing her to retract her comment. Instead he let out another deep sigh and settled back to his papers, draining his coffee before it got too cold and resigning himself to the fact that she was probably right.

PART THREE

Remember me when I am gone away,

Gone far away into the silent land;

When you can no more hold me by the hand,

Nor I half turn to go and turning stay.

Remember me when no more day by day

You tell me of our future that you planned:

Only remember me; you understand

It will be late to counsel then or pray.

Yet if you should forget me for a while

And afterwards remember, do not grieve:

For if the darkness and corruption leave

A vestige of the thoughts that I once had,

Better by far you should forget and smile

Than that you should remember and be sad.

Christina Rossetti, 1830-1894

Sixteen

The girl nervously rolled her fingers over the accelerator and the moped picked up speed, jerking forward as it did so. Immediately her hands tightened on the handlebars but the bike steadied itself and continued its journey up the shaded side of the hill away from the beach. As her confidence grew, she touched the accelerator once more - this time with a sharp twist of the wrist – and the bike again responded with its familiar judder just as it arrived at the first bend. Round the corner, the road straightened into a long stretch which funnelled the wind down the hillside towards the sea. SLAM! It was like hitting a wall of air. The bike whined its displeasure but the girl rolled her head back and laughed, her black hair dancing behind her, free from the dusty helmet safely housed in its container beneath the back of the seat.

The next bend was still 200 metres ahead and the gradient of the road levelled out, allowing the bike to pick up more speed. She started to sing, almost shouting the words to hear herself above the rush of the wind in her ears. 150 metres. A bird seemed to race her for a few seconds before veering off to the right and swooping down the rocky bank towards the coast road below. 100 metres. She changed gear and whooped with delight as the bike leaped forward in response, her confidence spreading to the machine. 50 metres. She looked down at her knee and frowned at the grease mark which the engine had left on her skin. With a lick of the fingers she rubbed the mark, managing merely to smudge it across her thigh. She was still looking down as she reached the bend and only glanced up when the bus was all but upon her. She knew she had no chance. There was no point even trying to take evasive action and, for the first time in her life, she accepted her fate unquestioningly. Her final thoughts were not of fear but of puzzlement – how had she allowed the bike to wander over onto the wrong side of the road? She died with a frown on her face rather than terror in her eyes. The impact threw her back across the asphalt and over the side of the bank. Her limp body bounced twice on the stony ground before snagging on the bushes halfway down the slope but the bike, upright and engine running like some riderless phantom, careered past her and slammed into the lower road, hitting the ground with a sickening crunch.

London, UK – 1996

Daniel started himself awake. His whole body was tense and his neck was sore. He wanted to rub it but his muscles seemed incapable of responding to instructions. He felt a brief flicker of panic and took a deep breath before systematically relaxing each part of his body, slowly and deliberately, until movement was restored. Even then, he found himself snagged on the sheets and unable to break free of their grip. It was not a hot night but he was coated in a thin film of sticky sweat which clung to the material and stubbornly refused to let go. Each attempt to escape seemed to entangle him further until, with one concerted effort, he shifted his body up and a few inches sideways. His exertions had been accompanied by a loud grunt and he turned his head towards his wife to see whether he had escaped notice. Sarah was peering back at him, her eyebrows raised questioningly.

'Bad dream,' he whispered in answer and nestled back into the pillow.

'Not a wet one I hope,' she mumbled.

He opened one eye and glanced over at her again.

'Chance would be a fine thing,' he grunted.

Sarah smiled and rolled over onto her back again, her hand resting reassuringly on her still-flat belly.

Daniel settled back down as well. He stared at the ceiling, struggling to replace the image of the crash with something less disturbing. Sometimes he wished he hadn't found out what had happened to Laura. It wasn't as though he had gone out searching for the answer. It was over a decade since he had last seen her after all. She had stood him up. It had bothered him at the time. He was young. He moved on. Or at least he thought he had. In the intervening years there had been the odd flashback but in the past few weeks, since hearing the news, he seemed to have thought of little else; some of it provoking warm memories but much of it painful.

No doubt he would have remained unaware and untroubled had he followed his original plan to give the law society dinner a miss. It was a Friday night after all and Sarah had long since given up playing the dutiful wife at these events, preferring an evening of TV and chocolate hob nobs instead. It wasn't as though Daniel always made it to the dessert himself, arriving home early enough to support his wife's argument that his career progression in chambers must be on pretty shaky ground if it relied on such a brief appearance to shore it up. 'Listen,' she'd told him, 'you're good enough and confident enough to turn these things down.' She had only mentioned it once but it had struck a chord with him and for several weeks, fully-persuaded that no amount of brown-nosing could justify such mind-numbing boredom, he had every intention of staying away. At the last minute though, something happened, something which seemed so inconsequential at the time but would end up transforming the direction of his life from this point on. He changed his mind.

As the rain hammered down on the taxi taking him to the venue, he cursed his weak resolve and resigned himself to yet another miserable and tedious evening. But this time things were different. This time one of the guests caught his eye. He watched her surrounded by a gaggle of junior barristers and admired the way she controlled the conversation of the group, leading her male companions on with an appreciative laugh and a flick of her ebony hair before putting them down with a raised eyebrow or a chiding wag of the finger. He was mesmerised by her. As he dutifully worked the room, making polite conversation with the people he was supposed to converse politely with, his eye would constantly be drawn back to her. He had a nagging feeling that they had met before, a long time before, but infuriatingly he couldn't put his finger on when or where.

The seating plan put her next to Daniel at dinner. If it hadn't, he would have sweet-talked the master of ceremonies into making the necessary adjustment anyway. For the duration of the meal, he concentrated all his efforts on her, refusing to get drawn into the various conversations which sprang up around him and which, in some cases, directed themselves at him.

He tried to gather clues with some degree of subtlety, teasing information out of her rather than jabbing questions at her. He wasn't sure whether she shared his sense of half-recognition but, if so, either her probing was several degrees more subtle than his own or alternatively she was deliberately giving nothing away to avoid him making the connection.

He wondered whether their paths had crossed on the legal circuit but she explained that her only connection with the bar was the friend who had invited her that evening and whose chair sat, unoccupied, next to her own.

'He's making his own connection with the bar at the back of the hall,' she added, nodding at the empty seat.

She seemed reluctant to reveal too much about herself – all he'd gleaned about her profession was that she was somehow involved in the hotel trade – but she appeared to have no such qualms about discussing her family, giving Daniel a run-down of her never-ending supply of siblings in such painstaking detail that he found it hard to stop his concentration wandering every few seconds. Suddenly he looked up at her.

'Sorry, what did you just say? About your sister?'

'What, the one helping my parents move house?' She had covered quite some ground during the time it had taken for her words to filter through into Daniel's consciousness.

'No, no, the one who was travelling round Greece. You said her name.'

'Laura? God yes, it was terrible. A moped accident on one of the islands. She didn't stand a chance apparently.'

'Which one? Which island, do you know?' Daniel was anticipating 'Mykonos' so her answer of Santorini momentarily threw him until he remembered that this may well have been the next step on her itinerary.

'Was she at Strathclyde?' he asked, trying desperately to dredge up any facts about his one-time companion from beneath the sludge of so many intervening years.

'Yes, that's right.' The reason behind this sudden barrage of questions finally dawned on the girl. 'Were you there as well? Did you know her?'

'No, no, I wasn't at college with her. But I think I met your sister in Greece. Dark hair, dark eyes….well, like you I suppose? We got pretty close. Did you actually say she'd died?'

Daniel hardly heard her response….or at least he heard it but didn't really take it in. He was shell-shocked. The girl asked how long he had known Laura and he was embarrassed to admit to just a handful of days. He tried to express how much she had meant to him, the passion and vitality which had lit up their time together, but, despite his best efforts, he still managed to make their relationship sound little more than a holiday fling, conjuring up images of drunken fumblings on package tours.

His reaction indicated a depth to their relationship which even he was surprised to discover. He had loved her and that's what he told her sister. He couldn't quite believe that, just days after he had last seen her, she had died, her life snatched away pointlessly and prematurely.

He had to adjourn to one of the QC's chambers when the ache in the pit of his stomach threatened to make him physically sick. The girl sat next to him with her arm around his shoulders, astounded by the power her older sister had exerted on him and desperate to find out how she had made such an impact. For several minutes she stroked his hair before moving closer and pressing her lips lightly against his cheek in a line towards his ear. He hardly seemed to notice but offered little resistance as she turned his face towards hers and bent forward to kiss him on the mouth. He seemed in a trance as she steered him towards the leather sofa and lowered herself on top of him. The only word he uttered was to call her by her sister's name but, far from taking offence, she encouraged him instead. 'Yes I'm here. Laura's here.' The room was lit only by the glow of the streetlamp through the window but the dead girl cast her dark shadow over the two figures before her: one lying with his shoulders braced against the arm rest and his eyes tightly shut, the other with her dress bunched up above her waist, grinding herself on to him with fierce intensity. While Daniel was struggling in vain to recapture the spirit and exuberance of that special time in Greece, the girl sitting astride him was trying desperately to bring herself closer to the older sister she never really knew.

He arrived home that night full of guilt and regret, the only time he had been unfaithful since he had met Sarah. She was asleep by the time he got home and he sat for several minutes in the bathroom, head in hands, watching a steady flow of tears drop to the tiled floor and wondering for whose benefit they were falling. That night he slept very little as he constantly replayed the chain of events in his mind, unable to blame drink but conscious that some powerful force had been drawing him all evening towards that inevitable conclusion. He was horrified by what he had done but also bewildered. He couldn't understand how he had been so weak. By the following morning, he felt even worse and readily surrendered to the over-powering urge to cleanse himself. His first shower took so long that it used up all the hot water but, so desperate was he to wash away any trace of the girl, that he used the pretence of strenuous exercise to take a second one later that morning. He would happily have opted for a third if he thought he could brave the chill water without arousing any further suspicion.

He was paranoid that Sarah already knew what he had done. Every question she asked him about the previous evening, apparently delivered out of politeness more than interest, seemed designed to trip him up. He knew that sounding too negative would simply heighten suspicion and prolong the interrogation so he tried to pitch his answers somewhere between casual indifference and mild enthusiasm. He took no pleasure in lying to her. He kept telling himself that he was looking at the bigger picture. There was nothing positive to come from admitting his stupidity and, as long as his indiscretion remained a one-off, Sarah was better off not knowing.

He felt uneasy about this position though and, over the

following days, his mistake seemed to hound him wherever he went. Adultery and political sleaze dominated the newspapers. Each policy issue, tragic accident or snippet of celebrity gossip seemed to have, at its root cause, some sordid love triangle or moral failing. Every television drama he settled down to watch with Sarah had a love cheat as its central character, convincing him that the TV production teams must have been a hotbed of extra-marital affairs. When he retreated from the media to the relative safety of the dinner table, he would sit, horrified, as Sarah ran through all their friends and acquaintances who were cheating on their various husbands, wives and partners in every conceivable permutation. According to Sarah, there was even one cheating on her lover with her own husband – a declaration which temporarily convinced Daniel that his wife was fully aware of his infidelity and was applying slow and deliberate torture until he cracked up completely.

What aggravated his guilt was the knowledge that they were trying for their first child. It had already taken far longer than they had anticipated and the monthly cycle of hopes raised and dashed had become depressingly familiar. There was a suggestion that something in Sarah's medical history was hampering their chances but, for all he knew, he could equally be the source of the problem. He was well aware how much she wanted a child and how loudly her time clock was beginning to tick. His own time clock seemed to operate on an altogether different setting and he was unable to generate the same natural sense of urgency. He wanted a child because his wife did. He wanted one quickly because he was desperate to present his mother with her first grandchild to dampen the twenty years of pain since his father had died and, at the same time, give her a renewed reason to live.

For several days, he couldn't help but wonder whether

the seed he spilled so pointlessly during that drunken evening just happened to be the one containing the magic ingredient at the heart of their search. It was only later, after Sarah had broken the news to him, that he worked out it was probably on the night *after* his disloyalty, during one of the most apologetic bondings he had ever experienced with his wife, when he had managed to provide the spark of life they had been waiting for. If he was right, it was an irony so delicious that it made a compelling argument for the existence of a higher being able to enjoy it fully.

Seventeen

Sarah found out about her pregnancy at roughly the same time that Daniel's conscience finally managed to out-wrestle him. She had always felt confident of success that month. She hadn't mentioned it to Daniel, not even on the morning of the test, but she was so sure she was pregnant that she would have been shocked if the blue strip hadn't actually materialised on the indicator. All afternoon she kept on looking at the thin tube to check that the reading hadn't disappeared.

As much as she was looking forward to telling Daniel the news, she couldn't wait to make the call to her parents.

'Marion, it's Sarah,' her father would shout away from the receiver. She would be able to hear her mother's anxious commentary in the background ('on my way', 'just a moment', 'nearly there') as she negotiated a route to the second phone, as though Sarah might get bored of waiting for her and hang up before she got on the call.

'Hello, love,' they would say in unison, 'everything OK? What's the news?' One of them would then forget to pause for an answer, leading to a drawn-out argument between the two of them over whether or not they were allowing their only child sufficient opportunity to update them about the recent events in her life. With their initial enquiry forgotten, they would then go on to ask after Daniel and several of Sarah's friends before finally remembering that they were yet to hear an update on their own daughter's adventures way down south in the big city.

Normally she would slowly run down the highlights of the week, slowly not out of choice but because of the frequent interjections which punctuated her commentary: 'Traffic? Don't talk to us about traffic. It's like Piccadilly

Circus at the roundabout heading into the village', 'How lovely. I think we saw that one ourselves at the local theatre....but I don't suppose it had your Simon Russell-Thingummy in up here.'

It was a ritual that was as familiar and comforting as it was frustrating. It was warm, irritating, predictable and reassuring. It made her feel ten years old, often driving her to mouth obscenities down the phone, much to Daniel's amusement. But sometimes, especially when she was on her own, it was exactly what she needed. Well, this time she wouldn't say a word until she'd soaked up every enquiry and they'd exhausted all possible small talk, no matter how long that might take, and then she'd hit them with her bombshell.

But first Daniel. She ran through how she would tell him. How long could she string it out for? Enough to let him get the moans and groans about his workday off his chest until he got round to asking her how her day had been. 'Oh you know, went for a run, took a couple of lessons at college, found out I was pregnant. The usual.' She let out a little yelp of excitement. This was going to be a night to remember, she was certain of it. In his tiny office in chambers, surrounded by stacks of case notes and encyclopaedic volumes of legal journals, Daniel shared his wife's view but for rather different reasons. After several days of agonising, he had finally resolved to tell his wife the truth before she found out from someone else. It was a risk but he felt that the episode had meant so little to him that he surely ought to be able to convey that fact convincingly to his wife. His plan was to give her the news that evening, as soon as he returned home from work.

He was later than usual – she had tried to ring him twice but his mobile was turned off – and so it was with huge relief that she finally heard the key in the door. She poured out two glasses of champagne and put them on the sideboard behind her, concealed from his view.

She hardly noticed the shifty look on his face when he came through the door of the kitchen and dropped his briefcase on the floor. He cursed quietly as the case slowly toppled over into the cat's bowl, sending lumps of congealed gravy splashing over the fridge door.

'Hello,' she beamed at him, unconcerned at his clumsiness.

He hadn't noticed her when he first walked in and nearly jumped out of his skin when she spoke.

'Christ! Sorry. Hi. Didn't see you there.' He could hardly look her in the face. 'Sorry about the…..er…..you know.'

'Don't worry about it. I'll clean it up later.' She studied the weary expression and the defeated slope of the shoulders. He must have had a bad day. She smiled to herself. This would make her news even better. 'Do you fancy a drink?'

'Yes,' he said slowly, 'I think I probably need one.' He put his keys on the table in front of him and put his hands in his pockets. 'There's something I need to tell you.'

Despite her best intentions, Sarah was too excited to stop, 'Well, don't worry. I'll more than make up for your miserable news.'

He was on automatic pilot, the conversation so well-rehearsed in his mind that he could simply turn the tape on and let it run its dreadful course with the minimum of involvement on his part. He had decided it would be better to make his admission of guilt straightaway rather than string it out in some torturous build-up. Better for Sarah but clearly for him too.

He got halfway through his next line, the one about how much he loved her and how stupid he had been, when deep in his sub-conscious, where he had scurried to hide as soon as he had pressed the 'play' button, he took in what she had said and paused. His instinct was to seize any excuse to delay the moment of truth but he was concerned that listening to her news would only serve to make his task even harder. For a split second, he determined to press ahead regardless but, for the second fateful time in the space of a few short weeks, his nerve failed him and he looked up at her.

'Sorry, 'he said, 'go on.'

She didn't need a second invitation. The champagne came out from its hiding place and Sarah spilled out her news, expecting to burst out laughing but dissolving into uncontrollable sobbing instead. And so they stood together in each other's arms, her face buried in his shoulder, dampening his shirt with her tears. It was a scenario not entirely unlike the one Daniel had anticipated....but with rather different consequences.

Over the following days, he felt liberated. More relieved than anything else. Clearly he was delighted by the news but it was almost as though her announcement had absolved him of all blame as well. He knew this wasn't true but it allowed him the opportunity for a fresh start and he felt a huge burden lift from his shoulders. His concern over careless talk evaporated as he reasoned that he knew no one quite unpleasant enough to inflict unsubstantiated and malicious gossip on a pregnant woman. Instead he focussed on the terrible news about Laura, about her death. She had surfaced in his thoughts very little since he had discovered what had happened to her, drowned out by the guilt of his own lapse, but now he found himself thinking about her during the quiet moments in the day, trying to piece together the memory of their time together. Some of the flashbacks he blocked out immediately, sensing the arrival of an unpleasant thought before it could fully break through into his consciousness. Many more were filtered out in case knowledge of the dreadful outcome contorted or disfigured otherwise warm recollections. From what remained, the experience which stuck in his mind most vividly was sitting outside the museum waiting for her to turn up again. It seemed callous to admit it but he took some genuine comfort from knowing the truth. He had been stood up many times in the past but never had he come across a better excuse for a no-show. "Public transport", "work commitments" and "forgetfulness" had all been used on him previously but, by anyone's standards, "sudden and tragic death" beat them all hands down. He hadn't been rejected, he had been denied. But what if he had asked her not to go, to forget about the reunion with her friends? Perhaps if she had stayed, things would have been very different. Perhaps she would have held onto a life which deserved so much more than the abrupt end it received.

And how on earth had she come off her bike? This puzzled him. She wasn't a novice. She owned her own motorbike. He couldn't remember her actually saying this but he felt certain it was the case. His thoughts kept travelling back to their last few hours together. It had seemed so natural at the time but, looking back, he was surprised how at ease they had been with one another. He expected to remember the sex but his over-riding memory of their final night was drifting in and out of sleep, wrapped in each other's arms. He couldn't recall any self-consciousness or embarrassment the following morning, just the warmth of their conversation and the gentle humour in their exchanges. At one point she had turned to him and stated, in all apparent seriousness, that they would obviously have to get married now for the sake of the baby. It took an admission of teasing on her part before he calmed down enough to take off his signet ring and place it on her finger, reciting a solemn vow of undying affection just as it slipped back off again. Was she really serious about meeting up again? Perhaps she had no intention of returning to the Peloponnese, preferring to move on to the next challenge instead. And all the time he had deluded himself with the romantic notion that the brevity of their encounter meant the flame of their passion had burnt that much more fiercely. Unfulfilled, and perfect as a result. But would she have come back to meet him if fate hadn't stepped in so decisively? Surely he would never know.

Then the dreams started. Not every night, sometimes not for days on end, but always the same sequence of events. Minor details changed – the distracting grease mark would become a swarm of flies or, more often, a lapse of concentration caused by her thoughts straying to Dan and their impending reunion – but the ending never altered, remaining consistent in its ugliness and inevitable in its outcome. Invariably, the moment of impact would wake him up and he would struggle to get back to sleep, unable to shake off an uneasy feeling that there was something more sinister about her death than his innocuous explanations appeared to suggest.

The broken nights were frustrating at the best of times but his pregnant wife had enough problems with restless sleep of her own without him helping. She knew something was bothering him. Initially Sarah assumed it was his work but eventually Daniel told her that he had read about Laura's death in the background of a case involving one of her old boyfriends. It gave him an excuse to talk about her to someone, even if that someone was his wife, and once or twice he would do so with a little more enthusiasm than was entirely appropriate.

'Look, she sounds too bloody good to be true,' she told

him one evening as he chose the end of a long day to recount the 'Psycho Killer' story, anointing Laura as the disco dancing queen of Athens in the process. 'Was there anything actually wrong with Little Miss Perfect?'

Daniel raised his head from the pillow and glanced nervously across at Sarah, realising that, even by his own impressive standards of insensitivity, he had gone too far this time. He began to backtrack furiously. He knew that the correct diplomatic response was 'yes of course' and dutifully gave it but he struggled to find any blemishes about Laura significant enough to satisfy his wife. In desperation he searched for some small detail which he hoped would suffice.

'She smoked. Like a bloody chimney.' He looked at Sarah expectantly.

'Well so do you, you hypocrite.'

'Yes, but I didn't then. And I only have the odd one now. Just like you used to. It's all a bit more stressful once you've got, you know, responsibilities.'

'Oh dear, how terrible life is for you.' She was clearly unimpressed. 'Anyway, is that it? She liked a puff every now and then?'

Daniel racked his brains for quite some time before unearthing a more suitable example. 'She was a bloody thief as well. Half-inched my Big Mouth T-Shirt.'

'What on earth is a big mouth T-Shirt?' She had been beginning to drift off to sleep. 'Was it the name of some prize you won?'

'Funny. Come on, Big Mouth Strikes Again. The Smiths. It's the cover you like, the preppy James Dean on a motorbike photo. Purple wash.' He checked she was still listening. 'You even like the song don't you?'

He took her grunt as confirmation and carried on. 'Well, it's my favourite song. And it *was* my favourite T-Shirt. She borrowed it for the treasure hunt and conveniently forgot to give it back to me again.'

Sarah raised herself back onto her elbow to face him. 'What treasure hunt? You've never mentioned this before. Didn't we even visit some of these places together?'

Daniel seemed genuinely surprised. It wasn't something he had deliberately kept from her.

'Are you sure? I must have done.' He looked at the slow shaking of her head. 'I *must* have done......didn't I?'

He took a deep breath and recounted the episode as best he could remember. This evidently was not too well as he transposed the Homeric verses from pottery jar to stone tablet and forgot about the mosaics altogether. Sarah picked up on the poetry straightaway.

'Wow, it was Homer was it? That's fantastic. Which part of the story was it from? Did you find it when you got back to college?'

He looked at her a little non-plussed by the question.

'Well, no, I didn't actually. I forgot all about it.'

'But you studied Classics at Cambridge bloody University! You *must* have been curious.'

He looked a little sheepish, 'Well yes, but I wasn't too hot at Greek. I studied it in English with the Penguin translation.'

'A tough course to get on, was it?'

Her sarcastic remark struck a nerve and he reacted more aggressively than was warranted.

'Yes, it was *bloody* tough. There's a lot more to a Greek degree than studying Greek.' He saw her eyebrow twitch upwards. 'Art, philosophy, history,' he stabbed the palm of his hand with his finger as he mentioned each of them, 'there are loads of papers you can take for the degree without being judged on how fluent you are in a dead bloody language.'

He settled back into the pillow and tried to calm down. 'Anyway, that was part of the reason I switched to Law before my final year. I was heading for a third otherwise.'

The conversation had nowhere to run and both of them accepted this last comment as a vaguely conciliatory note on which to end. He knew he had over-reacted. Perhaps it was the challenge to his academic credentials but there also remained in his mind the nagging doubt that he really ought to have behaved more inquisitively and tracked down the passage when he was back in college. If only he had been a little more studious in his first year, a few more nights in front of his desk instead of the bar, he might even have recognised the passage when he first examined it on that campsite bench.

He lay awake long after Sarah had drifted off, racking his brain to remember details of the day's diving but this time not for some long-forgotten mannerism or idiosyncrasy of Laura's but for the words and lines of the writing she helped find. The breakthrough came when he finally remembered that the words were not inscribed on stone tablets but painted on pottery. Moments later, he had slipped out of bed and was hauling a thick leather-bound volume from the bottom shelf of the bookcase out onto the landing. He ran his finger over the gold-embossed letters on the front cover. Liddell & Scott was the ultimate Greek-English lexicon. His edition was printed in 1869 and, according to an inscription inside, had passed through the hands of a pupil of Eton College sometime after 1893 before finally finding its way to Daniel, via a friend of his father's, just before he took up his place at Cambridge.

He lifted the front cover almost reverentially and slowly turned the heavy pages, releasing the musty smell of century-old paper. He quickly found the iota section and ran his finger down the page to find ἱδρώς, the one word he could definitely recall seeing – Laura had made a joke about 'cold sweat' being an apt description of their starlit encounter the previous night. Although there were one or two references to Homer, the primary example of literary usage was recorded as Sappho Fragment 2 Verse 13. 'Christ,' he muttered to himself, 'I was even going to major on Sappho.'

He immediately dived back into the bookcase and rippled his fingertips along the spines of the dustier books in his possession before pulling out the burgundy-bound essay on Sappho & Alcaeus by Denys Page. As he searched towards the relevant passage he gradually realised how little of Sappho's verses had survived from the sixth Century BC. After a while of searching for the Fragment, he became physically aware of his nervousness, the dry throat and shaking hands. He finally found Fragment 2, confusingly sandwiched between Fragments 31 and 5, but could see no words which meant anything to him, least of all ἰδρώς. He read through the text twice more before reaching the inescapable conclusion that, between Messrs Liddell, Scott and Page, there had been a significant difference of opinion over the numbering of Sappho's corpus of poetry. He decided to look up the word in Page's index and saw a reference to Fragment 31, one chapter earlier. He flicked to the front of the book with renewed optimism. The poem was about love and its powerful effects: Sappho was sitting at a banquet watching the object of her attentions across the table and suffering the symptoms of jealousy and desire. He scanned the translation on the right hand page, "A cold sweat grips me and a trembling seizes me all over, I am paler than grass, I seem to be not far short of death…..But all must be endured, since…." The poem stuttered and then broke off in mid-sentence. Daniel frowned and turned the page forward and back, trying to locate the last few lines, but there didn't seem to be an ending to the verse. Momentarily confused, he checked the page numbers in case one of them had been torn out but everything seemed in order. He flicked to the commentary, a little further on, and found the author's notes on the poem: "there was no means of determining the meaning (of the final words)," it read, "since the remainder of the sentence, and indeed the poem, is missing".

He turned back to the verse and read it again, alternating between the Greek words and Page's passionless English translation. He tried to picture the large piece of pottery. He thought he could see ἱδρώς ψυχρος in his mind's eye and perhaps τεθνάκην δολίγω a little afterwards as well. He desperately racked his brains but this was just one brief moment over ten years ago after all. A few minutes earlier he hadn't even remembered the pot itself let alone the words painted on it. But there were more lines, he was sure of it, and Page didn't have these lines. They were missing, lost to mankind for centuries, and he had seen them. It slowly dawned on him. He had seen the verse which completed one of the poetic masterpieces of ancient Greek literature. And where was it now? The last he saw of it was wrapped up in Laura's Smiths T-Shirt, *his* T-Shirt, and stuffed into her bag.

He knelt down by the bookcase and tried to get his head around this discovery. It was significant, really significant. Even the academic label 'important' would be rendered inadequate, to be replaced by more media-friendly descriptions; 'astounding', 'incredible', 'miraculous'. It was like finding a lost Shakespearean sonnet. No, it was like the world only knowing "Had I the heaven's embroidered cloths..." shorn of the last two lines until some librarian, chancing upon Yeats' original manuscript, was able to restore "but I being poor have only my dreams, tread softly

160

because you tread on my dreams" to a breathless world. He vaguely remembered one of the few lectures he attended – in body if not in mind – saying much the same thing.

He would be famous. Not fifteen minutes of TV game show fame but *real* fame. It had been so easy to track down the poem that he cursed himself for not doing so years before. Perhaps it had been too easy. He turned back to his giant lexicon and set about systematically checking all the other references to ἱδρώς. There were only a handful. Some of them he could find from his bookshelf and eliminate there and then, others required the slow whirrings of the internet to track them down. None came as close to fitting his description as the Sapphic verse had. It was her poem he had found, he was sure of it.

He heaved Liddell & Scott back into its resting place and turned to the computer. He spent the next couple of hours braving the ponderous speed of the internet and his unreliable connection to find out more about Sappho, jotting down notes on the back of one of his case studies. Despite living all her life on Lesbos, a small island far from the mainland, she was still the only woman recognised as making a significant contribution to classical literature. More than that, she was one of Greece's greatest poets. All the Latin greats – Catullus, Ovid, Horace – regularly quoted or referenced her. There were even plays written about her.

There was one particular quotation which he kept on re-reading to himself and eventually printed out, despite the danger of the noise waking up Sarah in the adjoining room. It was a quote from a John Addington Symonds and it really struck a chord with him:

"The world has suffered no greater literary loss than the loss of Sappho's poems. So perfect are the smallest fragments preserved that we muse in a sad rapture of astonishment to think what the complete poems must have been like"

'Fucking hell,' he whispered and reached for the orange highlighter pen, picking out 'no greater literary loss' and 'complete poems' before pinning the page to the noticeboard over the desk. It said everything about the enormity of his discovery. He hadn't heard of John Addington Symonds before but, with a quote like that, he hoped a number of other people had. It would be typical of his luck if the bloke turned out to be some amateur historian who paused from researching his family tree just long enough to write pompous and over-blown literary criticism for his local paper, only to find himself freely available on the world-wide web a century later. He made a mental note to check up on Mr Symonds at some future point.

The more he read about Sappho though, the more he realised that the relative obscurity of her writing nowadays had nothing to do with the quality of her verse but was purely down to the fragmentary nature of her extant poetry. It was pretty clear, even during his cursory research, that her whole corpus of work, nine books of poetry, was intact right up until Byzantine times, some ten centuries after her death. Presumably, at that point, the church intervened. It was classic 'Name of the Rose' stuff. Wary of any pagan movement or 'unnatural' activity which threatened to destabilise the natural order of things, an insecure and cowardly religious elite would have ordered that no further copies were to be made of Sappho's work and any current copies were to be destroyed.

He shook his head at the ignorance and stupidity of it all. She had claimed immortality through her verse but they had killed her off, long after her death but well before her poetry deserved to disappear. And all because of the lifestyle she led. Despite the brilliance of her verse and the emotional intensity it conveyed, she would instead be known to future generations purely for the appropriation of her name and the name of her homeland for quite different purposes. Even the plays which he assumed had been written in her honour turned out to be comedies, presumably full of tired and hackneyed references to her sexuality.

From what Daniel could remember from his own studies, it was by no means certain that she even deserved their misguided attentions in the first place. He looked up 'Cleis' in Page's book and, under the heading IRONY, scribbled some more notes on the paper in front of him: 'a creator of poetic masterpieces, largely unknown as a literary giant, instead finds fame as the inspiration behind the lesbian movement despite being married with a daughter celebrated in her own verse as "beautiful like golden flowers" '.

Daniel stared at what he had written for some time before adding a question mark to the end of the note. He had already come across far too many distortions of fact, deliberate or otherwise, for him to be entirely unequivocal about this latest piece of information.

He put down the book and padded downstairs to get a glass of water from the kitchen. He tried to take stock of the situation. Before this evening, before the unbelievable discovery he had just made, his focus had been on Laura and adding the full stop to his relationship with her. He had been searching for closure. He hated to admit his dependence on such an American concept but he could find no equivalent expression on this side of the Atlantic. He had wanted to know more about her, about her death. In truth, he had wanted to know whether she had been planning to come back to him after all. And why shouldn't she have done?

How different things would have been if Laura rather

than Sarah had walked down the aisle with him in that old village church. He drank most of the water and topped up his glass to take it back upstairs. At least it would have meant – he felt callous just thinking it – that he'd still be in possession of that bloody piece of pottery.

But that's not what had happened and 'closure' had just got substantially more complicated. He didn't have a clue where to start. He couldn't exactly waltz up to the front door of her grieving parents and announce 'Hello, I shagged your daughter. Sorry she's dead. Have you a broken old vase she took from me?' Well perhaps he could but it didn't seem the most fruitful approach. He pictured himself at the front porch as the door opened and quickly blocked the scene from his mind before it became too unbearable to imagine.

He had to find another route in. He knew what the answer was but he desperately racked his brain for an alternative plan. Try as he might he could only think of one option. Her sister. It had to be the sister. His groan was long and loud. He had only just managed to put this episode behind him and there would be a genuine risk of Sarah finding out this time if he got back in contact with the girl again. Besides, when he last saw her he was ushering her out of the chambers, pressing her knickers into her hand as she stumbled out of the door into the night.

He made his way upstairs and slumped back into his chair. He was exhausted. Rubbing his eyes with the palms of his hands, he began to think through the implications of putting his plan into action. Suddenly it didn't seem like the obvious answer after all. He couldn't jeopardise his marriage. Not again. Particularly now his wife was pregnant. It didn't matter that the motivations behind revisiting his earlier infidelity were this time entirely blameless. It would be a hell of a gamble. His head was throbbing with nagging doubts and he felt far too tired to dispel them. Reluctantly, he shuffled off to bed, hoping that a good night's sleep would bring some clarity to his thinking and perhaps present him with the sort of neat solution which was clearly beyond his capabilities right now.

As it was, the situation seemed no clearer in the morning and, after agonising about whether or not to involve his wife, in the end he decided to show Sarah his notes from the previous night over the breakfast table to see if she could help. At the first mention of Laura, she nearly threw her cup of tea over him, only holding back because she was enjoying it too much. As he explained what he'd uncovered though, she couldn't hide her excitement about the huge importance of his discovery.

'Christ, Dan,' she gasped, 'if you're right, this is massive. Absolutely massive.' She kept on shaking her head and mouthing the word. 'You've got to do whatever you can to track this down. You know that, don't you? Whatever you can. It's treasure, for God's sake!' She sat down for a couple of seconds and leapt back up again, unable to contain herself, 'Where are you going to start?' she asked.

For understandable reasons, he had stuck with his original story of how he'd heard about Laura's death and kept any mention of her sister well out of the frame. As long as he withheld this one decidedly important piece of information, Sarah was always going to struggle to add any value to their discussion. As a result, her suggestion of re-reading the old case notes to find names or addresses and contacting some of those involved, whilst meant positively and constructively, proved less than helpful.

The lack of enthusiasm which greeted her ideas was beginning to grate a little.

'You do realise don't you,' she said curtly, 'you've got to

find this thing before someone else does. What if they recognise what it's worth or at least wonder enough about it to take it to someone who does? They'll beat you to it. And it was you who found it after all.'

Daniel looked at her sceptically. 'If it hasn't surfaced in ten years, it's hardly likely to do so now.'

His tone had a sufficient lacing of condescension to make Sarah bristle. 'So how do you know it hasn't surfaced?' she snapped, pushing her chair back from the table and storming out of the room. Daniel stared after her, shaking his head at such a ridiculous comment until it slowly dawned on him that he didn't actually know an adequate answer to her question.

It was a Saturday but Daniel decided to go into chambers anyway. If Sarah was right, he might not have much time. He spent the afternoon wrestling with how he should contact the sister again. In reality he knew he had few options. After all he was missing one or two pieces of information, rather important information, before he could set any plan in motion; an address and phone number. Come to think of it, he didn't even have a name. He felt dreadful about this last point and literally hung his head in shame. He…didn't…even…have…a name. She had turned up on the invitation of one of his fellow barristers. He thought he had recognised the chap but he had only got a quick glimpse of him that night at the back of the hall. As for his name – Daniel shook his head in dismay at his increasingly poor retention of facts (not an admirable trait in his profession) – he couldn't even remember that either.

It was not a promising position and he imagined the shadowy figure of Fate poised at checkmate, waiting for his opponent's final futile move. By the middle of the following week, he had resigned himself to conceding defeat when a stroll along High Holborn and, unusually for him, a quick pint on his own in the Princess Louise challenged his atheism. Perhaps there is a God after all, he thought, as he walked in through the double doors and found himself face to face with his barrister who, by the looks of it, had spent most of the afternoon propping up the bar and was now being propped up by the barman in return.

He looked up as Daniel walked towards him.

'Hello, old boy. How's it hanging?'

Daniel responded to this unusual greeting with a rather more conventional, 'Fine, thanks.' And, with his offer of a whiskey being taken up with a show of gratitude normally reserved for last minute reprieves on death row, he began the painstaking process of holding a conversation with his inebriated colleague. Progress was slow and answers to questions were either unintelligible, tangential or simply absurd. Fortunately the man had a habit of talking about himself in the third person – 'John Reynolds is not the sort of bloke who accepts that sort of thing lying down', 'Old Johnny will come to the rescue' – enabling Daniel at least to put a name to the man with whom he was holding this torturous conversation.

'So, John, what about the girl you brought to the last law society evening. What was her name again?'

'Aha, you bugger you. Where did you slink off to, eh?' He aimed an elbow at Daniel's ribs and missed. 'Nice girl. Known her for years. Always badgering me to come to one of our dos. Not contravening the old rulebook was I?'

'No, I'm sure you weren't. And what about the girl? Where is she now?'

'Where isn't she now? She's a traveller you know. She's a nomad. A wanderer, eh? Feet so damn itchy......'

He took a slug of whiskey and managed in the process to lose what could charitably be called his train of thought, preferring to embark upon a eulogy of the pub, its beer and its bar staff. Daniel felt like throttling him.

'Listen, you twat, where the fuck is she now?' he hissed, bending close enough to his companion to spray his cauliflower ear with a fine mist of spittle.

The force of this interrogation and the sudden tight grip on his arm elicited the only lucid response which Daniel had managed to extract all evening.

'She runs the beauty salon in that hotel in Marrakech. Mammon, Moonia whatever.'

And with indecent haste, as though he was aiming to catch a flight to Morocco that evening, Daniel placed his colleague back into the care of the bar staff and headed out of the pub.

Eighteen

Sarah was sitting on the couch at her home in the warmth of the mid-afternoon sun, making notes in the margin of the typed script on her lap and pausing occasionally to take a sip from the coffee mug perched on the arm of her chair. After she had finished reading the essay and had scribbled some general comments and a grade on the bottom of the paper, she placed it on top of the small pile on the table in front of her and grimaced at the significantly larger, and unmarked, pile next to it.

There would be plenty more essays to plough through before she could take her maternity leave. The college was not overly-generous with their benefits and Sarah would need to leave it as close to the birth as possible if she wanted sufficient time afterwards to recuperate and spend quality time with her new baby. She hadn't even told the college authorities yet. Officially, she was sixteen weeks and was just beginning to show. A few of her colleagues had noticed, she was sure of it, but had been too discrete, or perhaps uncertain, to comment. She wouldn't be able to keep it quiet for much longer.

She bent over the bundle of fur curled up next to her and began scratching her cat behind his ears, smiling at him as he squeezed his eyes shut and pushed back against her hand.

'You're my little child substitute, aren't you?' Her fingers moved their attention to underneath his chin. 'What are we going to do with you when the baby arrives, hey?'

The cat seemed to understand the implications of the question and jumped off the couch, heading for its bowl in the kitchen. Sarah shrugged and returned to her essays. There were times, most notably meeting up with girlfriends from her Oxford college, when she felt slightly embarrassed by her line of work. They reeled off tales of back-stabbing and intrigue in the corridors of power in Westminster, high politics in the boardrooms of corporate giants or the cut and thrust of multi-million dollar deals in the investment banking community. In comparison, the latest developments in the staff room of her polytechnic seemed a little on the inadequate side. Officially it was called a university but she refused to refer to it as such ever since an excruciating exchange with one of her friends ended with the suggestion that Sarah had personally and unilaterally upgraded the status of the institution to inflate her own position.

She had originally seen the college as a springboard to greater things in the world of academia; papers published, a book even, a readership at one of the more illustrious institutions, all leading inexorably onto Emeritus Professor of English among the gleaming spires. But then she had met Daniel and, imperceptibly over time, her ambition had diminished as she began playing second fiddle to his own career. In her rational moments, she was happy to accept the situation. They only needed one major source of income and Daniel was probably best-placed to secure the necessary funds. As a result, any job location for her was governed by its accessibility from London and, in time, children were likely to over-ride even this consideration. Sometimes, though, she felt resentful of her husband's progress, that somehow it had been achieved at her expense, by sapping her own drive and transferring it to him.

Truth be told, this was a somewhat recurring theme for Sarah. She was no doormat and she had clearly landed some significant achievements of her own in her life, mainly (though not exclusively) through working exceptionally hard and making the most of relatively modest talent. But she conformed. She played by the rules, sticking to the same guidelines which others would bend or break to their own advantage, often to her detriment. Boys, sports teams, exams, auditions and interviews: in all of them, not every single time but at one point or another, she had lost out to others who hadn't felt the same compunction to adhere so slavishly to the rulebook as she had felt compelled to do.

But, if there were frustrations from her relationship with Daniel, there was much to be positive about as well. She thought back over their six years together. It seemed a long time to her friends but she could honestly say that the years had raced by. She had met him on the insistence of a mutual friend and remembered ruling him out fairly quickly as future marriage material. As she explained to her girlfriend over the phone the next day, he was wonderful company and very engaging but hardly likely to fulfil her every need considering he was obviously gay.

'I like a challenge' she told her friend, 'but this seems a pretty hopeless cause.'

Fortunately, she had been quick enough to hold the receiver several inches away from her ear to minimise the full effect of the bellow of laughter which erupted from the other end of the line.

'I don't think so, darling,' her friend had answered when she had finally pulled herself together. 'I slept with him off and on for two years. And I was after Liz. Yes, Liz, the netball queen. And just before Emma. Oh, and come to think of it, during Alison Johnson but for God's sake don't tell her that. Dan is many things but gay is not one of them.'

Despite such reassurances, Sarah had still made no effort to contact Daniel again, this time not because of his sexual preferences but his sexual history. He had slept with half her circle of friends and she had absolutely no intention of giving him a head-start with the other half.

As it was, they met by chance at a party a few weeks later and, despite her pride and best intentions, they had ended up spending most of the evening kissing drunkenly in the laundry room. From then on they were inseparable. Six years, a dozen holidays, a couple of cats, plenty of great sex and a rather painful appendix operation later, there she was; married and four months pregnant.

She was in her thirties now, but not by much, a little younger than Daniel at least – a fact which she reminded him every now and then but which generally solicited a dismissive 'if you can measure it in months, it hardly counts' in response. When she looked in the mirror, she still saw a pretty face. Not glamorously beautiful but attractive nonetheless. A short brown bob suited her far more than the long hair (flowing on a good day, tangled mop on others) which marked her years at college. And she could still do 'sexy' when she put her mind to it and was in the mood.

She put down her pen and settled back into the cushions, wrapping both hands around the warm mug and drawing her knees up onto the seat, feet tucked under her bottom. Her thoughts turned to Daniel's recent odd behaviour. His obsession with the dead girl had become decidedly unhealthy, even before this latest development. Long work hours and lack of sleep. It was not the ideal combination. And now this fragment of ancient writing threatened to plunge him even deeper into the past. Initially she'd been carried along with the excitement of the discovery. It was a wonderful notion but, the more she thought about it, the more she realised how unlikely it was. He called it an inscription so what were the chances of these two or three words actually being part of a sixth century poem? He had said himself that his Greek wasn't exactly up to scratch. It was probably a shopping list or something equally mundane. Nothing special. And anyway, this girl Laura would hardly have carried a few mucky pieces of old rock around with her. Not in a backpack the size of a postage stamp. There are more important things for a girl to keep with her than a lump of granite. But what could she do to take his mind off this wild goose chase? Perhaps he needed a break, a change of scene.

A knock at the door interrupted her thoughts. She looked at her watch, frowned and made her way across the hallway to answer it. In front of her was a young man with a Mediterranean complexion, obviously tall despite standing on the pavement two steps down from the doorway.

'Hi, hope I'm not interrupting anything,' he said, a little cautiously.

'Only essay-marking. It's slow progress.'

She paused to allow him to explain the reason for his visit but he shuffled his feet nervously and brushed the seat of his motorcycle with the leather glove in his hand.

'Do you want to come in then?'

He nodded enthusiastically. 'Essay-marking, yeah? Got to mine yet?' He followed her into the house. 'You'll love it. It's what you'd call a new interpretation, completely original. I read all your recommended list. None of them took my approach'.

Sarah gave him a weary look, 'In that case, Tony, as soon as you get your paper published, I'll pop you on the recommended reading list as well.'

'It's because I'm a bit older than the rest of the class.' He wanted to take control of the conversation again. 'You know, more mature, more experienced.'

She frowned at this last comment but had already turned

her back on him and was heading into the kitchen, flicking the switch on the kettle as she entered the room. Tony followed her obediently, padding a few steps behind.

'Coffee?'

'Yeah sure. Thanks.' He brushed the dark hair from his face.

Sarah gave herself a refill at the same time and took both mugs back out to the lounge, setting them opposite each other on the table by the settee. Tony was already sitting down and reached out for his mug with one hand just as he picked up one of the essays from the pile in front of him with the other. 'Hey, hands off,' she barked, a sharp slap causing him to drop the paper. He feigned injury, grinned and settled back into the seat with his coffee. Sarah walked over to the sideboard and thought about lighting herself a cigarette from the packet sitting on top. She had told Daniel that she had no craving for them at all since finding out about the baby but, every now and then, she could murder for one. She left Daniel's packet where it was, certain that he would have counted its contents anyway, and took a sip from her coffee instead.

By the time she turned back to the settee, Tony had got up and was standing in front of her, inches away from her. He bent his head slightly and leaned towards her.

'What on earth do you think you're doing?' She pulled her head back and away from him. 'I'm pregnant for God's sake.'

He reeled back and stared at her in astonishment.

'Pregnant? With a baby?'

'Yes, Tony.' She spoke slowly and deliberately. 'With a baby. That's how it generally works.'

'With *my* baby?' He looked at her with something approaching tenderness.

Sarah took a deep breath. She had been dreading this

174

moment. There was almost no chance that the baby could possibly be his. It had been a lecture trip. An important one. She had been incredibly nervous. There were so many people in the audience, including some senior members of the college committee. Most of her class had also made the journey to support her, several of whom insisted on taking her to the hotel bar afterwards to celebrate her success. She had got drunk. In fact she had got so drunk that, if she hadn't woken up next to Tony the following morning, she would have doubted his claim that they had even slept together. She was still slightly sceptical that anything had actually taken place but his reaction to her news made it clear what he believed to be the truth.

'It couldn't possibly be yours, Tony.' She tried to sound like his teacher. 'The dates don't match. There's no doubt it's my husband's.'

She watched his expression change. The tenderness was gone and, in its place, was something far less pleasant, something closer to a sneer.

'Bullshit.' He moved back towards her again. 'You can't be sure it's not mine. You might not think so but you can't be absolutely sure.'

She tried to hold his stare and not waver but, fatally, her eyes flickered down, just for a brief moment, and it gave him the answer he was looking for.

'Oh yes, Mrs Walker, I'm right aren't I?' He moved closer still and Sarah took a step backwards. His whole demeanour had changed. His confidence was recharged and his words had a menacing edge to them.

'You're not, you know.' She tried to sound strong and confident but the words came out with not much more than a whisper and she knew she hadn't even managed to convince herself.

She flinched as Tony stretched out a hand towards her

and he grinned as he reached behind her for the packet of cigarettes on the sideboard. He took one out and lit it, taking a long draw on the filter and blowing a smoke-ring into the air.

'So what are we going to do then, teacher?'

'Now listen, Tony, this is going beyond a joke. I'm prepared to pretend it hasn't happened but let's just…..' She half-turned towards the door but his hand snapped forward and tightened around her throat, strangling the rest of the sentence before she could give it voice.

'I'm not laughing,' he told her, holding his grip for a moment longer before loosening it and trailing his fingers down her neck towards her chest.

'Please, Tony.' She mouthed the words but they hardly made a sound.

'Hmmm?' He undid one of the buttons on her blouse and stared at the bare skin he exposed. He was beginning to enjoy himself. 'I wouldn't want your husband to find out. And if the college people knew then I guess you'd be in real trouble. I suppose you'd get thrown out wouldn't you? It might even make the local papers. All your friends would find out.' He slowly shook his head. 'Not good.'

Her heart was pounding so loudly it made her head hurt. She wanted to argue, to remonstrate, but all she could think of was one word. 'Please,' she whispered. It sounded like begging.

He undid a second button and a curve of white lace trimming slid into view as the blouse fell open a little further.

He watched her pretty face crease with despair. She was close to tears. Her future, her whole life, was in his hands. He knew it and the power sent a thrill racing through him.

'I'm pregnant,' she pleaded. 'Please.'

He snorted a laugh and reached down for his fly.

'Well in that case…' he said, pulling the zipper down.

Sarah stared at him for several seconds. She felt physically sick. Every nerve-ending screamed in protest but she felt drained of resolve, defeated. Nodding her head, she put down the mug on the sideboard behind her and knelt down in front of him.

'Good teacher.' He gazed down at her, a slight smirk on his lips. 'Good girl.'

Nineteen

It was only half past ten when Daniel's key turned in the lock after his evening out with Reynolds but, despite such an early hour and his comparative sobriety, he was full of guilt as he tiptoed along the hallway and into the kitchen. He poured himself a glass of water from the tap and noticed the two coffee mugs in the sink. Sarah must have had visitors he thought and took his glass into the lounge.

The radio was still on, softly, and Daniel walked across the room to turn it off. It was unusual for her to leave it on, especially as it appeared that she had gone to bed. What's more, the window was ajar as well. Daniel shut it with some irritation. Why didn't she just put a big sign outside inviting burglars to come in and make themselves at home?

He spotted the cigarette packet on the arm of the chair and cursed his forgetfulness. He could have done with a smoke tonight after wading through treacle with that prat, Reynolds. Out of habit he lifted the lid and checked the contents. He could have sworn he had more than four left from the weekend.

A noise from the room above interrupted his thoughts and he quietly made his way upstairs to the bedroom. As he approached the door, he could hear voices inside the room so he knew that Sarah hadn't gone to sleep yet. He took hold of the handle and gave it a gentle push, following it as it opened into the room. He looked down at his wife accusingly.

'What are you up to?'

Sarah wiped the chocolate from the corners of her mouth. 'A bit of comfort-eating I'm afraid.' She dangled the remaining stub of biscuits from the end of its uncoiled wrapper.

She was under the sheets but still fully dressed, pillows stacked up behind her to prop her up. She looked a little washed-out to Daniel.

'Are you OK?' he said as he sat on the edge of the bed and turned towards her.

She put her hand up to her forehead, shielding her eyes from him as she did so. 'Just a headache,' she replied, smoothing the sheets in front of her and brushing the crumbs off. 'Nothing much to worry about.'

Daniel was relieved and he began to get undressed, carefully draping his suit over the back of the chair before depositing the rest of his clothes in a pile by the door. He put on a dressing gown and sat down on the bed next to Sarah.

'You've been drinking haven't you?' She half-turned to face him.

'Just a couple.' He felt the truth was too close for comfort and so avoided it. 'How's our little one then?' He reached over and laid his hand gently on her stomach. His touch, so soon after her encounter earlier, made her shudder and she pushed his hand away quickly, masking her reaction with a small laugh.

'Oh, fine. You're not likely to get a kick yet.'

Daniel turned to watch the television and Sarah snuggled down into the pillows. She felt ill. She kept on wondering whether it was morning sickness. She even hoped it was. An excuse for some time away from the college, from him. She could see those dark eyes and the cold, steely glint behind them and the hollow feeling in the pit of her stomach ached a little more.

She had told herself that she had simply picked the wrong man for a one-night stand but this was not entirely fair. She hadn't picked him. She could genuinely remember

179

nothing of the night and how they had ended up in the same bed. She recalled exiting it quickly enough the next morning but by then it was too late. She had no doubt he wouldn't hesitate to hang her out to dry – with her husband, the college, the media. Giving in to his threats wasn't the answer but she had been terrified. It didn't occur to her that she had been the victim of rape. Not for a moment. As far as she was concerned, she had been the one to set this chain of events in motion the minute she had invited him back to her room. What she fully understood though was that responding to his blackmail would only prolong his interest. Her best bet was to steer clear of him in the hope that he would eventually grow bored and decide to seek out his sport elsewhere. Not easy when she was the one teaching his class three times a week.

She glanced up at her husband who was staring directly at her with a frown on his face.

'Well?' She looked bewildered by the question. 'I said, penny for your thoughts.'

She gave him an embarrassed smile. 'Sorry,' she said, 'I was miles away.' She patted his hand reassuringly. 'I probably am a tiny bit under the weather I suppose. Don't worry, though. It's fine….really.'

He took her hand and gave it a squeeze. He cared for her deeply. She was his soul-mate. He only hoped that the spark they had always shared would still be there once the baby arrived.

'What about you?' She asked. 'How are you feeling?'

'Tired,' he replied. 'Always tired. But that's the job for you'

She threw the spare pillow over the side of the bed and settled down to sleep, turning her back to Daniel so he could snuggle up behind her, moulding himself around her in an attempt to ensure maximum contact between their two bodies.

'You're working too hard you know,' she said after a while.

'Mmm, yes you're probably right,' he mumbled, not taking his eyes off the screen.

Sarah saw her opportunity. 'Why don't we have a break? Fly off somewhere exotic? While I still can.'

He shifted his gaze from the television and focussed on the back of her head.

'Marrakech,' he said firmly.

Twenty

The television fizzled and imploded inwards to signal the end of the evening's entertainment. For a moment, the only light in the room was cast by the streetlamp outside, dappling the backs of the chairs which grouped around the TV screen and silhouetting their occupants against the bare wall behind it.

Finally one of the figures pushed itself up from the seat with a slight groan and broke wind.

'Ooooh, beg my pardon. Must have been that apple crumble.'

The woman chuckled to herself as she hauled her heavy frame over to the light switch and flicked it on at the second attempt. The arthritis in her hip made movement difficult, particularly after she had been sitting down for any length of time. She was only in her late fifties but her face bore the scars of too much hardship and not enough love. Her husband was the breadwinner but she had probably worked more days than he had over the years, from check-out tills to office cleaning. This latest role, the genial landlady, was perfect for her though. She kept a clean & tidy house and she cooked a mean scrambled egg and bacon. Her fried bread, so she had heard through the grapevine, was generally considered to be the lightest and tastiest in the area. She liked helping people and hearing about their business. She *especially* liked that part. Often more than they did.

'Come on, Charlie. Up to bed.' She slapped the top of the chair with such force that the huddled little figure, who had been trying desperately hard to hide down the back of the cushion, popped back out again with a yelp of fright.

'You coming up as well, Tony?' Her tone with the guest

was far more polite.

'Not yet, Mrs G. I'll stay up a while longer.'

'OK then,' replied the woman as she manhandled her diminutive husband out of the door, 'don't forget to turn the lights out.'

Tony mouthed along with the words, not in malice but rather out of absentminded familiarity. As soon as he heard the right number of toilet flushes, door closings and floorboard creakings, he pulled a packet of cigarettes out of his shirt pocket and lit one of them by leaning forward and sticking it between the grill of the electric fire. He would need to remember to turn this off as well otherwise the old woman would charge it to his bill. And, no matter how much he sweet-talked her, she would not take too kindly to him smoking in the house either. He didn't suppose she was much different from all the other landladies in these faceless streets just beyond the London postcodes, swearing blind her determination to uphold the privacy of her tenants whilst, at the same time, constantly taking more than a passing interest in his comings and goings. Always offering to clear up his room, often suggesting he might contribute some of his tired old belongings to her car boot sale. Always trying to mother him. He took a sharp drag of his cigarette as this last thought loomed into his head.

He got up, wincing as he stood straight, and rubbed his right knee vigorously with both hands – a legacy of one too many tumbles off his motorbike. Slowly he walked over to the window and lifted the latch, giving the frame a sharp push and opening it a few inches into the night sky. The cold air sucked the smoke from his cigarette out through the gap.

He grimaced again, not this time from the pain in his knee but instead at the thought of his encounter with Sarah earlier on that afternoon. His actions had seemed so exciting at the time but now he felt dirty, soiled. He blamed her for leading him on. In her state for God's sake! Okay, he'd put a little pressure on but she wouldn't have done it if she hadn't wanted to. They said no but they meant yes. She'd be back for more, he knew it. It wasn't as though she got much support from her old man after all. If her marriage was so marvellous, she would never have agreed to let him in to her hotel room in the first place. Not that he gave her much choice, practically carrying her inside. But she certainly bent his ear about the bloke. The more drink he poured into her, the more she droned on about him. Some high-powered barrister, so wrapped up seeing to his work that he didn't realise someone else was seeing to his wife. Either that or spending too much time crying over some girl he'd lost in a motorbike crash. Poor bastard.

Tony blew smoke rings at the window and watched them explode against the pane of glass in front of him before disappearing outside. He could empathise with Daniel here. He had lost plenty of good biker friends over the years. It came with the territory. You didn't ride a bike if you couldn't handle a few accidents and injuries. Sometimes you were lucky, sometimes you weren't. When Tony wrecked his knee, his girlfriend broke her neck, the tree which their bike swerved into having a far greater impact on her than him.

And what had he achieved with his reprieve? Not far short of his thirties and still a student. And not a very good one at that. Floating from one course to the next, pausing from his pursuit of academic mediocrity only long enough to bed several of his fellow classmates and, occasionally, the odd teacher.

He had a horrible feeling in the pit of his stomach that his girlfriend would have made a better fist of the second chance than he had.

He took a final drag and propelled the butt out of the window with a flick, watching the glowing trail arc over the small front garden and land on the pavement beyond. He didn't know where he belonged anymore. He had been travelling for years, ever since he finished with school...or school finished with him. Travelling or searching. Or running. First around Italy and then across several borders, their stamps in his passport marking his progress. Just another way, he suspected, of the authorities keeping a watchful eye on him.

How many courses had he enrolled in now? And in how many countries? He paid his way with the money he earned as a bike mechanic and sometimes from less legitimate activities. He was no expert at securing grants or subsidies but they seemed to find their way to him anyway, especially in the UK. He looked out across the suburban street towards the rows of identical post-war houses. This was his favourite country and the one he had stayed in the longest. It helped him learn the language. It wanted him to stay. It looked after him.

He had made a deliberate attempt to snuff out any sign of his upbringing. His accent, by now, was only slight and his colloquialisms were far more natural than when he had first arrived. The colour of his skin gave him away but, in the multi-cultural melting pot of London, the distinction was lost. He belonged.

And he hadn't got into trouble here. Not serious trouble anyway, not yet, and certainly not more than the odd fight. His temper had always been a little quick to erupt but perhaps he was mellowing with age. Who would have thought that an English school teacher would be his type? Her old-fashioned attitude to discipline, punctuality and behaviour would normally have been impossible for him to accept so he must have pursued her, as clinically and systematically as he did, because he knew he would be able to apply a similar level of control on her outside of the classroom.

She probably didn't care very much for him. Not that this bothered him too much – she was hardly going to dictate terms to him in the tutorials again whatever happened - but things were different now. He had no idea whether the baby was actually his. In fact, he rather hoped it wasn't, what with all the responsibility.

His own parents had given up on him so easily. They would never have believed that he could get involved with someone of her experience, intelligence and maturity. The boy from the rough side of Naples and this well-educated English rose. He wasn't exactly going to surrender that without a fight, no matter who got in his way.

He lit another cigarette and gave a nod of acknowledgement to the man whose pack he had pilfered earlier on that day. 'Not even you, mate,' he muttered under his breath.

Twenty One

'It's marvellous, absolutely gorgeous.' Sarah drew back from the window of the hotel room and beamed a smile at her husband. 'The colours in the garden are fantastic. Just look at that mass of purple covering the wall down there.'

Daniel walked over to the window and murmured his agreement as his wife's enthusiasm bubbled on.

'Let's eat outside tonight. We could open the New Zealand sauvignon we brought over.' He was pleased to hear her in such good spirits.

'Only a couple of glasses for you, madam.' He wagged an admonishing finger at her. 'We have a baby to consider.'

She laughed and unconsciously cradled her stomach.

'Rubbish. It will probably do her some good.' Daniel glanced at her questioningly. 'Or him,' she added swiftly.

She wasn't sure about Morocco when Daniel first mentioned it a few weeks before but, after reading up about Marrakech and especially its celebrated hotel Mamounia, she was more and more interested. Now, seeing the hotel and grounds for herself, she was totally enchanted.

'It really is gorgeous,' she said to him again and leant over to kiss him.

The rest of the afternoon and evening passed in perfect fashion, yielding no hint of the events which lay ahead that night. They spent a couple of hours in bed – that drowsy afternoon sex, so much earlier than their normal night-time ritual that it marked out the holiday as something different, something special – before setting off on a tour of the hotel's facilities. He spotted the beauty salon early on in their wanderings and spent the next ten minutes manoeuvring Sarah away from it and himself towards it.

Finally when he felt that the saris and kaftans had

sufficient hold on his wife, he dived into the salon and folded his arms on the desk.

'Hi. I wonder if I can book a facial........for my wife that is.' Even as he grinned at the girl behind the counter his eyes had picked out their target a few feet away to the right. He raised his voice a little, 'When can you fit her in? Tomorrow? Great. Room 103.' Finally she turned round and looked at him. He caught her eye and executed what he intended to be an unconscious double take, although he had watched a few too many comedy programmes for it to be entirely natural.

'Wow! Hi, how are you?' He watched her smile as she walked towards him. 'You surely don't work here do you?'

'Hi,' she replied, 'I run the place...for my sins. Mimi, I'll finish this one off.'

She reached the counter and stood directly in front of him.

'On holiday?'

'Yeah,' he took the appointment stub from her, 'actually I'm with my wife. Do you want to meet up for a drink later?'

'Yeah, sure.' She brushed her dark hair behind her ears. 'How about the Piano Bar, eleven o'clock?'

'OK, great. I'll find it. Eleven o'clock. See you then.'

He flashed her what he hoped was a winning grin and headed out of the door, imagining the girl behind him shaking her head at the coincidence and settling back to her work. Instead, she had watched him every step of the way as he had left the salon, a playful smile touching the edges of her mouth.

Daniel looked at his watch. Nearly four hours to go. He wondered whether he could get through the rest of the evening without arousing suspicion. As it was, Sarah hardly seemed to notice his pre-occupation as they dined in the courtyard of the hotel and then later sipped cocktails in one of the rooftop bars overlooking the chaotic energy of the Djaama el Fna. She was like an excited child, pointing out the acrobats, snake charmers and story tellers in the square below but all Daniel could think about was how to elicit the requisite information from his clandestine meeting later that night.

The delicate task of making his way to the rendezvous unaccompanied went so smoothly it could almost have been rehearsed. On their return to the hotel, she wearily declined his suggestion of a nightcap but insisted that this mustn't put him off and he should go down for a last drink nonetheless. In the end he got to the Piano Bar a full twenty minutes before the agreed hour and spent most of this extra time deciding where to sit. The bar was almost empty and the surfeit of seating options was a great cause of concern for him. He moved places three times before settling on two chairs facing each other close to the unattended piano. Despite the abundance of waiters, no one seemed too eager to take his order so he wandered up to the bar and asked for the House champagne cocktail. He continued to wait at the bar whilst the concoction was prepared until the barman ushered him back to his seat with the polite but firm manner usually reserved for the very young or painfully ignorant.

He sat back in his seat conscious that, of the few people in the bar, all eyes were on him. Even the waiter who eventually brought over his drink seemed to tut disapprovingly as he placed the glass on the table. Daniel began to feel guilty, to see this secret assignation as an awful betrayal of his wife and marriage – far more so than his previous meeting with Laura's sister in London. There was nothing spontaneous or unexpected about this occasion. It was a calculated and well-planned act….and all the more deceitful as a result. He comforted himself with the assurance that nothing untoward was going to happen. It was just about information-gathering. The guilt failed to disappear though because, regardless of whether he liked to admit it, he was not entirely sure that this was actually the case.

It took him some time to unlock his gaze from the table and allow it free rein to roam around the bar. It was a wonderful room, beautifully decorated with jazz-age designs and filled with art deco furniture. Just as his examination had reached the painted sculptures of black slave boys flanking the entrance to the bar, he saw Laura's sister paused at the doorway, confidently scanning the room for a familiar face.

He half-rose from the chair and made a small wave which she acknowledged with a nod and a smile, setting off towards him and winding her way around the maze of green leather, blonde wood and geometric patterns.

'Hi, been here long?' she asked, kissing him lightly on both cheeks.

He shrugged as if to say 'Yes, but I forgive you.'

'Sorry, balancing the books. The annoying Texan woman in one four four had been filed under one fourteen by mistake. Took a while to sort out.'

Daniel greeted her explanation with a grave shake of his head. 'Don't apologise to me. Save it for the old widower in one fourteen who's going to get charged for a facial and bikini wax. Poor chap.' He gave her a broad grin. 'Anyway what do you want to drink?'

He was just about to get up and make his way to the bar when he saw one of the waiters heading towards the table with rather more alacrity than had previously been on show. After a brief exchange in French and a playful kiss on the hand, the waiter headed back to the bar, returning moments later with a shallow cocktail glass containing a bright orange liquid.

'Singapore Sling' she said in answer to Daniel's inquisitive look. 'They don't have it on the menu but they know it's my favourite so they indulge me.'

And what do they get in return?'

The sexual overtones of his question were obvious even without the raised eyebrows.

'Oh you know; pedicure, manicure or anything else which needs licking into shape.'

He laughed and shuffled in his seat, trying to maintain a relaxed and confident air but succeeding only in accentuating his discomfort. The hasty sip of his drink mutated into a loud slurp and he quickly blurted out a question to mask his embarrassment.

'So what on earth are you doing in Marrakech? I had no idea you were living here.'

She fixed him with a fiery stare. 'Yes you did.'

Any words which he might have used in response dried in his throat. The silence was deafening. It seemed that the whole bar had put its conversations on hold out of sympathy for Daniel's position. Finally he broke the deadlock.

'What do you mean?' He grinned awkwardly.

The girl's face softened at her companion's discomfort.

'Johnny wrote to me and told me that you'd been asking about me. He was worried that I would be cross that he'd given you my address.' She flashed him a mischievous grin. 'If you hadn't been in such a hurry at the law society do, you could have got hold of my phone number then. You only had to ask.'

Realisation dawned on him. She thought he was besotted with her. In fact she thought he was so besotted with her that he had tracked her down across two continents in an effort to renew their relationship. And she looked as though she would be happy to do just that. He smiled back at her. 'Oh shit,' he muttered under his breath.

Twenty Two

Sarah lay in bed, unable to sleep. She wandered out on to the balcony and gazed over the gardens, brilliantly illuminated by hidden spotlights dotted around the grounds.

She pondered whether to go downstairs and surprise Daniel. It was always so sad drinking on your own. Like a single ticket for the cinema or a table for one at a restaurant. She smiled as she thought of him propped up at the bar with only a Baileys for company.

She imagined herself gliding into the room, sliding onto the stool next to him and kissing the back of his neck as he leant on the polished counter in front of them. Then she remembered that she was not in much of a fit state to glide or slide on to anything and, once she had finally managed to heave her graceless bump onto the bar stool, any attempt to kiss even the most accessible part of his anatomy would send her sprawling onto the floor again.

The smile vanished as her thoughts turned back to Tony. She had tried to shut him from her mind for the duration of the trip but he kept surfacing. She hadn't seen him for some time now, partly as a result of some judicious lesson swaps with her colleagues but also because Tony himself had been away from classes, called back to Italy for the funeral of one his parents. She had heard from the teacher who had taken her lesson that he had been less than keen to go back home and she assumed his reluctance was down to her. She couldn't avoid him forever. Something had to be done. She wondered whether she could persuade Daniel to set up home elsewhere. They only had a small semi-detached, albeit in a salubrious part of West London. They hadn't needed anything bigger before but now, with the baby, she could perhaps suggest that something more spacious would be required. And preferably in a different part of town. His earnings were growing steadily and would soon reach the level where a larger property, even in London, could be affordable. They would lose her salary – as well as the maternity leave money – and she knew it would be difficult to argue the financial sense of making the move now. But she couldn't see another way out. That bastard would surely take the greatest pleasure in telling her husband the news. Her position in college would be untenable. It might even jeopardise her chances of getting a similar job elsewhere. Certainly she could forget the dreaming spires of university tuition. He may have been only a little younger than her but he was her student and she was his teacher. If she were found out, she could lose her job, her marriage, everything.

But there was something else, something more chilling. He frightened her. She was terrified about what he might do when she refused him. Not just who he might tell but how he might react if he lost control of his temper.

She could always tell Daniel the truth and hope that she would forgive her and decide to move on. That would certainly draw most of Tony's sting. Perhaps with her college supervisors, she could simply deny the accusation. Blame it on wishful thinking. It would be unpleasant for a while and she might need to pull forward her maternity leave but perhaps it would all blow over by the time she returned to work. If she ever did.

Did she dare tell Dan? The trust between them would be irreparably damaged and, without that, she wasn't sure whether the relationship could survive, child or not.

She sat on the side of the bed, head in hands, torn between the easier path of inaction and the high risk admission of guilt. Perhaps she should just go down and see him after all. She would know if she could tell him or not. She thought back to her earlier vision of tumbling off the chair and smiled. She was better off making a low-key and less dramatic entrance.

****

'How did you hear the news about your sister, about Laura?' He had decided that he neither had the time nor the patience for a more circuitous route.

'She was over with some friends from college. One of them phoned early in the morning.'

'Oh yes, that's right. I met them. What were their names again?' He spotted an early opening.

'It was Maureen Mackintosh who phoned up. They'd been good friends for years. Her own parents still live just down the road from mum and dad in Ballieston. Well, they did until recently. My folks are packed up now and ready to move. S'pose it always rubbed salt in the wounds when she came home to visit her parents. That's something Laura could never do. There's not a day goes by when they don't think of her. Not a *day*.' She checked to see whether Daniel comprehended the scale of their grief and the drain on their emotional resources. 'She would have been past thirty now.'

'I know,' he said, 'she was just a little younger than me.

He watched as she began to grow wistful and he knew he had to keep up the momentum before his probing became too obvious.

'What's Maureen doing now then?'

'Some lecturing job at Strathclyde. They were both at college there. You probably know.'

She was beginning to look a little bored with the conversation but Morocco was a long way for Daniel to go merely for one name and address.

'What about the other friend? What happened to her?'

'No idea. Can't even remember who she was. Anyway, that's not what you came over here to see me for is it?'

She leant forward toward him and Daniel seriously considered answering in the affirmative.

****

Sarah wrestled herself out of the baggy T-Shirt and slipped on a loose blouse and draw-string trousers. She went to the door before turning back into the room to pocket the key from the top of the chest of drawers. She took the lift down and wandered through the gallery of empty shops before spotting the bar at the far end on the right. For some reason, her pulse quickened as she reached the dimly-lit doorway – nerves from entering a drinking establishment alone and late at night or apprehension about the conversation she was likely to have. At first she struggled to make out anything in the shadows but, as she focussed on the room and took the whole scene in, she took a step back in surprise. The bar was empty. Not even a barman for decoration. She was momentarily confused until she remembered the piano bar back down the far end of the corridor.

****

Daniel made one last effort at information-gathering.

'How did you get all of Laura's stuff back?'

His companion threw herself back in her chair,

'For Christ's sake, Dan, will you stop going on about her. We brought her back in a bloody box didn't we.'

Daniel looked around nervously and saw that her raised voice had attracted attention.

'Sorry, sorry, sorry,' he hissed. She relaxed a little and he took the plunge. 'I'm really sorry but she had something which belonged to me and I really need to get it back.'

She fixed him with one of her sister's special stares.

'So that's really why you've come here, is it?'

Daniel began to get a little desperate, 'Look, you're really nice and I like you a lot but...'

****

Sarah mounted the small steps to the piano bar and entered the room just in time to see a striking girl with thick black hair deliver a resounding slap across her husband's face.

Twenty Three

It was true to say that the events of that night took a little of the gloss off their holiday in Marrakech. It was meant to be an early birthday present for his wife but turned out not to be quite the sort of surprise which Daniel had in mind.

Sarah didn't speak to him for the rest of the weekend.

In fact she didn't speak to him until Thursday of the following week, and then only to tell him to "fuck off and die".

She had no idea whether he was seriously trying to get the woman into bed. He told her he was just flirting. She probably believed him but he deserved the cold shoulder anyway. Not least because he had robbed her of the opportunity to clear her own conscience. In fact, because she had reacted so angrily, she had probably made it even more difficult to explain her own situation and ask for help. He would be up on his high horse so quickly she would hardly see him move.

Daniel accepted his punishment and resigned himself to a difficult week. He had always understood the risk he had taken in re-establishing contact with Laura's sister but he realised, on reflection, that his decision to embroil his wife in this plan was nothing short of suicidal. If that didn't deserve a couple of days in the dog-house then there was no justice in this world. And he was a barrister so he would know the odds of that.

What he didn't expect was his spell in the kennel to last longer than the entire holiday had. He assumed that all would be fine between them by the time of her routine scan at the end of the week but this momentous event was conducted in such a frosty atmosphere that the nurse decided against offering them the obligatory photograph of their baby in case they turned their sights on her rather than themselves.

It dawned on Daniel that putting things right would require something a little more proactive than simply the passage of time. He began putting all his efforts into making amends with his wife. He had always been thoughtful – relative to most of the other men Sarah had known at least – and he made sure he ramped up the subtle little touches which always proved far more effective than unimaginative alternatives like bunches of flowers and boxes of chocolate......although, for safety's sake, he showered her with those as well. He warmed her side of the bed with his feet before she got in and he left her post-it notes with funny or touching comments for her to find. He was already making tangible progress by the time her birthday arrived but still, on the actual day itself like many beforehand, he hid her presents around the house and gave her cryptic clues to their whereabouts, solving most of them himself in his over-excitement.

More than all this though, he flirted with her again and made her laugh. He forced himself to imagine he was in competition for her affections and began to recite poetry to her again, as he had when they had first started going out together.

It was strange. He thought he was doing it for her benefit, a selfless act or at least a calculated plea for forgiveness, but he realised how much he was enjoying it as well. It comforted him to know that it was quite possible to keep the spark alive but this thought was tempered a little by the recognition of how much effort it now took.

Not that Sarah was feeling quite the same sense of relief or renewed energy. Certainly she appreciated the effort he was clearly making and took great comfort that the warmth of their relationship was strong again but every touching moment, every poem and post-it note, reignited the guilt she felt and accentuated the hopelessness of her current situation.

She hid these feelings from Daniel with some ease. He believed what he wanted to believe, that things had returned to normal. He even contemplated following up on his fresh lead at Strathclyde University but decided that his re-stabilised relationship was perhaps not quite stable enough to risk another Marrakech moment. On top of this, no matter how intriguing he found the mystery surrounding Laura's death and the whereabouts of the missing verses, raking over the ashes of a dead girl, especially one who meant so much to him, was not a particularly appealing prospect.

Besides, he had a nagging suspicion, ever since Sarah had questioned whether someone else had beaten him to the prize, that he might already be too late. Perhaps it was even now in the hands of a dealer who was in the process of authenticating its provenance. For all he knew, another source had recently been discovered to solve the mystery of the missing verse – another gem, unearthed from the dustbins of Oxy-whatsitsname or scribbled on the bandages of some long-forgotten Egyptian mummy. Perhaps the find was already common knowledge in academic circles. If he was going to take this next step, he needed to make sure the prize justified the pain.

He hadn't lasted long enough on the Cambridge Classical Tripos to cover sixth century lyric poetry in any great detail, and certainly not to come into contact with scholars who dedicated their careers to it, but he knew a man who had. Richard Lewis, now Dr Richard Lewis, was an inspiration to him at college, largely as the source of lecture notes from courses he had been too hungover to attend but also as the provider of succinct summaries of books he had not been bothered to read. Despite the parasitic nature of their relationship, they had actually got on reasonably well and had exchanged a little correspondence in subsequent years – enough to legitimise Daniel's phone call suggesting a get-together. If anyone could corroborate the importance of his potential discovery, it was this man.

He arranged to meet up at the Cambridge college where Richard was now a fellow. Daniel had used as his excuse a request for funding from the Classics Faculty which had arrived through the post on the Friday and had been retrieved from the rubbish bin over the weekend when he realised its potential value in helping secure the meeting. He had also suggested, somewhat disingenuously, that they might use the opportunity to catch-up and reminisce over old times. He weighed up the credits and debits: on the plus side, some key insight into Sappho which could unlock fame and prosperity, on the downside, two hours of forced conversation and £50 a year for five years to buy sufficient books to replace those he stole from the Faculty library more than a decade before. It was a close call but the upsides just about won the day.

'So how's your wife? Sarah, isn't it?' Richard had asked after the initial pleasantries had been exchanged and the traditional sherry poured.

'Good, really good. Getting bigger. Our first.'

'Oh congratulations.' Richard raised his glass again.

Daniel was a little uncomfortable talking about his wife. He had told her that he was going to Cambridge but he hadn't mentioned the reason why and, though not technically an untruth, it echoed his recent misdemeanours rather more closely than he would have liked. 'And what about you, Richard? Married yet?'

Dr Lewis' response was equally uncomfortable. He was not recognised as the most eligible bachelor on campus and his attempts to dispel this theory had been so spectacularly unsuccessful that he had seriously considered whether switching sides would improve his chances.

They did indeed discuss the under-funding of the University and its key departments and they also ran through updates on their fellow graduands. They managed to cover the majority of people in their year with remarkable speed, principally because they had so few friends in common that their stories were of little interest to the other.

At every stage Daniel tried to steer the conversation towards Sappho, looking desperately to engineer an opening and even lying about the sexuality of Jane Bunting, one of the Natural Scientists in their year, in the hope of making a smooth transition to the most famous lesbian of them all.

Eventually Daniel's patience, not one of his most admirable virtues, wore too thin and, halfway through a discussion on Richard's current research into 'food and famine in the ancient world', he decided simply to raise the wholly unrelated question of how likely it was to rediscover classical literature which had been lost up until that point.

'What about someone like Sappho?' he continued, 'There's not a lot of her work around is there?'

'No, very little, very little.' Richard seemed slightly thrown by this change in tack. ' *"Few indeed, but those, roses"* '.

Daniel looked a little perplexed.

'Meleager, writing about her surviving poems' Richard explained. 'No, a new fragment of Sappho, why that would be a tremendous find. Extraordinary. Our own Professor Hodges discovered the last one though, didn't she.' He let out a sigh which Daniel took as a sign for a wistful smile and a whispered 'of course' in reply and dutifully provided both.

'How incredibly lucky we were to be taught by one of the giants of literary scholarship,' Richard went on. 'Just think of the years of single-minded dedication to one pursuit – the sacrifices and the disappointments. But think of the rewards too! She left her mark for the benefit of future generations and her name will live long in the annals of academia.'

Richard took a sip of his sherry. Daniel had sat unconvinced throughout the eulogy but was desperately trying not to show it. This last pompous comment was too much though.

'Oh come on, Richard. Does she really deserve such acclaim? Those other guys had done most of the heavy lifting. She just turned up for the applause.'

Richard's look of surprise gradually migrated to a smile. 'I know you're trying to see if I'll bite, Daniel. And I won't. You know as well as I do how tough the conditions were when she was working. There was that documentary about her on television recently. I think it captured the challenges she faced pretty well; painstaking research at home and, out in the Egyptian deserts, hugely difficult fieldwork in dreadfully inhospitable conditions. Years of toil. But that's what it takes to make such a mark on history. You're hardly going to pitch your tent, dust off your trowel and unearth literary treasure the next day are you?'

Save for several years of listening to classical music loudly through his headphones, Richard would have been able to hear the high-pitched squeak which escaped from Daniel's mouth. As it was, he saw the pained expression and wondered whether his fierce defence of the Professor, his mentor, had been a little over-zealous.

'Anyway, another find of that sort is not very likely

though.' His tone was conciliatory, in case he had overstepped the mark a moment before, and he glanced at Daniel with a look of uncertainty which Daniel managed to interpret as a suspicious glare. 'The Greek Lyric poetry in the pre-classical period, Sappho, Alcaeus, Simonides, was designed to be sung not read, as you know. These were singer-songwriters. The name of the oeuvre referred to the lyre rather than lyric sheets so words were rarely written down. Much along the same lines as the oral tradition of Homeric poetry, passed on by *rhetors* who travelled the Greek empire entertaining audiences with epic verse recited from memory. No, not likely. A lost play by Sophocles or Euripides on the other hand...'

'But surely someone committed Sappho's poetry to paper,' Daniel interrupted, still a little unnerved by Richard's earlier comment but determined to push ahead with his line of inquiry, 'otherwise we wouldn't have any of it available to us nowadays.'

'Well yes, of course. But then you have to find a path through the morality and religious beliefs of future generations. Someone of Sappho's purported lifestyle didn't stand much of a chance. Papal purges and book-burning would have done for her. Anti-paganism covered a broad spectrum of activities and inclinations and female homosexuality was definitely in-scope.'

'But she wasn't even a lesbian was she? She was married, a daughter if I remember rightly.'

'Well, strictly speaking she was a Lesbian from her birthplace.' Richard let out a small laugh and Daniel tried unsuccessfully to make a show of joining in with the joke. 'But besides, the sexual mores of the time were unlikely to preclude homosexual leanings simply on the basis of marriage. Love and marriage were often coincidental rather than compulsory bedfellows, as it were. The Greeks viewed marriage as a civic responsibility, an obligation almost. This was the job. Sexual activity was a leisure pursuit where the link to the job was ideal but not necessarily mandatory. So, despite Sappho bowing to the conventions of the time with her marriage, I don't think there's much doubt that she practised a type of love which could reasonably be described by the modern interpretation of the etymological phrase Sapphic.'

There was a slight pause as Daniel struggled to digest this comment.

'So she *was* queer after all?' he finally ventured.

'Well, yes, that's about the long and short of it' Richard replied.

Daniel sat for a while and pondered this information.

'I thought she was meant to have killed herself over a man, flung herself to her death off a rock? What's that all about?'

'Ah yes, Phaon. The tale's contained in one of Ovid's Epistles. We're in danger of taking at face value misinterpretations and deliberate distortions driven by the cultural norms of the time. Sappho was the subject of a number of Greek comic plays - unfortunately none of which have survived to this day – which focussed on her supposed heterosexual relationships like the Phaon example. As the audience would know her as a renowned homosexual, this seems like the sort of joke which comic plays are obliged to contain. I guess Ovid cemented the legend but missed the joke. Unusual for him.'

'So it was just a joke taken too literally?'

'Well, she may well have suffered a premature death. That would have been suitably romantic for a poet of her reputation. But, no matter the rights or wrongs of her reported demise and its subsequent manipulation by the media, there's been something far more insidious and poisonous than that over the intervening years. A number of later translators or commentators actually changed some of the pronouns in Sappho's work to make it seem like she was expressing her feelings towards a man rather than a woman.'

Daniel was genuinely surprised.

'Surely not. How could they get away with that? It would have been pretty obvious, wouldn't it?'

'Moral censorship has been flourishing far more recently than Classical times. John Donne, the sixteenth century English poet, wrote an interpretation of Sappho in a poem in which he makes her preference for same-sex relationships abundantly clear. That poem was excluded from his Collected Works until the turn of the twentieth century. And we could both surely think of more up-to-date examples than that.'

He got up and wandered over to the bookcase behind him while Daniel started to make a mental list of any recent cover-ups he was aware of in case Richard decided to test him on them.

'So that's why nothing much of her work has survived then?'

'Mainly.' Richard selected a book from the shelf and turned back towards Daniel. 'It would also depend on how strong the oral tradition is, how popular the poetry as well I suppose. On that basis, Homer was a more likely survivor than Lyric poets like Sappho or her contemporaries. However, she was certainly held in extremely high esteem by Classical commentators and thinkers. Someone – it might even have been Plato of all people – referred to her as the Tenth Muse. As you would know, that's quite an accolade.'

Daniel nodded his agreement while trying to work out whether Richard had called her tenth or tense. Neither seemed to make sense.

'And just nine books of poems, or at least that's how the library of Alexandria categorised them. Not a large amount but so much more extensive than the few sparkling fragments which we're left with today.'

He paused to take a sip of his sherry and Daniel pressed on.

'I suppose it might not just be papyrus where this sort of poetry would be recorded. Stone inscriptions? Pottery?'

'Hmmm,' Richard gazed up at the ceiling, the book unopened in his hand, 'inscriptions tended to be official or commercial. Wax tablets would be more likely. Perhaps educational, potentially correspondence between friends or lovers. Of course none of that would survive for any length of time. Pottery's a possibility though. There are plenty of Attic Black Figure and Red Figure vases which include a few lines of verse on them. It's usually Homer but, come to think of it, one of the Sapphic poems was found on a third century pot sherd. Probably written by a schoolchild, apparently it was riddled with grammatical errors.'

Daniel took a sharp intake of breath and tried to suppress a cough.

'Which poem was that then?' he finally asked. 'The only one I remember is her sweating and trembling with jealousy at some wedding.'

'No this one was a hymn to Aphrodite, "δεῦρο μ'εκ κρήτας".'

'So, nothing more recent? Nothing poised to take the literary world by storm?' He finished off his sherry after he asked the question but kept his eyes firmly fixed on his companion.

'No, no, just Professor Hodges' as I said...' Richard sat back down in his armchair. 'And the related piece in Cologne of course, hidden in the bandages of a mummified corpse of all places.'

'My God, you really are a walking encyclopaedia aren't you?' Daniel was barely able to hide his relief and raised his glass to his companion with an expression of thanks, bordering on undying gratitude, which wouldn't have looked out-of-place following an all-clear message from the doctor.

Richard blushed slightly at the back-handed compliment, if not the overly-enthusiastic response, and raised his glass in return. They sat in silence for a few moments until Daniel remembered that he had the niceties of a conversation to complete.

'But why do you think the rest of us know so little about Sappho?' he asked. 'Wasn't she recognised by her contemporaries?'

'On the contrary,' Richard replied, 'she was very well-regarded. She was obviously held in high esteem by the Roman love poets – Catullus imitates her closely in a couple of his poems, Horace copied her style and metre on occasions. And who knows how many other allusions we're unable to pick up because such a small amount of her poetry has survived? Look, it's taken only three centuries to shroud the details of Shakespeare's life in mystery. There have been more than twenty five centuries distancing us from Sappho so it's not surprising there's a little uncertainty about her life story.' Richard had been flicking through the pages of the book in his hand. 'Yes, you're right. Married to an official in Mytilene and a daughter, Cleis, named after her own mother.'

'Not quite in line with her reputation' Daniel muttered.

'Ah yes but most things are rarely as they seem,' declared Richard with a rueful smile. 'After all, I kissed dear Jane Bunting once. I was deeply in love. And look how she turned out.'

It was at this point that Daniel knew he had pushed his luck as far as ought and quickly made his excuses.

Twenty Four

This was the fifth day she had called in sick in the past three weeks, the second morning in a row. Her condition warranted some flexibility from the college authorities but she knew she wouldn't get away with many more similar phone calls.

It would be unreasonable of her not to grant the college some credit for the way they were handling her situation but she suspected it was less about the human face of the institution and more to do with the delicate legal position on discrimination which was driving their show of understanding.

She was well aware that her sick days would be putting pressure on other members of the teaching staff and she felt a pang of regret for making their lives more difficult. She assured them she was working from home when she felt up to it and made a big effort to e-mail over lesson plans and catch up with marking the submissions which she then sweet-talked Daniel into delivering to the college office in person.

Her husband was home as well this morning, having arrived back from Cambridge later than anticipated the night before. Whatever he had done there had obviously gone well because he was notably more upbeat than he had been in recent weeks, breezing around the house making her cups of tea and tidying up behind her without being asked.

She found him in the lounge, stretched out on the settee with one of her essays in his hand.

'What the bloody hell's this then?' He looked up from the paper as she walked into the room. '"The Shape of an

Apple is more real than its Taste. Discuss." Good grief. How many of these do you have to read?'

Daniel flicked through the stacks of essays in front of him.

'Well over half of them.' Sarah replied, a little wearily. 'I gave them the choice of the Apple one or "Characterisation" to practice for their General Studies paper. I didn't realise I'd get so many budding philosophers.'

Daniel picked up another one of the essays off the top of the pack and started to read it to himself. After a while he looked up at his wife.

'Hey, this is pretty good. But then it's not one of your apple ones so that might explain it.' He began to read aloud. "Nowadays, authors don't need to cope with characterisation. Advertising has conditioned the public to decode formulaic visual signals for a comprehensive understanding of social class, demographics and sexual history. And all within 30 seconds. This is the age of convenience characterisation, pen-portraits of the bite-size variety, sachets of stereotypes producing instant people."

'Wow, that's impressive. I thought you got all the foreign language students?' He looked at the top of the first page, 'There's no name on this one.'

Sarah wandered over and took the script from him.

'Oh that's one of the boys. There's Paul, Chris……Tony. That one's Tony I think.'

Daniel was in too good a mood to notice the pause which Sarah inserted before mentioning the name, an involuntary reaction as her mind registered the danger and scanned for signs of guilt before deciding it was safe to identify him.

'Well he's good,' Daniel continued. 'He's definitely got potential. What do you think of him?'

'Tony?' Sarah could hardly look at her husband. 'Not much. He's copied that quote from one of the books on the reading list. He must think I'm completely stupid.'

Daniel passed the essay back to his wife.

'Well, there's one thing you can say for plagiarism.' He sat up straight and slipped one of the cushions behind his back. 'It's less dangerous than making it up yourself. I only wish a few more of these celeb authors would follow suit. They all assume a few TV appearances, a couple of panel shows and, hey presto, they're William bloody Shakespeare.'

Sarah saw her escape route and ushered Daniel along it.

'What about you then, Samuel Pepys? Anything in your diary worth publishing?'

'Well, I've got a few travellers' tales.' Daniel replied quickly enough to suggest that he had given this some previous thought. 'They'd easily fill up a book. It could be some sort of compendium; "Travel Travails" or "Holiday Reading", something like that. What do you think?'

Sarah was unconvinced. 'Travel Travails? It sounds like some nineteenth century medical journal. And, as for Holiday Reading....' she shook her head without looking up at him '....they'll think it's just a list of trashy novels.'

Daniel was unperturbed. 'Did I ever tell you about my encounter with a dodgy Spanish lorry driver?'

'Yes.'

'That's a good one, isn't it?'

'It's unbelievable.' She scrawled a grade on the bottom of Tony's essay and slapped it down on the pile in front of her. 'Quite literally unbelievable.'

Daniel shook his head in disappointment. 'It's a traveller tale, my darling. They're not supposed to be accurate historical accounts. The clue's in the 'tale' part. Think of the Arabian Nights or Gulliver's Travels. My Spanish lorry driver is following in the tradition of Aladdin. In fact, remembering his fondness for young boys, myself included, I'd say he'd be following him pretty closely.'

It was probably just her current state of mind but his childish banter irritated Sarah when once it would have made her laugh. For a brief moment she remembered reading somewhere that this was one of the first signs of falling out of love but she blocked the thought before it could take root.

'That said,' he went on, 'they definitely make better reading if they're based on a real event. What about the boat trip to Egypt when we all ended up....'

Sarah was a little quicker to interrupt this time. 'Heard it. Hundreds of times.'

'It's another good one though, yes? And then there's the one when the police raided that flat in Venice?'

Sarah frowned. Now this one she hadn't heard before.

Daniel realised almost as soon as he had mentioned it that this story wasn't his but Laura's and back-tracked swiftly.

'Actually that one's not got an ounce of truth in it so probably wouldn't make the final edit.'

'Listen,' she put the paper down on her lap. 'You *can* write. You really can. I've always said that to you.' She stared straight at him as she would do one of her pupils. 'You might even have something with these travel stories. Base them off something you know – Laura, that Pedro bloke, the lot of them. Christ, it might even help you get her out of your system.

'You think so? I mean about the writing?' Daniel was loving this.

'Yes I do…..but you just need to get off your arse and do something about it.'

'Or get *on* my arse and do something about it.'

'Quite,' Sarah replied patiently. 'I've got some publisher

friends don't forget. They'd help. It would have to be good, mind, but I'm sure they could give you a head-start.'

'Understand. That would be fantastic.' He took a sip of his coffee and placed the mug back down on the table. 'Absolutely fantastic. I know I'm technically competent but that just puts me in the pot alongside everyone else with a turn of phrase and a decent idea. Unless you're out of this world, you've got to be on TV or the child of some literary superstar to get noticed. If your mates could pull a few strings….'

Sarah nodded and pointed her biro at him. 'Just pull your finger out though,' she tried to keep a stern face but couldn't help laughing when his boyish 'will do' came back in reply.

She turned back to her essay-marking and pressed her foot against the leg of the coffee table, inadvertently shifting the whole thing several inches sideways. Daniel grabbed his mug just as the contents threatened to spill over onto the carpet. It was a sharp reaction and he glanced over at Sarah, fully expecting an appreciative nod in his direction if not a full-blown round of applause. Nothing. She hadn't even noticed. By now the coffee was only lukewarm but he drained it anyway out of respect for the effort he had made in keeping the option open.

He settled back into the chair and, buoyed by their exchange, turned his attention to his book-writing ambitions. Of course, the Sappho discovery would be his first publishing breakthrough, the discovery which would rocket him to fame and modest fortune. He had visions of a nice property in Hampstead or Chiswick with electronic gates to keep the riff-raff out and a football pitch-sized garden where his son would develop the feints and step-overs which would one day grace Old Trafford or Twickenham.

Even if his sixth century poetic pot of gold didn't prove quite lucrative enough to put the house within his reach, he could surely use it as a springboard for future earning potential. Once he had made a literary name for himself, that would be the time to give those travel stories an airing. They were bound to sell reasonably well on the back of his earlier success. He thought back to the first time he had tried his hand at writing. A couple of years ago, he had begun to compose a classical detective story, an explanation of Ovid's exile from Rome and the mystery surrounding his abrupt departure. It was a subject which had fascinated him since school and he had bored plenty of people with an account of the event and his theories behind it.

He shook his head. Perhaps this one might prove a little too difficult to resurrect. As an attempt at novel-writing, he had given it up after the first few pages, as much for his un-readable writing style as the un-publishable subject matter. He had been full of hope after rattling several pages off in his first afternoon but had been brought back down to earth when he re-read them the following day. The prose, which had been so vibrant and alive the day before, had somehow deteriorated over-night. The plot suddenly seemed contrived, much of the 'action' was laboured and he was left with more than a slight echo of the stilted translations which punctuated his schoolboy Latin text books. A little better than 'Caecilius est in horto' but not exactly Ian McEwan. He had spent hours trying to salvage something from his efforts, toning down the classical language and spicing up the narrative, until his manuscript was riddled with deletions and amendments from his trusty red biro. Eventually though, he had been forced to accept it as a lost cause. He had never actually killed off the project, not officially. A copy of the amended introduction was still sitting in his Word file even now, condemned to gather cyber-dust on the shelves of his C-Drive. No, better to stick with the travel stories. More mainstream.

First things first though and the information he had gleaned from his Cambridge visit. His meeting couldn't have gone much better. Every concern was put to rest and all his hopes proved well-founded: the discovery was hugely important and there was nothing remotely resembling it currently doing the rounds of academic circles.

It had been decades since a discovery of this kind had been made. And by Professor Hodges of all people. The sly old bird. What had Richard called her? "A giant of literary scholarship". Well, the textbooks of the 21st century would be revised to include his own contribution, shoe-horning him into the seat next to her in the pantheon of classical scholarly greats. It was a place not entirely warranted, as Daniel was sufficiently embarrassed to admit, secured by a ten minute tussle with an ex-crustacean rather than a lifetime of hard work, sacrifice and dedication sifting through libraries of battered tomes and the sands of ancient sites. It had taken Hunt, Hodges and the team years to prise Sappho from her resting place whilst he had managed it in one morning during a post-coital dip. The only part which 'years' would play in his story would be the length of time it took him to appreciate the importance of his find and a while longer to get his actual hands on it again. Still, as long as he dialled up his own classical academic credentials and played down their propensity to go AWOL for long stretches, he should just about deserve his place at the professor's right hand.

He smiled warmly as he recalled the afternoon with her protégé. Despite initial reservations, he had actually quite enjoyed spending some time with Richard Lewis and all those years ago, when he was chief architect of jokes at the poor boy's expense, he never thought there would come a day when that was something he would say to himself.

He looked at his watch. It was nearly lunchtime and the case notes still sat on the table in front of him where he had placed them so purposely first thing that morning. He really didn't feel like running through them but it was a high-profile assignment and he would only have to work through the weekend if he ignored them now. Eventually he stretched over to pick them up. Just as he did so, as though waiting for the cue, the door bell rang.

He shot Sarah an expression of annoyance, as if cursing his luck to be interrupted in full flow.

'I'll get it,' he sighed. 'It's probably for me. I'm expecting a bike from one of the clerks.'

He got up and disappeared out of the door. Sarah saw through his little act and watched him out of the corner of her eye. 'What a load of bullshit,' she muttered to herself.

She settled back to the essays and continued to fill any spare space on the paper with constructive and helpful comments. Normally she would simply scribble a grade at the end but the guilt of so many sick days drove her to make more of an effort than usual. It was only after a few minutes that she realised Daniel hadn't come back in. She put down her pen and listened. She could hear him talking and wondered if he had made a phone call. It sounded like he was laughing…and he didn't do that very often with work colleagues or bike couriers. She levered herself up from the settee and headed out of the lounge. As soon as she stepped into the hallway she could see that he was not on the telephone but still at the door in an animated conversation with whoever had rung the bell.

She could hear the voice of a man and her pulse quickened as she walked towards the two of them. Her husband turned to face her. 'Ah, here she is.' He turned back to their visitor. 'Sorry,' he said, 'I should have invited you in. Dreadful manners.'

Sarah reached the door just as the man walked through it. She reeled back so sharply that she nearly fell over. Daniel was too busy moving discarded shoes out of the way to notice the expression of horror on his wife's face as she realised who he'd been talking with for the past few minutes. But the visitor noticed.

'Hello, Mrs Walker.' Tony grinned at her and gave her the hint of a wink. 'I've just been telling your husband how it was my fault that you ended up in such a state after your lecture in the Midlands.'

Sarah didn't know what to say. The confusion on her face as she looked at Daniel made him laugh.

'I wasn't surprised you know,' he smiled reassuringly. 'You were still worse for wear by the time you made it back the next day.'

Daniel let out a small laugh and then frowned. Sarah was acting oddly and he didn't know why. Perhaps she shouldn't have enjoyed herself quite so fully amongst her colleagues, students and the college top brass but a lecture in front of a sizeable audience was a big deal for her. She deserved to let her hair down.

Tony was also studying Sarah, revelling in her discomfort. He caught sight of Daniel's embarrassed expression and gave him a reassuring pat on the arm.

'Her secret's safe with us three.' He turned to the woman who had hardly stopped staring at him since she had come to the door. 'You know you can rely on me to keep quiet.'

She opened her mouth to say something and then, thinking better of it, shut it again. 'You go back to your work, sweetheart,' she said instead to her husband. 'I'll see what Tony wants.'

'OK,' Daniel replied, stretching out his hand towards the

man in front of her. 'Nice to meet you, Tony.'

'You too. I'll keep an eye on your wife at college. Make sure she doesn't do anything she shouldn't.'

'Cheers,' Daniel turned to wave as he walked back into the lounge. 'Good man.'

Sarah waited until the door closed before turning back to Tony.

'What the fuck are you playing at?' she hissed.

Tony took a step towards her. 'Aren't you going to invite me in?' He put both hands on her hips and stood up straight, towering above her. 'Sweetheart?'

She wrenched herself away from him.

'Get off.' Her forced whisper took much of the sting out of her words but the ferocity in her face made up for it.

He put his hands up in surrender and took a step backwards again, grinning at her all the time.

'Now, what do you want? Don't tell me you need some help with your work?'

'I've missed you at college. You've not been around much.'

'Neither have you.' She tried to take the upper hand. 'Sorry for your....,' she struggled to find the right word, '....for your loss.'

'Fuck him.' It had the opposite effect and the tone of his voice startled her. 'I only went back to make sure he was dead. Heart attack apparently. Should've been something slow and painful.' The sneer on Tony's face was particularly unpleasant. 'So, again, where have you been?'

Sarah mumbled something about being under the weather but Tony cut her short.

'Don't stay away, teacher, or I'll have to come round and see you more often. It might be nice to have another chat with your husband. We got on like old friends.'

She nodded and began closing the door. 'Alright, I've

got the message.' He kept his foot in the door for a moment but finally withdrew it. 'Good girl,' he sneered. 'See you soon.'

She shut the door and held her hands flat against it for several moments, her head bowed down towards the mat in front of her. She took a deep breath and headed back inside to Daniel. He looked up as she came into the room.

'That was quick.'

She hurried past him and dived back into her essays.

'He just wanted a pointer with his work. It wasn't difficult.' She sipped her tea but it was cold.

'Seemed like a decent bloke.' Sarah snorted at his comment but Daniel seemed not to notice.

'I've met him before haven't I? At one of your staff parties?'

Sarah stared at him blankly until she realised the misunderstanding.

'Oh God, no, he's not a teacher.' She almost laughed. 'He's one of the students. It was his course work he wanted to discuss.'

'Bloody hell,' Daniel replied, 'he must be nearly our age! He's either a slow learner or he's really keen not to get a proper job. Do his parents support him?'

Sarah shook her head slowly. 'No,' she murmured eventually, 'we do.'

'Oh right.' Daniel rocked back on his chair. 'I guess he's the kind of bloke your dad has in mind when he goes on about benefit tourists.'

Sarah sighed. Her father had seemed so modern and tolerant when she was growing up. Very 'with it'. All those exhibitions and theatre trips, all that travel to exotic places, embracing different cultures at home and abroad. Every time she brought friends round to tea, she would hope he was at home so that she could impress her schoolmates with her cool dad. But, as he got older, he seemed to grow less tolerant. Any balanced view he used to hold had become decidedly unbalanced: trades unions were exclusively bad, capitalism was generally good and professional rugby was so inferior to the amateur version that it wasn't even worth watching. Immigrants, who had once brought diversity to these shores, had now turned into scroungers.

But he was still her dad. Not quite so cool now but still just as important to her. Everything she had achieved at school, university and beyond, she had done for him. To win his approval and make him proud. So she couldn't help but wonder, as she agitated over her current situation, what on earth he would make of the mess his little princess had found herself in now.

'So where have I come across this bloke before then?' Daniel was talking to himself but it felt like an interrogation. 'It's nagging me. Does he live round here? Surely he didn't go to my school or something weird like that?'

'Doubt it.' Sarah butted in quickly. 'Unless you spent your formative years in the backstreets of Naples that is. Which you didn't. Now…..' she wanted to get him off the subject of Tony as quickly as possible '…..do you fancy another coffee?'

Daniel grunted a no and she was relieved to see him return to his case notes.

'Have a look at this.' She passed one of the essays over to him. 'It's one of the shape or taste efforts.'

Daniel took the paper and skim-read it.

'That's good,' he murmured. 'Reckons the question's ridiculous; that reality is defined by all the senses and it's pointless trying to prioritise one over another. Oh classic: "the least ludicrous way to distinguish between the senses is probably to rank them alphabetically". Like it.'

He shaped to pass the paper back to Sarah but she nodded at it.

'Keep going. There's more. She brings poetry into it. I'm not entirely sure why. I guess she's trying to draw parallels between emotional and physical reactions.'

Daniel frowned and took the paper back. He read further and then a broad smile broke out on his face. 'Oh yes, "How do I love thee?". Our song….well, poem.'

He reached over and squeezed his wife's hand. 'Remember that night?'

She smiled back at him, relieved to be discussing something genuine and warm. 'Of course', she replied softly.

'The pub was packed,' Daniel went on. 'Everyone was talking about the game or business. Office stuff, you know. And there were me and you, crammed into the corner sharing a bar stool, reciting poetry to each other.

"How do I love thee? Let me count the ways
I love thee to the depth and breadth and height
My soul can reach….." (Christ I can't even remember the words now)

Blah, blah, blah *"…I love thee with the breath,*
Smiles, tears, of all my life! – and, if God choose,
I shall but love thee better after death."

And we looked deep into each other's eyes, fell head over heels in love and decided to spend the rest of our lives together.' Daniel noticed the raised eyebrows. 'Least, that's how I remember it anyhow.'

Sarah sighed heavily. 'God, yes, I remember. We were in our own bubble oblivious to the world. Not a care, not a worry. It was really romantic. Everything was so….' she wanted to say 'easy' but it seemed defeatist, '…..so exciting then,' she opted for instead.

It was not the best choice of words and Daniel looked hurt, 'Exciting? It still is, isn't it? Sure, we've got a few more responsibilities now and it's always a little more exciting at the start. But we still get around to doing plenty of stuff don't we? Taking a few risks?'

Sarah's murmur of agreement was not entirely convincing, coloured as it was by her own more recent experience of risk-taking.

'Well I know things are different now you're pregnant.' Daniel was starting to sound a little desperate. 'It happens with every couple. We'll make sure the baby lives for us and fits in with our lifestyle and not the other way round. We'll still have fun won't we?'

Sarah remembered how she used to be such a fervent believer in rejecting the safe and boring middle ground in favour of a life of spice and excitement. But her current problem was so far from what she originally had in mind that it extinguished all positive thoughts about adventure and risk. All she could muster was a strangled 'sure' in response.

She knew that Daniel had taken her comment badly. They had talked about living life to the full too many times for him not to have sensed a change in her position. She also knew that the birth of their first child made him even more nervous that the carefree and spontaneous nature of their lifestyle would be drastically curtailed, ushering in an era of middle age ennui. It used to mean as much to her as it did to him but that was before she had experienced the downsides of 'living life to the full'. She hadn't the energy to explain or put him right. Nor the inclination.

Their exchange had left him flat. He contemplated cancelling the lunch he'd arranged with his old school friend but decided it would do him good to get out of the house. Sarah too probably. Better to inflict his introspection on someone other than his wife – far less dangerous. The worst he could do was dampen his friend's enthusiasm to put a follow-up date in the diary any time soon. Who knows, it might even cheer him up.

He had ended up at the restaurant half an early and had already got through half a bottle of Prosecco before his friend arrived.

'This whole concept of "one true love" just has such a hollow ring to it,' he'd suggested halfway through the salad starter. 'What if it's a load of bollocks? No soul-mate, no perfect marriage - every relationship fundamentally flawed, begging for some sellotape or sticking plaster to patch it up and eke a bit more life out of it. The thrill of the chase and the first few weeks of uncertainty can only last so long. After that, it seems to me it's all downhill.'

His friend had paused for a moment and placed his spoon back into his soup bowl. 'Of course it's bollocks,' he'd declared. 'My advice? Chill out and get used to it.' He'd lifted his spoon back to his mouth. 'Quickly,' he'd added, slurping loudly. 'For both our sakes.'

His friend had left early, unsurprisingly, but he had stayed to finish off the bottle and continue his introspection. Chill out and get used to it? Really? Is this all that he wanted from life? He gave a slight shake of the head as if in answer. 'Not exactly burning brightly' he muttered, drawing a cautious glance from the couple on the table next door. More 40 watt bulb than blinding super nova. Fine if each life was one leg of a relay race, with death merely the signal to pass the baton on. In that case, a contented and leisurely life could seem an attractive option. You could always pick up the pace in a later incarnation. But what if life was a 100 metre sprint instead and death marked the finishing line?

He tried to imagine death. The nothingness, the complete absence of thought or feeling. It was impossible. How could you imagine what it was like not to exist? He desperately searched for logical reasons why his spirit should continue to live on after its host body had given up the ghost. He could find none. Hawking and others had explained the Big Bang, Darwin had put together a pretty convincing theory of evolution and scientists had finally unmasked the inner spirit as a chemical concoction of DNA and a few chromosomes. Earth was not the centre of the universe but one tiny insignificant grain of sand in a desert of stars and planets. Strictly speaking, you had a greater chance of meeting an extra-terrestrial than you did your maker. In the absence of any shred of evidence pointing to the existence of a divine being, the only possible recourse was blind faith; a conscious decision to ignore all rational thought in the vague hope that there existed in this world some additional element that mankind was not yet capable of comprehending.

He couldn't accept such an arbitrary conclusion but, as the hopelessness of it all washed over him, he began to understand why so many people did. Was it a risk he was prepared to take? 'If it's one life, it needs to be a good one,' he thought to himself. But what about Sarah? Surely the role of dutiful wife and mother couldn't fill her with a great deal of enthusiasm either. What were the other options for them both though? How else could they keep the spark alive?

At least he had Sappho and the thrill of the chase. He would be forced to keep up the deceit with Sarah. It was nothing much more than a series of white lies but enough to give an edge to the pursuit. There was also the uncertainty about where the trail might take him and what he might find out. That came at a risk though. What if he was somehow to blame for Laura's death? That could destroy everything.

He only noticed the owner of the restaurant after he'd been standing beside him for a little while. 'Is everything alright, sir?' came the polite enquiry, anticipating a 'fine thank you' and a request for the bill.

Not this time though. Daniel seemed to consider the question carefully for a moment.

'I was thinking about death,' he finally blurted out. 'My wife's having a baby so, you know, new life and all that. I was wondering whether death really was the end or just the pause before a fresh start. Is this our only chance?' The restaurant owner wasn't sure whether he was supposed to reply so just carried on listening. So did the couple next door. 'Do we have to assume it is and grab everything we can from it while we have the opportunity? Or can we take it easy, safe in the knowledge that we'll have our chance again and again and again?'

The pause was so long this time that the man felt he had to offer some sort of answer.

'What I think,' he said with some reluctance, 'is that this is it.'

Daniel nodded his agreement. 'So,' he went on, 'we've got to go for it, yes? You only live once?'

'Well, yes, I suppose so.' The man was clearly embarrassed and glanced around the room. 'But you're allowed to have a breather every now and then you know.'

'Sure.' Daniel either missed his note of caution or deliberately ignored it in his haste to move on. 'But it's good not to have God passing judgement on us or an appraisal process to review our performance.'

He downed the last of the bottle and placed the glass carefully in front of him.

'After all,' he sighed, 'if there really was a God, do you think he would have allowed Kirsty MacColl to die before Shane McGowan?' he announced sagely and slapped his credit card on the table while the couple next to him desperately tried to suppress their laughter.

Reinvigorated by his lunch, and buoyed by the prosecco, Daniel stopped by the video shop on his way back and rented a tape of the English Patient for them to put on that evening. He had watched it before on a plane and, from what he could see when the stewardess wasn't standing in the way of the drop-down screen in the aisle, it was sufficiently romantic to make amends for his earlier exchange with Sarah.

Instead, the storyline managed only to stir up unfinished business. Long stretches of flashbacks were punctuated, every so often, with related events in the present, serving as a constant reminder that the reanimated characters were long since dead and buried. Daniel was struck by the hopelessness of it all, how brief and insignificant human existence seemed in the overall scheme of things. Millions of lives beginning and ending all the time, leaving a tiny trail of fading memories, a brief and temporary record of each happening. Neither Daniel nor Sarah were particularly religious, certainly not enough to accept the afterlife as anything more than an invention to keep doubters pious and the masses in line. As he watched the passion and pain played out on the small screen in front of them, the logic was inescapable. Rather than the slow smoulder of an unremarkable existence, better by far to blaze brightly and briefly with an intensity so blinding that, for one short, unforgettable moment, it would light up the millions of other ordinary lives flickering on and off alongside it.

He looked at his wife hoping desperately that she was thinking the same thing.

Twenty Five

'I told you it was good.'

'It was OK.'

'I knew you'd like it.'

'It was OK. Just OK.'

'If it was only OK, why did I get an A Minus?'

Sarah hardly paused from clearing the papers from the empty tables in the classroom. She marked him high as a bribe for his silence. Simple as that.

'Alright, it was more than OK. It was very good. But can you stop trying to pass off quotes from the reading list as your own? I've read these books a hundred times and I know them far better than you.'

Tony sidled up behind her as she bent over one of the desks and pressed himself into the curves of her bottom. She shot upright in an instant.

'Get off,' she hissed, 'remember where we are for Christ's sake.'

Immediately she reached for her stomach as she felt the muscles stretch. She caught her breath until the pain subsided again.

Tony ignored her reaction and walked over to close the classroom door, briefly checking whether anyone was lingering outside. If she says no, she means yes. At least that was one thing he had managed to learn from his father. A woman like Sarah got a thrill out of danger. That's why she was with him. The danger. The excitement. Ironically, his ex-girlfriend had even proved his point seconds before the collision with the tree that ended her life. Moments after she'd begged him to slow down, she was shouting "faster, faster" as the wind tore at their hair and roared around their ears. They say no, they mean yes. Everyone knows it.

'Rubbish, you love it.' He moved towards her again and grabbed her arm.

'Fuck off.' She hissed it again and the muscles in her neck etched themselves upon her throat.

His grip tightened on her arm. 'Go on, tell me it doesn't turn you on. Frightened I'm too big for you? Worried about our baby?'

He could see he was causing her pain and he felt a stab of excitement himself.

'Leave me alone, you *bastard.*'

All her frustration and anger erupted in this outburst and Tony stepped back, startled both by the ferocity of her words and the risk she was taking by shouting them so loudly. Sarah sat down behind one of the desks and begun to sob. It wasn't a deliberate action, not a calculated defensive measure to protect herself from further violence. Weeks' worth of pent-up fear and tension released itself in one great outpouring of guilt, self-loathing and despair.

She didn't stop until several minutes after he had walked out of the door and closed it behind him.

Twenty Six

Another evening in front of the television. The same routine. Landlady and husband. Don't forget to turn the lights out. This door, that flush. The window cracked open and the cigarette smoke escaping.

This night though, Tony found it difficult to relax. He felt humiliated and cheated. Her outburst had shocked him and knocked his confidence. A long time ago, he had been forced to see a counsellor, Dr Maria Esposito, after his mother had died and she had concluded that, although he rebelled against authority, he held a deep-rooted urge to abide by it. Apparently, he was desperately in need of approval and he demanded respect. So he would try to secure either or both by making a concerted effort to exert control in certain situations, especially those involving a woman in a position of power; a headmistress, a counsellor.....a mother.

After the first two sessions, his response had been to tell Dr Esposito to fuck off if she expected him to come back for a third.

He lit another cigarette and watched the drizzle melt into the pavement outside. His embarrassment was wearing off and he was left with that familiar anger, almost comforting to him now. He would make his teacher pay for what she had done. He had no choice. It was a matter of honour but also an entirely rational response. If anyone dared stand up to him, there was no recourse but to punish them. Otherwise they'd think it was acceptable. Everyone would. He had been as ruthless with the girl in his primary school class as he had with the pickpocket who pulled a knife on him. A cheating girlfriend, a love rival, a gin-soaked and belligerent father; there would always be a payback. Eventually.

Many of the books that he read, dismissed by some as conspiracy theories, had revenge as their core premise. It didn't bother him how long it took. He was extremely patient in this regard, despite the sense of injustice boiling up inside him. What he knew was that the longer it took for him to extract his pound of flesh, the more traumatic it was for his targets, always looking over their shoulder and clinging to the faint belief that they might just have got away with it. It was better to offer a little glimmer of hope because that meant the moment he finally confronted them was so much sweeter.

Only one person had ever escaped her due and she had put herself well out of the way of retribution. Instead, he had punished her by becoming everything she had wanted him not to be. But it was a hollow victory. A Pyrrhic one as his own national history would attest. He got nothing but misery out of his triumph. A lifetime of short-lived friendships, long-standing enmity and constant rejection from schools, colleges, clubs and even his own family.

Still, it made his life a lot more interesting than most. No one could deny that.

He finished his second cigarette as quickly as the first and made a conscious effort to savour a final one before he went upstairs.

He was beginning to unwind a little more now and ran through the various acts of compensation he would be prepared to accept from his teacher for her slight. More sex and money featured at the top of his list, high grades were just below. Who knows, if he played his cards right, he might just manage to secure all three. If not, there was always the consolation of a little violence to make up for it.

Twenty Seven

It was already getting dark by the time Sarah came in through the door. She walked into the kitchen just as Daniel's arm reached the apex of its third rotation as he slapped his air guitar along to 'The Boys are Back in Town' on the radio.

'You've come a long way from your synthesisers and jangly indie guitars,' she said sarcastically, popping her keys down on the table beside her.

'Yeah well, when you really want to make one of these babies scream,' Daniel shouted above the ear-splitting music and pointed the neck of his air guitar at her, carefully fingering the air strings along its air frets, 'you can't beat a bit of heavy.'

Sarah shuddered at his words and turned to go upstairs. Daniel found her half an hour later soaking in the bath.

'Wondered where you'd got to.' He knelt down beside her and leant over the edge of the bath to trail his fingers through the water.

She kept her eyes tightly shut. He noticed a fleck of foam clinging to one of her eyebrows and reached over gently to wipe it away. Still she didn't look at him.

'Bad day. Very bad day,' she said in explanation.

'Why? What happened?'

'Oh, you don't want to know. It was just one of those days.'

She sat up and ran her hands through her damp hair. For the first time he saw the dark bruise on her upper arm.

'Christ, what's that? What did you do?'

She hadn't noticed the mark before now so at least her reaction of surprise was entirely genuine.

'God, that's bad. I didn't think it would leave a bruise.'

'What did you do? Does it hurt?'

'It's a bit tender but you know what these things are like. They look a lot worse than they really are. Only takes the slightest knock as well. This was just getting into the car. I was carrying loads of books and jammed my arm in the door. Bloody stupid.'

His gentle touch on her arm hurt almost as much as Tony's earlier grip and she winced in response.

'I thought you said it didn't hurt?'

'I said it was tender! Must be a little more sore than I realised though.' She sank her shoulders below the water again.

'Do you want a drink? Tea, coffee? What about a glass of wine?'

She thought about it for a minute. 'Better not,' she decided until she noticed the disappointment in his eyes and relented. 'Oh, what the hell, go on. Just a small one.'

She watched him disappear through the doorway and listened for the heavy footsteps on the stairs before she felt comfortable enough to subject the bruise to closer inspection. She put her head in her hands and groaned quietly. The sooner she plucked up the courage to sort things out with Tony the better. It might even help to take her maternity leave a little earlier than she had been planning. Just as long as he didn't turn up on her doorstep again. A clean break. A new baby. A fresh start. She felt a brief surge of optimism at the thought of such a positive future but the moment proved short-lived as she remembered what needed to happen to make it a reality. She glanced at the purple imprint on her arm and her fragile confidence evaporated. It wasn't just his vicious temper, it was his unpredictability. No plan of action, no considered approach could take that into account. Despair squeezed a solitary teardrop over the lip of her eyelid to trace a slow path down her cheek, the final trickle from a depleted reservoir.

She heard Daniel pull the bottle out of the fridge and wiped away the tear, forcing herself to allow more upbeat thoughts to fill her mind again. A few years ago these would have revolved around nights out and weekends away but now it was the idea of lazy days at home with the baby which cheered her up. Her husband was a good man. He would always provide for her and ensure they would live out their days together, happy and comfortable. Safe.

She dreaded to guess what her friends would make of her thinking like this. At least she would soon have a glass of wine in her hand. Some people were surprised that she was still drinking so far into her pregnancy but her friends would have been horrified if she hadn't been. She enjoyed going out with them but it wasn't as though she even wanted to drink most of the time. She joined in to keep others happy, to prove to them that she wasn't 'boring' or 'stuffy' or hadn't become a middle-aged mum overnight.

She knew she should be strong enough to stand up for herself. In fact, she was surprised that she found it so difficult. Surprised and disappointed. How ironic, she thought, that she of all people should worry in case her companions accused her of betraying their shared doctrine of living dangerously. Accused *her*? She was being blackmailed by one of her students, for Christ's sake, one she had shagged whilst pissed out of her head. That surely ought to grant her enough brownie points to see her through several years of humdrum domesticity and motherhood.

She still had the sneer on her face as Daniel wandered back into the bathroom.

'Good grief,' he muttered, 'who's getting the brunt of that expression? I wasn't that long was I?'

'Just thinking about work,' she replied. 'I'm not always thinking about you, you know.'

He leant forward and placed the two glasses of wine on his pregnant wife's rounded tummy where it broke the surface of the water like an island in the ocean. He held them there for a moment, admiring his composition – two palm trees on pristine sand.

'Oh well,' he sighed, 'let's have a drink on the baby – literally by the look of it – and forget about work and stuff.' He picked up both of the glasses and clinked them together before handing one to her.

Sarah smiled and took a sip of the wine. 'Mmmm, that tastes good.' She noticed his eyes light up in response. 'I hope this little rascal approves.' She looked down at her stomach and patted it reassuringly. 'You've been wide awake all day haven't you?'

'You've had a good kicking then have you?'

Sarah caught her breath and turned it into a deep sigh before replying to Daniel, 'Yep, pretty active. All arms and legs for most of the afternoon. I'm not sure if this child will ever sleep.'

'I read somewhere they can listen and respond to music, even at this stage in the pregnancy,' she said.

'Oh Christ.' Daniel looked alarmed. 'I should have turned down the Thin Lizzy track. The poor kid will be scarred for life. In fact I'm feeling a little traumatised myself.'

They sat in silence for a while before Daniel announced he was going down to watch Sportsnight. He took the bottle of wine with him and didn't appear again until it was well and truly finished and she was in bed, fast asleep. The next morning, despite the alcohol intake, he still woke early enough to beat the alarm clock but Sarah had suffered yet another sleepless night and was already watching the breakfast news downstairs. He reached down by the side of the bed and picked up Denys Page's treatise on Sappho from the carpeted floor where it had taken up permanent residence for the past few weeks, leaving a book-sized impression on the flattened pile. As he lifted himself back on to the bed, he caught sight of the box of tissues which had enjoyed far more gainful employment than the book as Sarah's pregnancy had developed. He paused momentarily, fingers hovering over the narrow opening, before reluctantly settling on Page's Sappho and the slightly more cerebral pleasures which lay within.

Flicking guiltily past the first few pages with their pencilled reference numbers and the damning library stamp, he hurriedly found his way to Fragment 31. *His* poem. The one which would make him famous.

He tried to read from the original Greek but ended up relying heavily on Page's English version. Even in the translation it was obvious how bitterly Sappho's jealousy dripped from the first few lines and he could almost picture her spitting out the words as she gazed at the object of her infatuation across the table.

"I think that man has the luck of the gods on his side,
sitting opposite you, so close to you, and listening
to your sweet voice and lovely laughter"

He started as the radio alarm made a belated appearance, re-set for an extra hour by Daniel the night before when he realised he had an empty diary the following day. For once, the DJ was sparing his grateful audience the usual inane babble, inviting them instead to 'Guess the Year' from a string of familiar refrains.

"Living on the ceiling, no more room down there.
Things fall into place, you get the joke, fall into place"

Daniel collapsed back onto the pillow and sighed. Marie Crawford, Xmas 1982. He had asked her out on a Friday, got a better offer on the Saturday, gone out with the other girl until Thursday and then asked Marie out again on the following Tuesday. Unsurprisingly for such an ominous beginning, it was a short and not entirely successful relationship. He had eventually given up on her after three weeks when he finally realised he was unlikely to get any further than stroking her majestic breasts through her school blouse. It was a full two years later before he discovered that she had slept with his best mate on day 3. And days 6, 7 (twice), 11 and 17. His own best chance had been in her bedroom in December 1982 until a line on one of her records had made him burst out laughing and spoil the moment.

He flicked off the radio. Blancmange was a crap name for a band anyway.

He turned back to Sappho's poem and painstakingly picked his way through the Greek words. Her description of her own suffering was a remarkable piece of writing, each word so sparingly employed that the rich conciseness of her poetry was impossible to capture in another tongue. He mulled over the list of love-sick symptoms; the burning flesh and humming ears, the clammy sweat and fierce trembling, speechless, blinded, paler than grass and close to death. He thought back to the first few weeks with Sarah.

It was some time since he had experienced the ache of early love but he recognised the physical pain which the poem described and remembered how he had literally gasped for breath as he plucked up the courage to phone her up after the party.

He had met her for lunch soon afterwards and had deliberately played it low-key, concentrating on making her laugh and keeping the conversation light rather than trying to pick up where they had left off at the party. It felt the right thing to do at the time – to take the pace down and get to know each other better – but it also helped that, despite his nerves, he was fully confident of getting her into bed by the end of the week.

It was only months later that he found out how uncertain his prospects had actually been as he coaxed out of Sarah an admission that she had been looking for any excuse to confirm the dreadful mistake she had made. He was shocked to hear her say that any hint of embarrassment or brash over-confidence, let alone an assumption that they were moments away from diving on each other again, would have been sufficient to see her head straight for the door.

He put down the book and pulled the duvet back over him. That ache of first love was always so real, so genuinely painful. If anyone felt the same symptoms at any other time, they would immediately book an appointment with their GP in case they were experiencing the early signs of some noxious and life-threatening disorder. And this was love! A positive emotion. One which people yearned for, the cornerstone of literature and song. No wonder the language associated with love was so often martial. Someone captures your heart and then they break it. Love conquers all. Eros even shoots you with a bloody bow and arrow! It was positively brutal. But so powerful that it stayed with you for years afterwards.

That mixture of excitement, nervousness and fear, which characterised most of the first few weeks with Sarah, was exactly the same concoction of emotions he had experienced so often during his school years.

He could clearly recall Rachel Morris in Form 4 and the trepidation he had felt before asking her out. Rehearsing what he would say had appeared to have such a severe effect on his breathing that his mother feared he might be asthmatic. Oddly, he had felt the same extreme reaction the following week when Rachel Morris in Form 4 had decided to go out with Simon Mansfield in Form 6 instead. Sadly he couldn't remember any moment during the intervening week which had made these two bookends of asphyxiation worthwhile. He frowned. There was something else. It had been his birthday. She had finished with him on his birthday. He was inconsolable at the time but could smile about it now. She had promised him a present to remember but the packet of condoms, which this comment had encouraged him to spend several minutes at the chemists plucking up the courage to buy, had ended up sitting in his drawer for a couple of years longer than he had anticipated.

Mentally he scrolled down the calendar of his 4th and 5th form years and tried to chart his sexual progress along the way. He was surprised which memories remained with him most strongly from those years. He vividly remembered a marathon of Christmas kissing in the under-age sanctuary of the Frog and Spade and the one embrace with Jackie Stirling, a friend of some long-standing, which he could almost taste today. It had blown his mind at the time and the thought of her consumed him for days afterwards until the intervention of the Xmas holidays and the stately Julie Turner, a sixth former and prefect no less, allowed him to move on. He could hardly picture the face of the girl who had taken his virginity but he could recall every second of the kiss which Jackie Stirling had given him.It was a regular source of frustration for him when his memory failed to identify people, names or events in his life, often from the previous week as much as from the distant past. So, it was fascinating for him to find out which episodes stood the test of time, surviving in such sharp focus over fifteen years later. Some of the moments had seemed so innocuous and yet they had somehow embedded themselves into his sub-conscious and clung on while so many others had slipped away and disappeared. The ones which survived still managed to muster some of the same effects he experienced at the time. He could feel the butterflies in his stomach even now as he relived them. Fresh and exciting, painful and nerve-wracking – spikes of emotion marking themselves out above the rest of the flotsam and jetsam.

For Daniel, the logic was compelling and inescapable. Why on earth wouldn't you look to fill your life up with as many of these episodes as possible? What did you have to gain from any of the sludge which settled between them? A tick in the box for making it through another week? Presumably its only purpose was to fill in the gaps between the spikes – what did that bloke call it, a breather? Something to stop yourself from having a heart attack.

He sat up and remained motionless for several seconds, deep in thought. He heard Sarah pottering about downstairs and thought back once more to those first few days with her. If only he could fall in love with her every few months. How much more exciting and fulfilling than simply being in love.

It was unfair to compare Laura and Sarah but he couldn't quite work out how he could have fallen in love with two such different people. Laura was the risk-taker. She sailed close to the wind and lived life in the fast lane. He decided that she also loved life and, as well as the fast lane, she lived it both to the full and on the edge. There were so many bewildering expressions describing her lifestyle that either there were far more risk-takers than he had previously imagined or they generated far more interest than their numbers warranted.

And Sarah, was she really so safe and boring? Only in comparison perhaps. She had a wonderfully dry sense of humour and was fun to be with. She liked a drink but couldn't hold it too well, which sometimes made her even more fun to be with. But it wasn't what she did which defined her but what she didn't do. There was always a strong, sensible side which invariably took over at key decision points. If in doubt, she would tend to say no. With Laura, there was always a sense of spontaneity, always the hint that anything might happen. What did she call it? Carpe Diem? It was exciting and dangerous. He accepted that he had got to know these two women at very different stages in their lives – there was a big difference between the responsibilities of a student and of someone in their thirties earning a living. It didn't occur to him that his memory might also be a little suspect and that he had added a degree or two more spice to Laura's approach to life than she had actually shown him.

'We're back to burning brightly,' he thought. The descriptions of risk-takers were so familiar because they were distributed liberally throughout the obituaries which particularly caught his eye, the ones for younger people dead long before their four score and ten. This wasn't a movie and it was difficult to justify this outcome in real life when Laura hadn't even made it past her twenty first birthday. Sarah's less dramatic outlook may not generate quite as many thrills but at least it was likely to last a whole lot longer.

He heard the kettle whistle and flick itself off. 'Christ,' he thought, 'I hope I haven't jinxed her.

He picked up Sappho's verse again and re-read her own description of love's devastating impact, a moment she had managed to keep alive for over two thousand five hundred years. He thought about the scene itself. It was difficult to work out the relationships between the three characters in the poem. He had always assumed that the girl was a bride at her own wedding, indeed most ancient commentators had supposed the same thing, but this assumption was far less clear from a fresh reading of the work. And the man whose proximity to this girl so inflamed Sappho, was he the groom or simply a fellow guest? And what about Sappho? What was her connection with the girl? Teacher and pupil? Lover? The surviving fragment of the poem tailed off just as Sappho seemed about to reveal why she was forced to endure this terrible love-sickness in silence. The concluding lines were lost and, with them, the key to the poem's interpretation.

He slumped back on the pillow. It was just a piece of clay, an innocuous lump of pottery, but this find would change his life forever if he could get his hands on it again. But where on earth was it now? He tried to put himself into the shoes of Laura's friends, of Maureen MacKintosh. Presumably she would have collected all of Laura's belongings together and handed them over to the parents. Or even kept one or two for herself. Either way, they had probably been put in a drawer or in a box up in the attic, too painful to discard but then, over time, simply forgotten and left to gather dust. He couldn't imagine her parents suddenly deciding to sift through their daughter's belongings and, even less, taking some precipitous action on the basis of the faint markings on a fragment of old vase. The only time it could possibly surface was when the couple died and their family had to sort through the accumulation of papers, keepsakes and detritus which had been stowed away.

Daniel took some relief in recalling from his various conversations with Laura's sister that her parents seemed distinctly alive and well. But that wasn't all. A frown creased his forehead. She had said something else about them, something which might encourage dusty drawers to be opened and lofts to be cleared. A look of horror crossed his face. They were moving house.

'Oh shit,' he muttered, 'I might have less time than I thought.'

Up until this point he had tried to fit the search around case-work as well as pausing out of sensitivity for Sarah's condition but he couldn't put it off any longer. He knew what he had to do. He jumped in the shower and got dressed before Sarah had even finished her cup of tea. Despite his appointment-less diary, he made his way into work with significantly more alacrity than he usually demonstrated. Once comfortably settled behind the desk in his office, he immediately rang up directory enquiries and was put through to the main switchboard at Strathclyde University. It took a number of redirected calls for him to be connected to Maureen Mackintosh but eventually a woman's voice chimed her name down the phone at him.

'Oh hi,' he said, assuming an air of innocent politeness which he often used when adopting an economical approach to the truth. 'I'm trying to get hold of one of your members of staff called Laura. Unfortunately I don't know her surname but she's from Baillieston and went to college at Strathclyde, ooh, quite a few years ago. I'm afraid I've been transferred to most of the departments in the building so I'm hoping you may be able to help me out. I was told you might know her.'

There was a brief silence at the end of the line. 'Who are you after again?'

Daniel pressed on. 'Her name's Laura. I heard she was working at Strathclyde although I must admit I've not seen her since college days. Good looking girl, early thirties, long black hair. At least I assume it's still black – we've all gone a little grey since those days. Lots of brothers and sisters. But anyways, I'm planning to travel up to Glasgow next week on business and I thought it would be a great idea if we could meet up. I know it's a bit of a long-shot but she was very special to me some time ago. I don't suppose you know where she is, do you?'

Again, silence. 'Who is this?'

His tone evolved seamlessly into polite confusion. 'Er, my name's Daniel, Danny. I met Laura when she was travelling in Greece. In Athens. Years ago. She turned up with two friends and then she and I spent some time together. Alone. Look, perhaps I've made a bit of a mistake. It was just an idea you know, meeting up with her again.'

'Christ.' He could picture the girl on the other end of the line desperately trying to work out what she should say next. 'Danny, hi, I'm Maureen. I was travelling with Laura around Greece when we were at college together. At least I think that's who you mean. Are you the boy she met in Athens? You talked to us on the train when we were just getting in.'

Innocent politeness, polite confusion and now confused amazement. 'Wow, you're joking! Maureen, yeah I remember you. You and Laura refused to stay at my hostel. After all the effort I put in as well. How on earth are you?'

'I'm fine, Danny, fine. But I need to tell you about Laura. Something terrible about Laura.'

'Look, Maureen, I don't expect her to be sitting there pining for me after all these years. I'm married myself.' Daniel knew this was a little mean and felt slightly guilty for saying it.

'No, it's worse than that. A lot worse. She's dead. She died in an accident soon after she left you.'

It's difficult to know how to feign shock or grief. Despite what might be supposed, the actual reaction tends to be unnatural calm, the real thunderbolt striking much later when the numbness has worn off and the brain has finally registered the enormity of the news. Daniel opted for stunned silence followed by stammering incomprehension.

'God, what terrible....I mean, Christ, that's unbelievable. How did it happen? I mean, God, I can't believe it.'

He could hear her own voice quaver as she interrupted him.

'Look, if you're up next week, why don't you pop in. We can chat about it. It would be good to talk about her again.'

Bingo.

'Sure, sure. Let's do that. That would be nice.'

'When are you up?'

'Tuesday.'

'OK, Tuesday. Say 11 o'clock?'

Daniel murmured an acknowledgement.

'Come to the main desk and they'll give you directions. Sorry to give you such dreadful news over the phone. Nice to talk to you, Danny.'

'Yes, you too.'

'See you Tuesday.'

Twenty Eight

'We need to talk.'

'We do? What about?'

'About everything.'

'Everything?'

'Yes, everything.'

'My grades?'

'No, of course I'm not talking about your grades, Tony. I'm talking about us.'

Sarah stared at the receiver as if she was connected up to a complete moron.

'Oh us, OK then. Sure. Look, I'm still half asleep. When?'

'Next week. After the tutorial session in the afternoon. Your place.'

'Tuesday, yeah?'

'Yes, Tuesday. You'll need to give me directions and an address.'

'Why?'

'Because I've not been to your place before, Tony. That's why.'

'I'll give you a lift on the bike.'

'Don't be so bloody stupid. Just give me the directions and I'll meet you there.'

'Just watch out for Mrs G.'

'Who's Mrs G?'

'The landlady.'

'I'll be your Auntie Sarah come to visit.'

'But I haven't got an Auntie Sarah.'

'Goodbye Tony.'

Twenty Nine

Daniel was a junior barrister. He earned a living arguing a point of view and he had been accepted into one of the most prestigious sets in London because he had proved that he was rather good at it. So, why was he so worried about convincing Sarah that he needed to take an overnight trip to Glasgow? He had agitated about broaching the subject for so long that he had convinced himself that he would need some well-choreographed phone calls with a work colleague, loudly conducted within Sarah's earshot, to rescue the situation after he had no doubt ballsed it up initially. As it was, Sarah was keen to use his absence as an excuse to visit an old school friend so it couldn't have worked out better.

Ironically on the train up he began to get cold feet himself about the mission and wished he had followed his initial gut feeling after all. Surely he couldn't expect any greater success than he had met in Marrakech? In fact the chances of an equally humiliating outcome seemed pretty high. At one point in the journey he had decided to ditch the Strathclyde idea altogether and spend his time in the city touring art nouveau Glasgow instead. Some Rennie Mackintosh earrings or a brooch would make a suitable peace offering to present to Sarah on his return. Ultimately though, he knew he had to go through with his original plan. Turning back now, he would spend the rest of his life wondering what might have happened if he had held his nerve. He really had no other choice. When he arrived at the station, he asked the taxi driver for the University without even thinking. The College of Art could wait for another day.

Maureen had been expecting him. In fact she had been expecting him for the previous few days. She had been very close to Laura and it had taken a number of weeks to get over the shock of her death. At the time, her coursework had begun to suffer and her tutors, initially sympathetic and understanding, grew more impatient the longer it took for her to snap out of her depression. But she had eventually pulled herself together and learned to live with her loss, principally by burying any thoughts of Laura and suppressing the hurt. Then came the phone call from this boy, this man now, and the memories of her friend came flooding back, all the more vengeful for their long period of neglect.

She took the call from reception more calmly than she expected but she could feel her heartbeat quicken as she went downstairs to collect him. They shook hands so formally that Daniel was embarrassed enough to attempt a clumsy kiss which caught the side of her head as she turned away to lead him to her rooms. All the way back, they exchanged well-prepared small talk – how had the journey been, had he been to Glasgow before, what did she teach at the University, was the weather always this bad. Neither of them listened to the replies but both followed the social etiquette unquestioningly. Daniel pondered this strange but accepted practice. It was like foreplay he decided; not unenjoyable but there's always a feeling of obligation, of going through the motions out of convention more than choice prior to the main event. His mind drifted off as she talked him through the previous week's weather, day by day. She was aware that he was only half-listening to her and knew he had been as consumed by Laura over the previous week as she had been. She turned to look at him as they arrived at her door and felt a sudden strong empathy with him, a genuine understanding that they were

248

on the same wavelength. Daniel smiled at her as if in confirmation. 'Or perhaps more like the qualifying rounds of the FA Cup,' he thought to himself.

He followed her into the sitting room and she motioned him towards an armchair diagonally across from her own by the fireplace, an arrangement which had taken her a few attempts to perfect. She poured cups of tea for them both, placing hers on a side table next to her chair, and sat down on the edge of the seat facing him. It was a signal to end the preliminaries and move on to the reason for his visit.

Daniel leaned forward, towards her. 'How did it happen then, Maureen? How on earth did it happen?'

He had tried not to rehearse this opening in his mind so that it would sound more genuine but he was horrified at how artificially it had come across. Luckily Maureen hardly heard the words because she knew what his question would be and was desperately trying to deliver her answer without breaking down.

'A moped accident. No helmet. We always suspected that the car coming the other way was on the wrong side of the road but that's not what the authorities decided.'

'Why, what was their verdict?'

Maureen hugged the sides of her coffee mug for comfort.

'The official view was that they took the corner too fast.'

Daniel's jaw dropped and he looked at her stunned. He hadn't been prepared for this.

'They?'

Thirty

Sarah scanned the titles of the books on the two shelves. They read like a who's who of cult heroes, all characterised by the obsession their deaths had encouraged in predominantly adolescent young men. Punctuated by the odd novel or reference book, these conspiracy theories filled up most of the space in Tony's modest library. "Is Elvis really dead?", "Was Marilyn silenced by the CIA", "Jim Morrison: where is he now?" "Who killed Mama Cass?". Sarah thought she could have saved further rainforest destruction by fitting the answers onto a single page of A5 instead; yes, no, Pere-Lechaise cemetery, a ham sandwich.

Tony noticed her interest. 'What do you think?'

'About what?'

Tony nodded at the books. 'That lot.'

She was about to give him a fairly candid response when he carried on.

'Something pretty fishy's going on. How come so many high profile deaths in such unexplained circumstances? Huh?'

She was going to suggest 'drugs' but she didn't want to antagonise him any more than necessary. 'So what do you think then?' she said instead.

Tony lit a cigarette and opened the window behind him.

'It's obvious. It's a conspiracy isn't it? Pop stars and actors, all high profile personalities, mixing with politicians and statesmen, other high profile personalities.' He paused and slowly nodded at Sarah, waiting for her to catch up with his thinking. 'Yes, you've got it. Names get dropped, secrets get spilled and the CIA have a lot of cleaning up to do to stop the public finding out.'

Sarah had been worried that her husband had chosen these couple of days to be away in Scotland. His trip had given her the space to tackle this problem and she had seized the opportunity but she was nervous that he wouldn't be there to support her when she got home. Or if something went wrong. But Tony's views were so laughable, so childish, that she found her confidence growing the more nonsense he spouted.

'Take Mama Cass for instance.'

'Oh yes?'

'Her and the other Mamas & Papas...' Sarah's concentration wandered to her ante-natal classes, '...they were into everything and anything. Believe me. Sex and drugs were just for starters. What they did made sex and drugs look like shoplifting. Or speeding, careless driving...something like that.'

Sarah realised what meagre small talk she had shared with Tony since she had first known him and was almost grateful that he had concentrated on the threats and menaces instead. He was far more adept in that particular field.

'And they hung around a lot of famous people. People with an awful lot to lose and the means to do something about it.' He shook his head sadly. 'No wonder she had to go. There was even a suggestion that John Lennon was involved at one point. She was carrying his baby after all.'

Sarah's groan was almost audible. She desperately searched for the positive attributes which must have attracted her to him that evening at the hotel. There must have been a good reason to put her marriage at risk. Not just a bucket-load of alcohol. He was certainly a good looking young man, a beautiful olive complexion which came with the Italian genes and muscle tone which had years of working with heavy motorbikes to thank. The T-

Shirt he had on looked a size too small for him, presumably a deliberate ploy to accentuate his well-developed physique all the more. She noticed the image on the shirt for the first time. It looked strangely familiar, a faded print of a motorbike rider. She thought she recognised it from a cover in Daniel's music collection and looked in vain for the name of the band. Typical, she thought, that the sort of groups Daniel liked wouldn't stoop to anything as crassly commercial as advertising their name on the merchandise.

'Who's the band?' she said, pointing at the shirt.

'The band?' He looked down at the sepia splash on his chest and laughed. 'Oh no, I don't think so. I got it from an old girlfriend. It's one of those early biker rallies. It hasn't got a date on but it's original you know. She said she got it from someone who'd been there. Probably worth a fair bit.'

Sarah nodded, convinced that whichever ex had fed him that line was having one last laugh before finally dumping him. She smiled in solidarity with a true sister.

* * * *

Although he was anticipating a difficult discussion when it came to the whereabouts of Laura's belongings, Daniel had expected to coast through the first part of the story without too many alarms. He might well have braced himself for a touch of sadness or a rush of nostalgia but he wasn't prepared for the bombshell she unwittingly dropped in just one casual aside. He had imagined Laura's final journey on numerous occasions and had run through a variety of different scenarios in his mind but never had he considered that she might not be riding the bike alone.

'Who was she with then?'

He had tried to sound casual and relaxed but had barked the question rather sharply. Maureen was a little surprised by his reaction, especially since he seemed to have taken the rest of the news so relatively calmly.

'She'd met up with him just the day before. She was on the back. It should have been him that died but somehow she took the impact.' She gave an involuntary shudder. 'Apparently she wouldn't have felt a thing,' she added hastily.

Daniel doubted this very much but, rather than sadness or horror at the manner of her death, his over-riding emotion was anger. She had betrayed him. He tried to shake off the feeling but it had a firm grip and demanded answers: who was this 'friend' and how close had their friendship actually become.

'Well, who was he? A local? Showing off to his mates?'

Maureen began to feel like the conversation was slipping out of her control. 'No, no, nothing like that. He was a traveller too. From Italy, somewhere down south. I think Laura had met him in Athens.' She paused to check whether it was safe to continue. 'She mentioned that you and he had got into some sort of fight? Over her?'

Daniel stared at her. Was she playing a game with him? Pay-back for his own disingenuous phone call? He asked whether she was sure and she nodded. It couldn't be. Not that bloke. That was Athens not Santorini. What had he done, stalked her?

'Was he drunk? Is that what happened?' He managed to sound calmer than he looked.

'He assured us he wasn't – that's what he said at the time anyway. Laura on the other hand……well, it was an impromptu beach party and she was always the life and soul.'

Maureen realised what she said and caught her breath. She took a tissue from her sleeve and blew her nose quietly.

'He was taking her back to the campsite. Perhaps we should have stopped him.'

'What do you mean?' Daniel leaned further forwards to within touching distance of her chair. 'Why would you have wanted to stop him?'

'He was angry. With Laura. I didn't really know him but he seemed a little…..you know…..hot-headed. They reckon he took the corner too fast.' She started to sob. 'For God's sake, she wasn't even twenty one. She had so much still to live for. So much.'

Daniel was not a natural in these situations but he knew the right thing to do at this moment regardless of the churn he was experiencing in his own stomach. He got up and knelt by her chair, taking her hand in his. He didn't say anything – he didn't know what to say and he was too much in shock himself to find any words for her – but she just needed a source of strength to anchor her grief. They stayed like that for several minutes, Daniel desperately trying to recall the face of the young man who had stolen his soul-mate away and Maureen replaying the decisions, so inconsequential at the time, which had led to her friend's death. For a while she was oblivious to his presence but finally she looked up at him, smiled and wiped her eyes.

'That's better.' She coughed out a small laugh. 'God, I haven't done that for years. Thanks for being here.'

* * * *

Sarah turned her attention to the mantelpiece, the only other area of the room which could shed much insight on the man who had been making her life hell for the past few weeks.

It supported a bizarre collection of personal ephemera. A photo of two young boys – brothers judging by their similarity – in a heavy wooden frame, a vase which presumably he had made at school out of other bits of vases, a miniature motorbike made from a kit and a small tin of coins, tokens and stamps, none of which appeared to be legal tender in Britain.

She turned to look at him and raised her eyebrows. She wasn't sure how to start this.

'Why the big meeting then, Sar? The kid's mine after all then?'

She knew she could rely on him for inspiration.

'Listen, Tony, it's time to call it a day.'

She noticed his expectant leer. 'Not go to bed, Tony. That's "call it a night". I mean end this charade.'

She consciously adopted her school mistress tone. 'No, the baby is definitely not yours. But you'd probably guessed that anyway. And you can forget about your childish blackmail threats. I've already told my husband the truth and I don't give a shit about the college. In fact, I might even tell them it was rape unless you go away quietly.'

The look of horror on his face made her wish for a camera to preserve it for posterity.

* * * *

He had accepted another cup of tea and settled back in his chair. Holding her hand and sharing her tears had allowed him to compose himself a little but he still felt bewildered by the story she had related. It was enough of a shock to find out that Laura was not riding the bike on her own but to hear that her companion was someone he had known, someone he'd had an altercation with, that was even more alarming news. It raised a whole new dimension to the accident and one which sickened Daniel even to consider it. What if the fight in Athens – so trivial, even funny at the time – had been the catalyst for the train of events which culminated in that terrible final night? What if the argument on the bike was about him, sparked by jealousy or pride....or perhaps revenge? In other words, what if he had ultimately been the cause of her death? Her blood on his hands, no matter how innocent his involvement appeared to be. He tried to push the dark thoughts from his mind. It might not even have been the same man after all. The description Maureen had given him drew a complete blank and the name she had mentioned meant nothing to him either. He decided to concentrate on his search instead.

'What did you do with all her stuff? Did her parents come out to collect it.....?' He paused slightly, '.....and Laura obviously.'

'We made sure we sorted out her belongings first. We didn't want her parents to see everything.'

Daniel was a little puzzled, 'What do you mean?'

Maureen gave him a knowing glance. 'She was an adventurous lady. You know that. Her bag contained one or two things she wouldn't have wanted her parents to see. To them she was their precious little girl. You know how it is.'

Daniel nodded knowingly, hoping she would go on to explain.

'We went through everything before handing it over. We threw away some of the more risqué material.'

Daniel decided to go for it. 'There was some stuff we'd collected together. Some finds from the bay near the campsite. Bits of pottery and stones. Junk really. Certainly not risqué. Did any of that make it back? You didn't keep any of it did you? It would be great to have a souvenir of her.'

This was roughly the same question he had put to Laura's sister and he held his breath as he waited for her response. This time the reaction was altogether different.

'Oh God, sure, I understand. But I didn't keep a thing. It was only one backpack after all. Everything we positively vetted went back with her parents. We travelled light as you know. She had a knapsack with her at the time of the accident but that was lost at the scene. I don't remember your pottery and things, I must admit. They might have been in that knapsack. I think I would have remembered them if I'd have come across them but, Christ, it was years ago after all.'

They sat in silence again, this time more uncomfortably than before, aware that there was suddenly little else for them to talk about.

'So have you got any mementoes of her?' he finally asked. 'Photos, that sort of thing?'

'I've got some photos. I dug them out after you phoned. There are none of Athens but I've got one or two from Mykonos.'

She walked to the bureau and picked an envelope off the open top. She handed it over to him and squeezed his hand as he took it. He slid the photos out, four in total, and looked through them, slowly and deliberately. He was bowled over. His only images of Laura had been held in his memory and now suddenly it was like being back in Greece with her again. He realised how differently he had remembered her. She had taken on mythical status for him and, in his mind's eye, her appearance had altered accordingly. He could immediately recollect the smells and sounds of their time together. He could even just about hear her voice. He studied her face in each of the photos. She was more than simply plain but not as radiant as he had remembered her more recently. Younger too. Her true

257

beauty was genuinely in her personality, the smile which lit up her face and the eyes which carried most of her conversation.

Daniel shook his head, a tear threatening to spill down his cheek. 'We talked about marriage, everything. I only knew her for a few days but it felt like a lifetime. She was coming back to the Peloponnese to meet me before she...' he wiped his face with the back of his hand. 'Well, you know.'

Maureen put her hand on his arm.

'Look, Danny. She was very fond of you. I remember her saying so. She really liked you. But she was Laura. She loved life. She loved men. And they loved her. It was all the little tricks she played on them.'

Daniel didn't like where this was heading and wanted her to stop but she carried on.

'The trick with the knickers? Oh it's alright, Danny, I knew she tried it out on you. She told us. It was her party piece. She'd done it on the night of the accident as well. I shouldn't think she'd got round to the big reveal this time though.'

She started to cry again. Daniel wished he had left well alone. He far preferred his own flawed, incomplete memory of Laura and the rose-tinted view of their love for each other. He had been looking for the final piece in the jigsaw to complete the picture, make it perfect, and instead his truth had been shattered, finally consigning the notion of 'one true love' to the dustbin. He picked out one of the photos of Laura and showed it to Maureen.

'Can I have this? It would mean a lot to me.'

She nodded, relieved that she had made a point of getting copies of all of them in case he asked for one. Daniel put his jacket on and slipped the photo into his inside pocket. Maureen collected herself one last time and put her hand on his arm. She knew she had upset him but she felt it was for the best. Otherwise he would have carried on with a romantic notion in his head and a burning desire for closure. She kissed him on the cheek.

'I believe everyone has a finite amount of heartbeats when they start off.' She smiled at him warmly. 'Laura had just used up all of hers, that's all.'

****

He lay back on the bed, hands behind his head, and stared straight at her. She avoided his gaze and lowered her eyes. The image on his T-Shirt was beginning to get on her nerves, nagging away at her. She began mentally to flick through the CDs in her husband's collection, as much as anything to distract herself from the penetrating stare.

Suddenly he jumped to his feet and walked towards her. His frame seemed to fill the small room, blocking her way to the door and pinning her against the bookshelf. Her earlier confidence completely evaporated in a split second and she was scared. Really scared.

'So you think it's down to you whether we're finished, do you?' His tone had a sharpness to it now, thick with spite and menace. He moved a step closer and bent down towards her.

'Do you?'

She glanced at the vase on the mantelpiece, weighing up whether she could get her hands on it before he reached her and, even if she did, whether it would inflict sufficient damage to allow her time to slip past him and out. She tried to remember if he had locked the door.

He was just inches away from her now.

'So you told your old man did you?'

He prodded at her stomach. 'Don't please' she croaked.

'Bet you didn't tell him that he might not be the father. I expect he'd pay a fair bit to keep that quiet wouldn't he?'

He hardly listened to her reply and carried on talking over her.

'You lot think you're in control don't you? You think you make all the decisions and us men just fall into line.'

Sarah tried to think of some response but she didn't understand what he was saying and she didn't want to antagonise him by getting it wrong.

'See him.' Tony spat the words and thrust a finger towards the photo on the mantelpiece. 'That's my brother. He's dead. His own mother did it. My own bitch of a mother.'

Sarah could see that he was losing control. 'God I'm sorry, that's terrible. That's just terrible.' Her voice was soft and soothing. 'That must have been awful for you.'

'She left me.' He was shaking with anger. 'I didn't do anything wrong but she just fucking left me. Her son. Her own flesh and blood.' He wiped away the spittle from his mouth and slowly looked back up at Sarah. 'And now you think you can do the same, do you?'

She froze. For several moments the silence became a buzzing in her head. Finally she managed a whisper.

'Come on, Tony, we can still be friends.' She knew it sounded pathetic but she just wanted to ease the tension and calm him down. It had the opposite effect.

'Friends?' He was almost shouting. 'Friends?' Now laughing, a bitter hollow sound which seemed to grow louder as it bounced around the walls.

She didn't hear the knocking at first, drowned out as it was by the echoing laughter, but Tony did and he stopped abruptly and wheeled round to face the door.

'Tony? Do you have company, Tony?'

The voice came from right outside his door and suggested that its owner had been listening in for more than a little while. Tony's menacing sneer fell away in a split second and Sarah stared in amazement as he transformed into a little boy before her eyes. He turned to her alarmed. 'Oh Christ,' he hissed. 'It's the landlady. She'll kill me if she knows I've had a cigarette in here. I'm not allowed guests either. Can you do something about the smoke?'

He turned back to the door, 'Hi, Mrs G. Just coming.' He opened the door a mere fraction and somehow managed to slide through it and, at the same time, keep the cigarette smoke and his illegal guest firmly inside.

Sarah slumped to the floor and took several deep breaths to calm herself down. Seeing him revert to his childhood had put her back in control again. She could finish this now. She knew she could. She got up and walked around the room, enjoying the freedom and ignoring his plea to clear the smoke. She would be delighted if he got into trouble and wondered whether marching out of the door puffing away herself and pointing an offending finger at him and the baby would help bring about the conclusion she was looking for. She sat by the bed and opened one of the drawers. His diary stared back at her, daring her to pick it up and have a quick flick through the pages. She took it out, turning it over and over in the hope it might drop through her hands and fall open at a particularly revealing page. But it stuck steadfastly in her palms. If she wanted to read it, she would have to do it the hard way.

She walked over to the door. She could hear the two of them outside and swore she heard Tony answer the woman's charge of 'you know the rules don't you' by describing Sarah as one of his aunt's friends who had come over to help clear up his room. 'I could have done that for you,' came the slightly hurt reply which seemed to sting

Tony into persuading her to take the job instead and offering to make her a cup of tea to say thanks.

Sarah knew she had a few minutes more now. No matter what she thought about him though, she didn't feel comfortable prying into his personal diary and reluctantly returned it to the drawer. Instead she pulled out a photograph album which had been sitting below it. She had no compunction about scanning through this particular volume. There was a real mixture of photos in the book and there seemed little continuity from page to page or even picture to picture – all different people and different places. They were obviously taken at vastly different times as well, judging by the change in Tony's appearance as she got further through the album. Suddenly she realised that all the pictures were of girls and that most of them had their arms round Tony or were sitting next to him. Quickly she flicked to the back of the album and caught her breath in surprise. There it was, a photo of her in the centre of the page. It was a pretty recent snap. She racked her brain to think when he had taken it before slowly realising that it had nothing to do with Tony and had been taken by Daniel at Xmas. It was one of a set which had been lying around the house. She sat down on the bed and started to shake. He must have stolen it when he was last round there. Worse than that, she remembered that the original had caught Daniel's reflection in the mirror behind her. Tony had trimmed down the photo to cut her husband out.

She turned the pages back towards the front and looked at all the innocent young girls who had fallen for Tony's charm. She stopped at one in particular, a tattered photo which looked like it had spent a number of years crammed into a wallet before being returned to his book of conquests. It was of a pretty girl with dark hair and her arm round a grinning Tony. She was wearing the same T-Shirt he had on today, less faded and not sepia but purple. It suddenly dawned on her.

'Big Mouth Strikes Again' she whispered.

Thirty One

He felt like the life had been sucked out of him. Sarah thought it was an unsuccessful case in Glasgow which had made him so depressed on his return and diplomatically left him alone in his study while she headed into college. After her own experience she was glad for the space herself. She brought him in coffee before she left – as a show of support – but otherwise she thought it best to let him work through his disappointment on his own.

Daniel sat staring at the wall. He replayed the conversation with Maureen over and over again. The phrase "she was very fond of you" constantly jumped into his head. "Fond". It was the worst possible thing she could have said. Everything about it indicated what she *didn't* feel about him. It wasn't "besotted" or "enthralled". It wasn't even "in love". She was simply toying with him. With him, with Antonio, probably with half the male population. And he had sat outside that blasted museum for the best part of a week waiting for her to turn up. What a mug.

He was pretty sure he knew what had happened on that bike. Maureen didn't, the Greek authorities didn't but he knew. He had pieced it together on the train back from Glasgow, using what he had learnt from Maureen, his own experience with Laura and a basic understanding of human nature. He remembered the effect her little party trick had made on him before he found out she was teasing. How would a hot-headed Latin react in the same circumstances?

Daniel re-ran the whole episode. He pictured an incensed Antonio dragging Laura away from the object of her flirtation and hauling her onto the back of the bike. Within seconds they were racing along the beach road, a stream of swear words pouring out from driver to

264

passenger, Laura just laughing and grabbing him tighter and urging him to go faster. Perhaps he'd misunderstood her trick and assumed she'd already betrayed him. Normally she would have put him straight by now but the thrill of her deception grew stronger as his temper increased. Every time he appeared to flag, she would egg him on with various snide comments and asides, blind to the fact that she was hastening her own death.

His invective grew louder until he was turning round and screaming the words at her. The bike started to veer violently from one side of the road to the other. Suddenly the thrill wasn't there anymore and excitement was replaced with terror.

'Look where you're going, for Christ's sake,' she shouted. 'Turn round, you idiot.'

She was no longer in control. When she saw the car coming towards them, she knew that he wasn't either.

Five seconds later she was dead.

He swerved to miss the car but hit the tree side-on instead. Was this the truth? Is this exactly what happened? He drained the coffee mug and put his head in his hands. He couldn't shake off the feeling that there was something he was missing, something not quite right. It was odd that this guy should turn up again, especially after getting the brush-off in Athens. Really odd. Was it just a coincidence or had he followed her? The longer he thought about it, the less likely it seemed. It was more than a little unlucky for the passenger to come off worse in a crash than the driver. He tried to picture various scenarios but eventually shook his head – it must have been the helmet missing. That and simply bad luck. No one would be fucked-up enough to do this on purpose.

It was late afternoon before he emerged from his den, soon after hearing his wife return home.

He wandered into the kitchen where Sarah was unpacking groceries. She gave a slight start when she noticed him standing by the door.

'Good God,' she said, 'you look a right mess. Did you get locked in or something?'

He looked a little sheepish and sat down at the table.

'Sorry,' he said, 'I didn't realise what the time was.'

'Have you had any lunch?' He shook his head and she opened up a packet of cereal bars, throwing one of them over to him and accompanying it with the sort of stern expression which she usually reserved for students who forgot their homework assignment.

'Thanks,' he muttered, avoiding her stare but guessing there was one directed at him.

'I've just boiled the kettle. Do you want a coffee?'

He nodded and sat in silence until she placed the mug in front of him.

'Do you want to talk about it?'

He didn't answer, watching instead the steam rising from his coffee and waiting for it to cool.

Whether it came naturally to her or not, a few years of teaching had reinforced the benefits of patience and persistence. She pulled out a chair and sat down opposite him, leaning towards him. 'I've never seen a case affect you so much.'

It took him a while to respond. 'It wasn't a case,' he said finally, still not looking at her. 'I found out what happened to Laura.'

Sarah hadn't quite understood.

'What, you bumped into someone during the trial? She came from up there didn't she?'

He took a sip from the mug and continued to hold it close to his lips. 'There wasn't any trial,' he said quietly. 'It wasn't a case. I arranged to meet one of Laura's school friends to find out what happened. She told me everything.'

Sarah wasn't sure whether to be angry, shocked or hurt but, having recently discovered Tony's connection with Laura, she wanted to hear more. She stayed silent for several moments.

'Why did you lie to me, Dan?' She spoke softly, the calmness in her voice having a far greater impact than angry words. 'Couldn't you trust me?'

'I don't know, I'm sorry. I didn't want to rub it in, that's all.'

He looked almost pathetic. She knew there were two different paths she could go down – an explosion of righteous indignation or a supportive approach which would secure further truths and insight. She made her decision quite consciously and leaned forward to take his hand in her own.

'I could have helped,' she said gently. 'You should have told me.'

For the first time he looked up at her, relieved to hear a conciliatory note in her voice.

'But I didn't want to drag you into it. It could so easily have been a wild goose chase. If I hadn't found out anything then....'

He left the sentence unfinished but she picked up on it.

'And what did you find out then, Sherlock?' She tried to lighten the tone, encouraging him to tell her more of the story.

'Well, she wasn't on her own when she died in that motorbike crash.'

Sarah's throat felt dry and she stared at him in silence for several moments. In the end she had to cough out her question.

'Who was she with?'

'It was my fault. I started it all off in Athens. I got into a fight.'

'What are you talking about?' The colour drained from her face. 'Who was she with? One of her girlfriends?'

Daniel shook his head slowly.

'No, a bloke. Her new bloke. The new me.' The irony of this description wasn't lost on Sarah. 'We had a fight over her in Athens. He'd obviously....'

She broke in over him. 'Who was he? What was his name?' She tried to sound calm but the questions snapped out of her. 'Where was he from, Dan?'

She knew the answer even before Daniel confirmed it. She had been expecting it ever since he mentioned a second person on the scene but, when she actually heard his name and where he came from, she felt her whole body deflate as though some of the life-force had been let out. She thought back to the photo in Tony's room. The T-Shirt had been a memento...or worse still, a trophy. She shuddered to think how close she had to come to suffering something similar, were it not for the intervention of an unlikely angel. She had not stayed in Tony's room any longer than necessary. After waiting for him to return from appeasing his landlady, she clarified her earlier comments about terminating their relationship in no uncertain terms, leaving precious little room for misinterpretation. He was given no opportunity to interrupt as she let flow such a torrent of vitriol and hate that she doubted he would ever dare speak to her again let alone use his threats to unsettle her.

After she had left him shell-shocked in the house, she went straight to her college and asked the principal for immediate maternity leave, apologising for the short notice but hinting at medical problems which so disconcerted her manager that he agreed to her request without challenge.

The relief she now felt sat uneasily alongside the heavy burden of her knowledge. Her husband was frantically trying to put together the most important jigsaw in his life and she was holding one of the key pieces back from him. She kept on telling herself that Tony wouldn't have been much help anyway. Laura probably meant nothing to him. He had hardly spent the rest of his life in mourning. There were plenty of completed pages in his photograph album following this girl's brief and early entry after all.

'I think he was after revenge.'

His comment suddenly made her feel sick. 'What do you mean?' she stammered, the words catching on the phlegm.

'Laura had rejected him. This bloke. A few days before in Athens. I'd even got into a fight with him myself.' He put his head in his hands. 'Christ, I really do think it might be my fault. I think he followed her. I think he saw it as unfinished business.'

He looked up at her and stared straight into her eyes. 'And he certainly got his retribution didn't he.'

Sarah put her hand over her mouth. For a moment, she was sure she was going to faint. She leant on the table to steady herself. Daniel might be right, in a way he couldn't possibly imagine. What if this relentless hunger for revenge had not ended with Laura's death?

'So what are we going to do?' she finally whispered.

'About Laura?'

His question jolted her out of her state of shock and she pulled herself together.

'No,' she said hurriedly, 'let her go. About Sappho. Are there any other leads? What about the second friend?'

Daniel shook his head.

'No, that's the lot. That's the end. It's probably better off unfinished.' He looked at her and smiled. 'More perfect somehow.'

She smiled back at him with little warmth, not totally understanding what he meant.

'I could always go to Santorini. Search out the hedgerows for a dirty old T-Shirt wrapped around a few broken bits of pottery.'

Sarah stared at him.

'Pottery? You didn't tell me it was pottery.' She almost shouted the accusation.

Daniel looked shocked. 'OK, calm down. What did I say then?'

'A tablet, a stone inscription, something like that. Not bloody pottery.' She was beginning to sound hysterical.

'Christ, OK. Sorry. What's the big deal? It was definitely a pot or a vase. I thought I told you that at the time.'

Sarah's mind flicked back to Tony's bedsit. The airfix kit bike, the family photo and the patchwork vase. The bloody vase. She tried to remember what it looked like. Those marks. She thought they looked odd at the time. They were writing. Oh Christ, he's still got it. The bastard stole it from her as she was lying there dying. And now he's glued it together and stuck it on his mantelpiece like some sort of prize.

She was about to break the news to Daniel, triumphantly and dramatically unveiling her discovery, when the realisation hit her. How on earth could she tell him without him finding out about Tony, about all the lies and deceit? She thought through her other options. She couldn't quite imagine Tony simply handing it over either. Not after that recent episode. Not without negotiating something fairly substantial in return.

'Look, I'm still not feeling right.' She spoke slowly and quietly. 'I'm going to lie down.' She kissed him on the top of the head and made her way out of the kitchen, steadying herself on the bannister as she climbed the stairs to the bedroom. Daniel was puzzled by her abrupt exit but any concern was overshadowed by his relief at managing to unburden himself with such apparent inconsequence.

She hadn't stormed out. She was just unwell. That would explain the slight outburst earlier too. If the only thing she was upset about was what format the poem had been written on, he was a lucky man. He settled back into the chair and breathed out slowly. After everything he'd been through in the past few weeks – the deception and the disappointment – he couldn't quite believe it was over. And no repercussions from Sarah either. Clearly he didn't fully deserve such an outcome but he recognised his good fortune. He had dodged a bullet there.

Thirty Two

She lay on the bed on top of the sheets for some time. The irony of the situation was almost laughable. Betraying her husband had found him the thing he longed for the most but at the same time stopped him from ever obtaining it. She let out a short and hollow hoot. There *is* a God she thought. Some sick bastard who's got so bored of playing his celestial games that he's turned his attention to fucking up ordinary people's lives instead.

'Haven't you got more important things to do?' she whispered through gritted teeth.

But this god-fearing trick of passing responsibility upwards for anything the faithful found too difficult to deal with just didn't work for her. She knew it was her fault. In fact it could have been so much worse. What if Daniel had found out? Would he have left her to bring up a child on her own? She had been so stupid to risk so much for one drunken mistake. And then allowing herself to be intimidated for so long afterwards. She cradled her unborn baby. Her child needed him. She needed him. Over the past few weeks, she had grown to appreciate the importance of a safe and secure environment, a strong and stable family background. No more dissatisfaction. No more risk-taking.

Her conclusion was comforting but she still couldn't shake off the uneasy feeling that she had been used, an instrument of revenge in a hunt spanning over ten years. She couldn't believe that he could be so calculating. Not Tony. How could he have known who Daniel was and how she was connected to him? She kept telling herself it was just a coincidence.......but the nagging suspicion remained.

She wondered whether she had truly seen the last of him. Deep down, she doubted whether he would ever fully accept her word on the paternity of her child. Her own calculations proved it was highly unlikely that he could possibly have been responsible but she suspected that his grasp of mathematics might not help him come to the same conclusion. If he did show his face again and threaten to disrupt her life – for revenge, blackmail or whatever – she would just pay him to disappear. This, after all, was a language which Tony was bound to be all too fluent in.

She wriggled under the duvet cover and pulled it over her tummy. Life shouldn't be 'endured' or 'survived' she thought but it needn't be a series of fairground rides either. She remembered musing about the meaning of life with Daniel soon after she had met him and smiled as she recalled how he had looked around, leaned close to her and whispered, 'I'm not entirely certain,' and then with another furtive glance sideways and a nod back in her direction, 'but I'm pretty sure it's not 42.'

There were worse people to spend the rest of your life with, she thought. She listened to her own slow breathing for a moment and felt her eyelids flicker before turning onto her side and going to sleep, ignoring the sharp kicks inside her and the slightly duller twinge lower down which she assumed was simply another symptom of her current condition but which would grow no less quickly but far more malevolently. Less than two years after giving birth to her first and only child, a healthy baby girl, it would bring her own existence to an abrupt end. Another life snatched away. Prematurely. Pointlessly.

Downstairs, Daniel poured another glass of the wine and settled back down at the kitchen table. The bottle was already open when he went to the fridge earlier but he had still drunk well over half of it as he mulled over the clutch of revelations which his trip up north had secured. He wished he hadn't tried to complete the jigsaw and had been content to leave it beautifully flawed. Far better for him to fill in the gaps with his own doctored version of events. It hardly mattered though. In every single scenario, she still ended up dead.

He took little comfort in remembering that she believed in life after death. He didn't. Even if she was right about people living on as their bloodline preserved remnants of their DNA, he couldn't imagine that her surviving chain would prove particularly strong, filtered and diluted by so many siblings and with no children of her own to contribute to the cause. Equally, the alternative, his own brand of nothingness, meant that she was gone forever.

But there was one other option. He had half-jokingly suggested a compendium of traveller's tales to Sarah but there was an idea there. Rather than a compendium, why not attach the stories to a single person who would provide a consistent narrative thread to the otherwise disparate tales? Laura could be his heroine and, if he could persuade someone to publish (and Sarah had promised to use her connections for him), he would gift her the life after death which she so firmly believed in, however modest his book sales turned out to be.

Daniel jumped up and began rummaging through the kitchen drawers for a pen and notepad. He knew that half a bottle of wine would have no trouble robbing him of any pearls of literary wisdom as soon as his head hit the pillow......and he had every intention of uncorking another before that point. For the sake of the discerning reading public, he decided, his ideas needed to be consigned to paper. Fully-armed, he sat back down at the table and began drawing frenzied little circles in the top corner of the page to get the ink flowing. He then marked every second line with a numbered bullet-point, reaching a rather optimistic double-figure tally before beginning to jot down his notes. They read like the blurb on a dust-jacket; like many in his profession, he liked to believe that the natural empathy with people which had encouraged him to take up a legal career in the first place had also deprived the world of a consumer champion and marketing guru.

His opening point was sufficiently long to spill over its allotted space and render the rest of his numbering system immediately redundant: *transport Laura around the great civilisations of the world – to Egypt and China, Italy and Greece – in a series of adventures full of danger, intrigue and amazing discoveries*

Daniel watched the wine chase around the glass, clinging to the sides, as he twisted the stem round and round. He re-read his first line. 'Very good,' he murmured to himself. He scratched a line through '*amazing*' and scribbled '*earth-shattering*' above it. He read it again and smiled. 'Very good indeed.'

His second bullet point was belatedly pithy: *And romance.* He felt he owed her that.

Drawing on his well-versed travellers' tales, he could pretty much draft the first instalment of the series there and then and proceeded to outline a plot which saw Laura survive shipwrecks and police raids before finally wresting the literary treasure from its underwater hiding place, a little deeper this time than a few feet of water and guarded by a sea creature slightly more intimidating than a dead crab.

Next he made a note about using Laura's DNA theory to identify significant ancestors who had helped shape the places she was visiting. That was a nice touch, he thought. Fitting. A mark of respect. He wanted to include Pedro as well – not Pedro the accountant but the swashbuckling adventurer he was destined to become in an alternative reality – and so jotted his name down as his final point.

He leant back in his chair and put his hands behind his head. This project felt like a fresh idea to him. He had no recollection of the confident prediction he had made to Laura during a drunken night in an Athens bar. 'Mark my words,' he had boasted, 'I'll get the stories published.' But his subconscious had dredged up the memory and issued the challenge.

In the years to come, following the birth of their daughter, he would manage to complete his project and, after Fate had delivered his crushing blow, Sarah's friends would do the rest and pull enough strings for him to see his work in print, just like she had promised. Like Daniel, they would hardly expect a bestseller, their motives rooted in pity rather than belief, but the first book would be a notable success and, from that, a series and even a minor franchise.

For now though, as he drained his glass and refilled it with what was left of the bottle, his aspirations were a little more down-to-earth, focussed primarily on whether he would be able to shift a first print run. He felt confident. His mother, he reasoned, would buy half of them at least.

Sappho had kept the memories of her lovers alive for over two and a half millennia. Whilst he couldn't promise Laura such longevity, he would do what he could to give her a life back and allow her a prolonged and vibrant youth. No growing old gracefully….or even disgracefully. No grey hair, sagging body or failed eyesight and hearing. Life after death.

He raised his glass and nodded in approval. He suspected that she would have done the same.

'Vivid and in your prime,' he whispered.

Thirty Three

The door was locked and the woman knocked for some time to ensure there was no one at home. Satisfied that the room was empty, she pulled a set of keys from her pocket and, a few seconds later, she was inside the room.

She walked to the window and looked outside. There was no sign of Tony's bike and she assumed that he was still tied up with college lectures. She knew she was taking a risk and half-closed the curtains so that she couldn't be seen from outside.

The room seemed slightly different from the last time she had been in there. It was still messy, clothes strewn over one half of the floor and folders full of paper spilling out over some boxes in one of the corners, but this time a strange smell seemed to hang in the air, the faintly sour and unpleasant odour usually associated with young boy's bedrooms. She wrinkled her nose slightly and considered what a small amount of air freshener could do to improve matters.

She thought back to the argument which had erupted between the two of them and felt her anger rise again. They had not seen each other since and the memory of their exchange was still vivid. His behaviour had been quite a shock to her but, as she considered her response, she wondered whether she had over-reacted.

Suddenly she heard footsteps making their way up the stairs to the landing. She froze where she stood, catching her breath and straining to hear whether the footsteps would turn left into the bathroom or right towards the room she was in. She heard a lock snap shut and the toilet seat lower and knew that she was safe for a few more minutes.

She walked over to the mantelpiece and picked up the vase from the shelf. The glue welding the different pieces together showed up as thick yellow ridges up close, clumsily applied and partly obscuring the writing. There were not just cracks but gaping holes and, even with her untutored eye, she could see that a number of the pieces didn't actually match up. Some of them didn't even belong to the same vase. She ran her hand over the dappled surface and traced the faded letters with her fingers. For a few seconds she stared at the pot before dropping it into the Laura Ashley carrier bag she had brought with her.

Mrs G shook her head. Such a dreadful, horrible old thing she thought. How many times had she told him that?

She pulled a block of bubble wrap out of the same bag and unpacked a brand new pastel blue vase which she placed proudly on the shelf where the previous pot had stood. She looked at her purchase with some satisfaction. Tony would be delighted that she had finally replaced that monstrosity with such a beautiful and classy alternative. It was a peace offering. She would obviously charge the cost to his rent but she knew he would be more than pleased to pay it. After all, he had given her permission on that awful afternoon to help clear up.

She walked out of the room, locking it behind her, and took the steps down to the kitchen and out of the back door. She pulled the lid off the dustbin and dropped the Laura Ashley bag, complete with redundant bubble wrap and patched-up vase, into the black bag of rubbish, wiping her hands on her apron as she made her way back into the house.

Printed in Great Britain
by Amazon

33242311R00166